PRAISE FOR
The Long Wait for Tomorrow

★"[A] thoughtful exploration of free will versus predestination. Dorfman's prose is magnetic."

—*Publishers Weekly*, Starred

"Dorfman spins brilliant sentences, packing big ideas, philosophy, the sounds of jazz and pure energy into the dialogues. . . . A wild, thought-provoking, heartbreaking jolt of a ride through astrophysics, friendship, Armani suits and heartache."

—*Kirkus Reviews*

"[Dorfman's] infectious, last-day-of-school vibe effectively clears the way for a conclusion every bit as unexpectedly ferocious as the opening chapter."

—*Booklist*

"[A] fresh take on the politics of high school. . . . An action-packed, well-paced plot that veers off in surprising directions; the flavor is similar to Tharp's *The Spectacular Now*, with profound insights about causes and effects at play among the banalities of high-school drama."

—*The Bulletin of the Center for Children's Books*

Also by Joaquin Dorfman
Playing It Cool

By Ariel and Joaquin Dorfman
Burning City

THE LONG WAIT FOR TOMORROW

JOAQUIN DORFMAN

RANDOM HOUSE 🏠 NEW YORK

All rights reserved. Published in the United States by Random House Children's Books, a division of Random House, Inc., New York. Originally published in hardcover in the United States by Random House Children's Books in 2009.

Random House and the colophon are registered trademarks of Random House, Inc.

Visit us on the Web! www.randomhouse.com/teens

Educators and librarians, for a variety of teaching tools, visit us at
www.randomhouse.com/teachers

The Library of Congress has cataloged the hardcover edition of this work as follows:
Dorfman, Joaquin.
The long wait for tomorrow / by Joaquin Dorfman.
p. cm.
Summary: North Carolina high school senior Patrick's life is a mess, but when his best friend, star quarterback Kelly McDermott, suddenly begins behaving very strangely, Patrick must do what he can to try to save everyone in the present and the future.
ISBN 978-0-375-84694-6 (trade) – ISBN 978-0-375-94694-3 (lib. bdg.) –
ISBN 978-0-375-84695-3 (trade pbk.) – ISBN 978-0-375-89297-4 (e-book)
[1. High schools–Fiction. 2. Schools–Fiction. 3. Family problems–Fiction. 4. Mentally ill–Fiction. 5. Conduct of life–Fiction. 6. Time travel–Fiction. 7. Steroids–Fiction.] I. Title.
PZ7.D727477Lo 2009
[Fic]–dc22
2008027273

Printed in the United States of America
10 9 8 7 6 5 4 3 2 1
First Trade Paperback Edition

THE LONG WAIT FOR TOMORROW

YESTERDAY

YESTERDAY

Kelly held the kid's arms fast from behind the flagpole, didn't have to tell the rest what to do. Zack, Cody, and a few of the other players were ready with the duct tape. Starting at the shins, they made their way up past his crotch, large hands surprisingly nimble as they wove Edmund into a gray, opaque cocoon. Edmund's piercing cries were greeted with laughter and hefty catchphrases, lifted live and direct from any given football practice:

> *Go, man, go!*
> *That's it, hustle!*
> *Let's move it!*
> *Come on, one, two, you got it!*

And above that, the rip of duct tape unfurling. Soulless and dry, it seemed to fill every inch of the stadium. Empty bleachers, finely shorn blades of grass, all of them echoing with that same, rasping familiarity; even as Edmund's screams lost traction, turned to meaningless, choking pleas for mercy.

High above them, the Stars and Stripes whipped soundly along with the wind.

It was late spring, and Patrick stood to the side, laughing along. Not from any substantial delight in the situation, but more out of an unspoken duty toward it. High school had its rules, laws, hierarchy, and food chain. Absolute, and non-negotiable, Edmund was simply part of what was and always would be.

And Kelly was on top of it all.

It took less than a minute and a half. Kelly's teeth bit down, severing the roll of tape from its winding tail. Edmund was now strapped, immobile against the iron pipe. Patches of rust rubbed off on his neatly ironed white button-down shirt. Tears ran down his eyes, eliciting further peals of derision.

And Patrick was more than happy to join in.

"Yeah, that's it," Kelly announced, arms folded across his chest. From beneath well-toned muscles, the number 13 peeked out, green numbers against the white football jersey. He tilted his head, addressing Edmund directly now. "You can cry all you want, Eddie," Kelly informed him. A frenzy of similar statements arose from his teammates as they fed off each other. "Believe it or not, we're about to do you a real favor."

The sprinkler system came to life, a resonance of soprano helicopters accompanying the spray of water.

Each one of Kelly's teammates flinched.

Patrick did his best to take it like a man, but only Kelly truly stood fast against the drizzle. Dirty blond hair catching a bit of the water, letting it fall against his lightly sunburned face; blue eyes unconcerned. Steadfast; letting the water do what it had to do, splashing both him and Edmund; it was as close as they would come to being equals.

"We know what you saw," Kelly informed him with calm,

easy words. "In case you were wondering what this was all about."

Edmund must have guessed as much, launching into his defense: "I didn't see anything! Believe me, I didn't! Nothing!"

"Well, that's just not true."

"It is!" Edmund's voice wheezed out, already sensing the futility. "It's true, Kelly, I swear."

"Hey!" Cody barked, stepping out just a bit from the rest of the group. His body was all muscle, almost incompatible with his short stature at a mere sixteen years of age. Detonation eyes under a mop-top haircut. "You keep lying, Kelly's going to skin you alive, got that?"

"OK, thanks, Cody," Kelly sighed, pinching the bridge of his nose, squeezing his eyes tight while shaking his head. "I'm not going to skin you alive, Edmund. And sorry to insist that we *do* know what you saw, though I like what you're trying to say. It's a good step. I also figure you haven't told Principal Sedgwick yet–"

"I haven't!" Edmund insisted. Grinned manically, frantic hopes surfacing. "I haven't!"

"Because if you had, we probably wouldn't be having this conversation. Which is also good." Kelly gave Edmund a strangely reassuring smile coupled with eyes that didn't quite agree. "Still, though, I'm afraid that's not good enough. . . . We could really use your help here."

A knowing chuckle was shared by all.

"Boys . . ."

Kelly didn't have to say another word.

The rest got to work, though the next part wasn't as easy as planned. Their tape job had been a solid one, efficiency exemplified, and getting to Edmund's belt called for an almost brutal display of force. He was wearing shorts, and as they reached under the web of duct tape, some leg hair had to go, brutally torn from its roots. Edmund screamed as Cody and Zack reached under, crawling upward, working against the adhesive. They unbuttoned his shorts, at which point Edmund must have realized what was about to happen, as he let go of all punctuation. Each shriek became a natural extension of the one before, not a breath taken anywhere between.

Patrick was struck with a sudden awe, his first time witnessing circular breathing.

Charlie Parker in his nightmares, his angels whispered.

Edmund's shorts were yanked down around his ankles. The white briefs beneath would have been enough to embarrass anyone, but this situation required something beyond the whole nine yards.

Something damaging.

They sent his underwear down to join his shorts, and Edmund's screams cut out all at once. One last dying echo was heard by the in-zone and then the helicopter sounds took over once again. Edmund was exposed. No way around it, though the rest did all they could to make sure he knew it. Pointing and laughing, doubled over in exaggerated delight, it was open house on Edmund's private parts.

Splash, splash, Edmund shut his eyes tight as the sprinklers continued to make rainbows in the afternoon sun. His breath began to slow, jaw working, as though trying to summon an invisible, ultimately imaginary force within himself; a desperate comic-book wish gone unanswered.

Kelly extended his arm toward Patrick.

Patrick complied instantly, moved with swift motions to ensure the camera's safety.

"We're going to take a little picture now, Edmund." Kelly took a few steps back, positioned himself...no chance of the camera getting wet, screwing up this priceless moment. "You don't have to smile or anything, just be yourself."

Edmund's eyes snapped open, and Patrick almost took a cautious step back. The fear was still there, the terror. But upon this traumatic foundation, something unexpected had taken hold: a pitch-perfect rage that seemed to radiate from Edmund in toxic waves. It was pure hatred. A dark plague that couldn't possibly be coming from the same pathetic creature who moments ago could barely find it in him to scream at his own captors. And now his voice barely trembled under the weight of his own fury.

"I'll kill you," Edmund told them, Adam's apple working. Grinding out the threat with little compunction. "I swear to God, I'll kill you all."

All at once, Patrick felt his resolve weaken. And, somehow, he could sense this same uneasy relapse poisoning the rest.

All except Kelly, of course.

"I wouldn't blame you if you did," Kelly replied, improvising gracefully through this unscripted moment. "Do what you're told, Edmund, and none of us has to die."

He held the LCD screen up to his eye, and the deal was sealed with a click.

Edmund's face regressed into its previous incarnation as the others returned to the fundamentals. Cocky smirks, unchecked swagger. Hyperactive taunts bringing comatose tears to Edmund's eyes, allowing Patrick's angels to bless him with their reassurance:

Everything as it always was and should always be.

"Cody!" Kelly called over his shoulder.

Cody ran over, grin painted with a fresh coat of excitement. He watched with wet lips as Kelly removed the memory card from the camera and handed it to him.

"Keep it secret, keep it safe," Kelly ordered. "Like we discussed. No uploading, no test runs, even between us."

Cody's eyes narrowed. "Kelly, this is the only copy we have."

"That's just the point," Kelly said, half turning to address Edmund, encapsulating all of them into the pact he'd forged. "It's a matter of good faith."

"Kelly..."

"He has to *trust* us, Junior," Kelly insisted.

A sour expression flickered across Cody's eyes at the word *Junior.*

Kelly gave him an apologetic look, a compensatory slug on the shoulder. "Run home now, Mad Dog."

A spoonful of sugar, and once the medicine went down, Cody did as he was told. Ran across the field, did a few rapid hops, spins, all the while clutching at an imaginary football. He charged past the in-zone, bleachers, and over the chain-link fence, taking a shortcut to the parking lot.

Kelly turned back to Edmund.

He extended his hand toward Patrick, who quickly reclaimed his camera.

"There you have it," Kelly said. "Cody's gone. That picture belongs to him now; you're never going to see it again. And neither will anyone else...."

Edmund began to struggle madly against his bonds. From fear to anger to pure, unhinged denial. With each fresh turn, the sprinklers offered just enough lubrication to aid in his final struggle. A few of the others allowed for worry, but as far as Kelly was concerned, it was all over.

"Tell Sedgwick what you saw, Edmund"—Kelly spelled it out with terrifying ease—"and that picture gets posted online faster than you can blink. We find out you told anyone else... you even tell *me* what you saw, and it turns up in everybody's mailbox *yesterday*, understand?"

Kelly didn't wait for the OK.

Edmund's thrashing had done its job. The water had sufficiently weakened the adhesive, and he broke free with a pathetic sob. Ripped through the duct tape and ran across the field, barely managing to hold up his shorts and white cotton briefs.

"Leave it," Kelly said, raising his arm in response to his followers, assuring them there was no need to give chase. He watched as Edmund stumbled his way toward a caged freedom, strands of duct tape streaming from him like an unraveling matinee mummy. "It's all right ... now he knows it."

High fives and congratulations all around.

Kelly turned to Patrick and gave him an approving smile.

Patrick grinned in return, everybody's watches set to the afternoon sunlight.

Kelly slipped out his fifty cents.

One quarter, then another, a ceremonious moment amid the swath of afternoon shoppers. Patrick stood to the side, watching with parallel reverence. Taking care not to stand too close, to give Kelly his moment with the fountain.

Kelly's eyes narrowed, stared across the wet expanse dotted by jets of cascading water. Alongside the miniature geysers stood statues of frolicking children: pure bronze, elated expressions frozen in time. Scores of submerged wishes, quarters, nickels, dimes, surrounded their russet brown sneakers. Arms extended; chasing after each other, or perhaps an unseen bronze puppy that lay just beyond the boundaries of their wondrous bronze world.

All along the outdoor promenade of South Point Mall, people continued to stroll by, oblivious.

A conclusion was reached, and Kelly slipped one of the quarters over his thumb with rehearsed dexterity. He flicked his thumb in an extension of that same movement. The twenty-five-cent piece was sent through the air, glinting head over tails, a perfect arc resulting in a satisfying, isolated splash.

Patrick waited for a moment, then launched into their traditional follow-up: "What'd you wish for, Kelly?"

Kelly smiled slightly. "What would you have wished for?"

"I don't know."

Kelly pretended to consider this, then handed Patrick his second quarter. "How about you give it a shot?"

Patrick turned the coin over in his hand, regarded Washington's head with suspicion. "What do you think I should wish for?"

"How about getting your ass off that wait list, and *into* Ohio State?"

Patrick paused. He knew the drill, what was expected of him. Even in his own head, he could see it playing out: him nodding, concentrating, and casting the suggested wish onto the waters. Just as they always had, since they were young enough to sacrifice penny bubble gum for the sake of a wish.

Instead, he found the quarter glued to his palm.

"Patrick?"

"I don't know..." Patrick coughed. "I mean, you know..."

"No, I don't," Kelly replied, annoyed. "You want to come with me to Ohio State or not?"

"Of course..."

"So?"

"I'm just saying." Patrick shrugged, then began to negotiate. "How about the game? State championship on Friday, we've been waiting all year for this moment. How about I wish for—"

"Look, maybe if the season had actually happened when it was supposed to. Back in the fall, when a loss might have actually *swayed* a scout or two. But the season *was* postponed, I got into Ohio State, and *you* got wait-listed. Now which one of us needs a favor from God? You or me?"

"Well..." Patrick tried to match Kelly's irritated tone. It came out sounding meek, almost wounded: "Maybe I don't want any divine intervention in my life."

"You don't really get to choose that kind of thing."

"Then what's the point of the wish?"

"There is no *point*. It's just something we *do*, something we've always *done*."

"Then you do it," Patrick told Kelly, holding out the coin with a conciliatory raise of his eyebrows. "OK? Will that—if you do it, make the wish for me, can we just drop it?"

Kelly took the coin, muttering: "Consider it dropped."

"I'm sorry."

"One wish coming up," Kelly mumbled again, voice already losing its edge. Slipping back into the well of concentration, focusing. "This one's for Pat."

Patrick gave a relieved hum of approval. He kept his hands folded in front of him, a diminutive five-eight bodyguard to Kelly's six-one stature. Watched as Kelly prepared himself; going through the motions as though he'd lived it all before, seen it all before. A tradition stretching so far back, Patrick didn't even know if it had ever meant anything. Didn't even know why they had come so close to fighting over a world neither of them even believed in.

Patrick was still wondering, so lost in the fountain's rush of water that he didn't notice Jenna approaching.

Neither of them did, probably the only two who hadn't seen her exit from the main shopping mall at their backs. It was a rare occasion when Jenna didn't manage to turn every head within sight. Attention wandering, necks craning from text messages and iPods, it was the moon and the tides with her. Even after a full day of school and work, hair tied up in a simple ponytail, black-and-white Foot Locker shirt doing all it could to ignore the subject of her breasts, she could still make the air-conditioning sweat.

Round lips, almond-shaped eyes shimmering despite the lengthy shadows of surrounding buildings, she made her way over the red tile sidewalk and snuck up behind Kelly McDermott.

Patrick caught her in the act, unnecessarily tiptoeing as she inched her hands around Kelly's head.

Too late, no time to react, and Jenna's palms swept in, locked themselves over Kelly's eyes.

Kelly's mouth turned to a nauseated grimace of astonishment, his arm jerking up in a spastic salute to nothingness. It was a mere split-second reaction, but just enough to send the spirits scampering as the coin went flying, ricocheting with little grace off the bronze eye of a capricious child-statue.

The quarter landed with an unceremonious plunk in a nearby garbage can.

"Damn it!" Kelly barked. He reached up, clamped down hard on Jenna's wrists, and spun around. "Jenna, what the *hell*? I was in the middle of something, you couldn't see I was *doing something?*"

Jenna backed up two steps, alarmed. "Kelly, what's wrong with you?"

"I just lost my quarter there."

"Hell, I'll get you another one, here—"

"It doesn't matter!" Kelly yelled, exasperated. The stares that had followed Jenna over there now promptly retreated to their own business. "It was that one, that's the one that mattered."

"What difference does it make?" Jenna sniped, tearing herself from Kelly's grip.

"It's never going to be the *same*," Kelly insisted. *"Goddamn* it, Jenna."

"Kelly..."

"Never mind," Kelly said. He leaned back against the rim of the fountain, pinched the bridge of his nose, and shook his head clear. "Just, never mind... You done with work, baby?"

Jenna blinked, unsure if this was the same conversation. "Yeah."

"Tell you what, we'll grab a bite to eat, how's that sound?"

"Yeah, sounds good."

Kelly turned to his wingman, smiling now. Almost encouraging... "Patrick, you in? Know you love that double cheeseburger, onion, pickles, mayo... 57 Sauce, amigo."

Patrick hadn't caught up quite yet, managed a pert nod. "Gotta get my stuff first."

"Gonna get some money from the ATM." Kelly bounced himself off the fountain and swooped in to give Jenna a quick kiss on the lips. "It's good to see you, honey."

And Kelly was headed across the promenade, stopping

only to pick up a doll for a clumsy five-year-old, who then went on her way without a single thank-you.

Patrick saw Jenna looking after Kelly. Her face was awash with the honest confusion of a misfired prank, unable to give in to her livid instincts. She turned to Patrick, as though expecting an answer from him. Patrick shook his head, as he frequently did when apologizing for Kelly.

These were times Patrick wished he had it in him to act.

Put Kelly in his place.

But neither Patrick nor Jenna was entirely certain where that place was.

There were times, it seemed, when Kelly McDermott was simply eternal.

They left Jenna in the car, out on the street.

The pair trotted across the front yard, stepping nimbly from stone to imbedded stone, the uneven path leading up to Patrick's house. It was evening now. Just the smallest suggestion of daylight smudged the clouds, purple hues preparing for black skies and starlight. Crickets singing in the bushes, even the occasional bat flapping overhead, punching its time card and getting to work.

Illuminated windows were sent along the house like shrieking eyes.

A quick squint, and Patrick could see his parents in the kitchen.

"You always do this," Kelly casually informed Patrick.

"Yeah, Kelly, I know."

"Nobody else in this neighborhood comes in the front way except you," Kelly marveled. "Hell, nobody in *suburbia* comes in through the front door—not what it's there for."

Patrick yanked on the glass storm door, glanced back into the thick twilight.

Up and down the street similar houses all stared each other down. Two-story, slanted roof, aluminum siding colored an off-white in accordance with standard community code. Lawns rolled out like carpeting, all the way to the curb, engulfing what space should have been left for sidewalks. Driveways stretched all the way back to hungry garages and back-porch doorways.

Kelly was right.

Cookie-cutter houses, and everyone made the same cookie-cutter entrances.

Patrick dug into his pocket, procured his keys, and went in.

His parents called him into the kitchen.

All current endeavors ceased as soon as the two of them stepped in. Patrick's mother, seated at an overused wooden breakfast nook, stacked and filed papers from her office in one fluid motion. She brought her hands up to her mouth, large brown eyes blinking behind ringlets of graying hair. Patrick's father set down his bottle of Bass Ale and tossed the opener on the counter. His red cheeks, two plum-shaped islands on a round white face, seemed to lift off as a smile turned to a grin, and that grin turned into a laugh. . . .

"Hey-hey-hey!" he announced, pointing with pride. "Mr. Starting Quarterback!"

"We just heard yesterday . . ." Patrick's mother pushed out

from the table, almost knocking her chair onto the brown linoleum. Her voice wavered like notes from a musical saw: "ConGRAtuLAtions!"

Patrick's parents descended on Kelly. Rough hugs, pinches, handshakes, and firm, friendly caresses, it was just the cover their real son was looking for.

"I'm just going to get my stuff," Patrick said, not expecting an answer.

All expectations proved correct, and he slipped out of the kitchen, upstairs. His bag was already packed, a red and white duffel lying on the bed. He slung it over his shoulder. Took a look around his room, all the years gone by since childhood without a single adjustment to show for it. A white dresser with a couple of plastic toys, pictures of himself and his parents. A couple of just-for-trying trophies, cheap plastic all painted gold. White wallpaper, multicolored animal shapes floating about in confused positions. Even his bookshelves had remained as always, crammed to capacity with the Hardy Boys, Betsy Byars, C. S. Lewis, R. L. Stine, and Beverly Cleary.

Even the bunk beds, still waiting for a second body to come home.

The only thing new under the sun was a poster of Miles Davis at Birdland–half cast in shadows, smoke blurring in a black-and-white backlight. That unique pose, body leaning forward in a slanting stoop, lips lowered to meet the trumpet's mouthpiece. A foreground table full of empty glasses, and a lone woman, watching, hand pressed close to her neck, because who could ever believe being that close to Miles Davis.

"And we don't even play the same instrument," Patrick murmured, turning to the closet.

He opened the door, reached in, and pulled out his saxophone case.

Took another last look around the room that time forgot, a little displeased with himself.

Patrick took the stairs two at a time, relieved to be on the move. His momentum carried him into the kitchen, where he slid to a stop. No need to stop the presses, his parents were still playing bumper pool with Kelly's attention. Patrick's father had opened a fresh beer for Kelly while his mother proudly showed off a framed photograph of their first date together at an OSU pep rally. The three of them had already performed this song and dance a few months before, but there seemed to be no end to the cards up Kelly's sleeve, always something new worth celebrating.

"How many freshmen can say the same thing?" Patrick's father boomed rhetorically. "How many freshmen can say, *Oh well, I'm not technically at college yet, but I'm already the starting quarterback for a Big Ten school!*"

"Just got lucky," Kelly assured them. Perhaps believing it, perhaps not.

Patrick's father waved his hand dismissively. "Ah, so the Buckeyes had a little shakedown."

"It was *you* they chose," Patrick's mother insisted. "*Your* talent, so *nuts* to luck."

Patrick's father looked up from the festivities, tilted the bottle in his son's direction. "You heard anything yet?"

"I'm at school when the mail comes," Patrick replied, brushing his shirt absently.

"Sometimes they call," Patrick's father insisted.

"They do call, sometimes," Patrick's mother echoed, making it law.

Patrick knew better than to argue. "Nothing yet."

His father turned back to Kelly. "You going to take care of our boy next semester?"

"You bet . . ." Kelly pretended to take a swig of his beer, nodded to accentuate the point.

"Jenna's in the car," Patrick announced, wrapping his thumb under the bag strap, as though shouldering it for the first time.

Kelly got the hint, set his beer down. Macheteing his way through continued compliments and congratulations, he made it to Patrick's side. Said his farewells and began to follow Patrick out of the kitchen.

"Where are you going, Patrick?" his mother asked.

Patrick frowned. "Over to Kelly's for the week. His parents—"

"I mean, why are you going out the front door?"

Patrick's father nodded. "Everyone else goes out the back."

Kelly gave Patrick a quiet smirk, pat on the shoulder.

And in the end, Patrick did as he was told.

Kelly finished off his patty melt on Texas toast.

Patrick took his last morsel of burger, dipped it into a blob of Heinz 57, and followed suit.

"Patrick..."

His head shot up, a common side effect brought on by the sound of Jenna's voice.

From her seat across the booth, Jenna smiled slightly, head tilted to the side. Only halfway through her waffle, a small triangular piece still stuck on her fork, resting on her plate. Jenna was a slow eater, a slave to her good manners. *Never talk with your mouth full, don't focus on your next bite until you're all done with what came before.*

Chew slowly, and Patrick found himself doing just that, right cheek bulging slightly.

"You've got something," Jenna told him, finger brushing lightly against her chin.

Patrick's eyes widened, and he resumed his chewing, double time. No longer able to relish the last of his mayonnaise-soaked burger, he reached for the napkin dispenser. Pinched a little too tight, came out with twelve or so more napkins than he had intended. Swallowed hard, despite not being done chewing, and haphazardly dragged the napkins across his chin.

"Thanks, Jenna," Patrick croaked, taking a few more blind swipes. He felt the partly chewed burger making its way haltingly down his esophagus. He lowered his hands slightly, examined the handiwork. "Christ."

Jenna laughed. "I'll say."

Patrick felt himself turn red. "There was, like...onion and half a pickle slice on my chin."

"Yeah," Jenna giggled, picking up her fork.

"You want a take-out box for that, Patrick?" Kelly offered,

prompting Jenna to drop the fork back onto her plate with a loud clatter and throw her head back, laughing. Kelly raised his knee, resting his foot on the edge of the seat, arm snaking effortlessly around Jenna's shoulders.

Patrick watched Jenna lean into him, resting her head against Kelly's chest.

Laughter ebbing, fine brown hair spilling down the front of his shirt.

They had to be the best-looking couple in that whole joint, no question. Not to say that Waffle House was where supermodels came to hibernate between runway gigs. The majority of regulars, older locals for the most part, would be the first to admit time hadn't treated them too kindly. Younger clientele might not be ready to admit as much, but their eyes didn't carry enough interest, anyway. Red and bloodshot, wandering empty stares, either stoned or drunk.

Newports and Pall Malls burning through all hours of the morning.

Patrick hurriedly folded the contents of his napkin, tossed it aside.

Jenna rolled her eyes up at her boyfriend. "I'm going to try and finish my waffle now. That OK with you, Mr. Ohio State?"

"Go right ahead, *Mrs.* Ohio State. . . ."

"Hey now, they still got me wait-listed," Jenna insisted, picking up her fork. Dipped the waffle piece in some syrup and pointed across the table. "You, Patrick? Anything from the Buckeye State?"

"Nah, nothing," Patrick said, quickly reaching for his Sprite.

"Mmm . . ." Jenna was obviously planning to say something else, but there was a mouthful of waffle and proper etiquette to navigate past.

While she chewed, Kelly jumped in: "They accepted me and my SAT. They've got to accept you, Pat."

"You're going to be their star quarterback."

Kelly thought about it, blue eyes admitting an easy defeat. "Yeah, that's also true."

"Did you check?" Jenna finally swallowed. Reached for her water, left lipstick stains on the straw and tried again. "Did you check the *mail* today, Patrick?"

"Parents did."

"How about yesterday, did you check yesterday?"

"*Two cheeseburgers!*" came the cry from behind the counter. "*Double hash browns, smothered, covered, diced, and peppered!*"

Patrick glanced over at the sudden rise in activity and grill-top sizzle. "No. Nothing yesterday."

"Quit bothering Patrick," Kelly told Jenna.

"I'm not *bothering*."

"You are."

"*You* just don't want to think of a game without Patrick in that horn section."

"Don't have to," Kelly stated. "Patrick's going to get in."

"You know the future all of a sudden?"

"Yes."

"Neat." Jenna resumed slicing up her waffle.

Patrick had retreated from the conversation. Turned his head toward the curved floor-to-ceiling windows. There wasn't a hell of a lot to see out there. Ten p.m. traffic lights along the Scarborough Road overpass, changing their colors more out of principle than anything else. An occasional taxi pulling into the parking lot. Cabdriver raking his fingers through a salt-and-pepper beard, waiting for the witching-hour calls of drunken barflies unable to get home on their own. Gas station across the road, another farther down the way. Shopping outlets mingling with pawnshops, Mexican-owned convenience stores, fast-food marquees dropping low as ninety-nine cents, burger outlets outbidding each other in the race to see whose egg-and-cheese biscuit was the most worthless. Far in the distance, the crimson sign shining high and bright just beyond the railroad tracks—white letters reading BOXXX CAR VIDEO.

Verona was a town both alive and dead in many ways, but outside wasn't what concerned Patrick. Simple focus, ignoring the orange streetlights and simply staring *at* the window. Watching the secret reflections of Kelly and Jenna. Narrowing his sights even further, Patrick locked out all that lay beyond and around Jenna's face, hair, body. He watched her smile, chew, never let on when she caught herself talking with her mouth full, hand shooting up to cover her mouth, eyes wide, mortified that someone might have noticed. The window was Patrick's sanctuary, a bunker for nuclear testing. It was a looking-glass world where Patrick could give his eyes the liberty of gazing, even as he saw Jenna look across the table and ask someone a question.

That someone was Patrick, and reality came complete with two quarters sliding across the table.

"You want to put on some tunes?" Jenna asked.

Patrick glanced down at the change resting by his arm, an eagle and founding father awaiting their fate.

"Pat's just going to put on the same two songs he always does," Kelly announced.

"That's what I like about Patrick." Jenna smiled reassuringly across the table.

Kelly shrugged. "I just don't see why all the suspense."

"I don't, either," Jenna informed him. She gave Patrick another smile, head jerking once in the direction of the jukebox. "Another thing I like about Patrick."

"Whatever," Kelly said playfully. "I liked him before you did."

"Can't change history," Jenna lamented.

"Or the future," Kelly added, turning to Patrick. "Go on and play your songs, Patrick. I can dig it."

Patrick picked the two quarters up off the table, scooted his way out of the wooden booth.

Kelly handed him twenty bucks and a yellow slip of paper, grease stain on the top left corner. "And get that for us while you're up, will you, Pat?"

Patrick nodded, walked across the black and gray tiles. There wasn't a soul around, it seemed sometimes, who could make it across that floor without shuffling. Something about the noise, the white fluorescent weight from above. The secret knowledge that it didn't matter how many times a day they mopped up, or how high the sanitation grade got with every inspection, nobody truly *believed* that floor was or ever would be truly free from that invisible layer of grit.

And the jukebox was no exception to an unchanging world. Pale pink and yellow track labels faded by the shine of 24/7 service. No MP3s or Internet connections; and although old-timers might laugh at the thought, the CDs stacked within were Patrick's old-school. They were the happy constants, the familiar threads woven into the fabric of the security blanket, keeping the world at bay.

Patrick slipped in his fifty cents.

One quarter, then another.

Glanced over to the table, saw Kelly whispering something in Jenna's ear.

Patrick shifted his focus, out to the window. Caught Jenna's reflection.

Eyes lowered with a demure beauty, unable to stop herself from smiling.

Patrick absently placed a hand over his abdomen, turning to the jukebox.

Punched out the numbers from memory, and turned to pay the check.

Patrick had parked his ass out on the back deck. Sitting on a green iron-crafted chair, legs stretched out, listening to 90.7 FM, a couple of cuts from Lester Bowie and the Brass Fantasy. Behind him, kitchen windows joined forces with outdoor floodlights, cast long shadows on the deck, past the deck. Out into the backyard, where shadows grew thin and disappeared, darkness stretching out into a singularity.

Patrick tapped his pen against the sheet music in his lap, blank lines awaiting his touch.

He closed his eyes, searching for it. Listening for the sound of crickets, the only evidence that there even were such things. Listening for their message, feeling his hand move across the page, a slow-motion printer. Filling in notes without thinking, without looking. Rescuing all that was lost in translation.

The sound of crickets, mercifully commonplace, and Patrick felt his face flush. He opened his eyes, glanced back to the brick façade of Kelly's house, up to a dimly lit second-story window. No way to tell if they were still going at it, Patrick's ears had found their sanctuary. Guilt-ridden thoughts, wondering if he'd left the house because the sound of Kelly and Jenna was too much to bear, or if maybe the sound of Jenna's cries was simply too good not to listen to.

"You're a disgusting person," Patrick muttered, trying to countermand images of Jenna's eyes and lips, both half closed, hair sprawled over Kelly's pillow.

That's right, came the voice of his angels. . . . *Kelly's pillow.*

Patrick sighed, lulled into a melancholy state. He sank uncomfortably into his chair, craned his neck back, and strained his eyes for some small hint of starlight. Each distant dot originating years before he could witness it, nothing more than what was once upon a time.

"That one dot," Patrick murmured, unconsciously transcribing its position along with the others', "that one dot could be seven years ago. Seven years ago is right now, so we've all gone back."

"And they say we all come from starlight," Jenna added, her face now floating over him, eclipsing Patrick's entire vista. He might have jumped, startled, might have found it in his heart to cry out. But there was too much to like about this one interruption. Jenna's upside-down face grinning an upside-down smile. Tousled hair reaching down to tickle his face, mascara smudged into tiny raccoon ringlets. The faint understanding that she was wearing one of Kelly's button-down shirts, still open and revealing a black underwire bra. "So truly, seeing that we all come from starlight, where *have* we finally gone?"

Patrick smiled stupidly, a common side effect brought about by the sight of Jenna's face. "I don't know."

"Good night, Patrick...," Jenna whispered.

She darted down the wooden stairs, toward the driveway.

"You going home?" Patrick called after her.

"I don't want my dad to worry...." Jenna turned, hands clenching both sides of the shirt together. Black work pants and bare feet skipping backward. "I'll see you, Patrick."

"Tomorrow!" Patrick managed to call out.

Jenna waved and disappeared around a corner.

Patrick looked down to find every line filled with the notes of starlight and Jenna's voice.

It wasn't more than four seconds after her car started up when Kelly stepped out onto the deck. He stood behind Patrick, allowing his shadow to join ranks with the rest for just a second. Not a lot said, and for that one second, the Brass Fantasy continued with their rendition of "I Only Have Eyes for You."

Then Kelly took a few steps, reached down, and snapped the radio off.

Waited for the whirr of the CD player and pressed Play.

The latest from 50 Cent belched out into the night, crickets gone silent, unhappy.

"Sorry, Pat." Kelly lowered the volume to adjust for the music. "Just not in the mood for jazz."

He sat down amid the beats and single-track sample. Took a sip of water, biceps bulging reflexively as he brought the bottle to his waiting lips. He kicked his legs up onto another chair, adjusted his boxer shorts, and raised his eyes to the sky.

"Jenna took off," Patrick offered.

"Yeah, her father's car..."

"Her pop's a good guy."

Kelly nodded. "Sure is."

"What time is it, anyway?"

"Eleven-forty, last I checked."

Patrick nodded. Not that he really cared. The day had been a long one, with or without the aid of Father Time. And here he was, sitting with Kelly McDermott, watching the stars while 50 Cent let them have a tiny taste of the thug life.

"Kelly?"

Kelly kept his eyes skyward. "Yeah?"

"Have I congratulated you yet?"

"Huh?"

"On OSU? Have I said, you know, actually said, congratulations?"

Kelly thought about it. "Don't bother...not till you get your letter."

Patrick didn't budge one way or another. Decided maybe a different approach would serve them best, and asked: "Were you this certain you'd get *your* letter?"

"Well, no sense in pretending anymore..." Kelly rocked his head left and right, cracked his neck, and straightened out. "I was accepted to OSU way back in the fall."

Patrick didn't say anything.

"I mean, you knew, Patrick," Kelly insisted. "When we went to visit and they had me work out with their team. Didn't have another way to make the final check, what with the NC season pushed back to spring. ... So yeah, they offered it to me. So did Florida State, Michigan, a couple others. Had to keep it quiet, of course, but ... I mean, who do you really think got me that new car?"

Patrick felt a twinge of jealousy. "I guess I knew you knew. I just didn't realize just how you knew it was all going to work out."

"Well ..." Kelly shrugged, though not in any dismissive way. He took another swig of water, relishing the purity. "The world was made for people like me. It doesn't matter what I do, what I say. Why do I get a car, while you get wait-listed? Nobody gets extra credit for guessing the sun's going to come up tomorrow, that's just how things have been fashioned. There's a Kelly-shaped hole in the universe that needs to be filled, that's been hollowed out specifically for me to fill. . . . It's like floating on an inner tube down the rapids, I am already there. It's just plain old run-of-the-mill destiny."

Patrick reached out and grabbed Kelly's water from the table. "Sounds nice."

"It's not as though I like it, Pat. It is what it is."

"Destiny."

"And you're coming with," Kelly insisted. "It may not be fair, the way the world bends toward certain people. But as long as it does, there's no sense in letting the opportunities slip by. I'm going places, and I want you there with me. You're *going* to be there with me, Pat. We'll make headlines."

"Has Jenna gotten her letter yet?"

Kelly didn't answer.

"You going to marry her, someday?" Patrick asked.

Kelly waved his hand before his face. "You sound like an old bitch nagging."

"I'd marry her if I were you," Patrick said. He stood up, tried to take a pull of water. Found less than a drop left in Kelly's bottle, and that was that. "I'd wise up and marry her fast."

"Before what?" Kelly asked.

"Before she wises up and realizes she just might have a choice."

It was close as Patrick ever came to cracking on Kelly.

Kelly's reaction was a quick laugh as he stood up. Turned his chair around to better face the backyard, catch sight of all that was waiting in the dark. "We're all going to be just fine, Patrick. . . . You'll see."

Patrick didn't answer.

He turned, opened the back door, and paused.

Patrick took a look back, one of those moments. Maybe it was that these days were numbered, moments where it felt as though life was quietly stalking them one by one. Moments Kelly would dismiss as weakness, and so Patrick kept his mouth shut.

Though he did look back, maybe because it was one of those moments. He took a look back at Kelly, sitting with his back to the floodlights, awaiting his destiny.

One last look before closing the door on tonight.

That last look, last glimpse of the young Kelly McDermott before tonight became yesterday, and tomorrow turned to today.

TODAY

#1

His eyes opened, and for a moment, Patrick didn't know where he was.

He blinked his way out of sleep, let reality tighten its grip as the guest room came into focus. Antiquated floral patterns along the walls, framed paintings that hadn't made the cut for any of the *important* rooms. White lace curtains, complete with delicate patterns sewn into the near-translucent material. A desk, easy chair, dresser, miniature bookcase; all of which had lost their jobs around the house to updated versions of themselves.

From somewhere nearby, Patrick heard a door slam.

He grunted and stretched his toes, heard them crack under the stiff sheets.

Felt as though he should piss.

Patrick stepped out of the guest bedroom and into the hallway, down to the end, only to find light emanating from beneath the closed bathroom door. He changed his bearing toward the adjacent doorway, poking his head into Kelly's room.

Lil' Kim, 50 Cent, T.I., Eminem, and an oversized Jimi Hendrix stared down at Kelly's bed from the rectangle walls of their poster prisons. The purple/blue comforter lay in the middle of the room, crumpled and confused on the off-white carpet. A pair of black panties hung from a nearby chair, awaiting Jenna's long overdue return.

Patrick glanced back to the bathroom, saw a pair of stilted shadows from under the crack.

"Getting some juice," Patrick announced, words aimed through the door.

"Patrick?" Kelly's muffled voice sounded oddly cautious.

"Yeah. Getting some OJ. You want anything? I could cook up some eggs."

No answer.

Patrick shrugged.

He took slow steps down the stairs, bare feet making sticky, smacking sounds on the polished wood beneath. Down another hallway and into the kitchen, where gray morning light robbed the room of depth, shone dully off the white counter-tops.

Glancing out the windows, Patrick saw the stereo stuck on the deck. He scampered out onto the damp wood, already hot in anticipation of another broiling day. Collected the radio and returned it to the kitchen, wiping the soles of his feet clean on the indoor mat.

Patrick opened the door to the fridge, procured some Tropicana Pure Premium. Poured a hefty helping and guzzled it down, all the while staring blankly out the window. A jazz bass line, compliments of Paul Chambers, did loops through his head. He hummed along through his nose, paying close attention to how the notes changed as his stomach grew in circumference.

Patrick set the empty glass down, smacking his lips.

He wiped some crud from the corner of his eye, blinked.

OK, now he definitely had to piss.

Patrick jogged up the stairs and was once again confronted with a closed door between him and much-needed relief. He didn't want to bother, but his options were few; the downstairs was broken, and Kelly's parents never left town without locking their room.

Good times all around.

He sighed, fist raised and at the ready for a little knock-knock action, when the door opened. Opened hard, practically swinging off its hinges, enough force to make Patrick jump at the sight of Kelly's body filling the entrance.

In the ensuing silence, Patrick went from believing he'd done something wrong to simply wondering what could possibly *be* wrong. Kelly's eyes were wide. Wide with what, exactly—surprise, amazement, bewildered fear, perhaps all of the above—that would have to wait. Patrick was more alarmed that Kelly should be in the grip of *any* of those emotions. It was the unspoken urgency of it all, the way Kelly stood poised with one hand on the door frame, the other fast on the knob. There was also the glaring detail that Kelly, fond of sleeping in the buff, hadn't bothered to cover up before heading to the bathroom.

Letting it all hang out, just standing there in his birthday suit.

Patrick found his voice, coughed. "Everything all right, Kelly?"

Kelly looked as though he was actually considering the question. Not so much considering, it was more than that. He narrowed his stare, leaned close toward his best friend's mouth, as though wondering if Patrick had even *asked* the question.

And Patrick thought maybe it was worth repeating: "Everything all right–"

"Patrick?"

A fairly simple question, although the uncertainty in Kelly's eyes, the honesty of the inquiry, left Patrick at a loss. Unable to answer, and for a moment, it seemed as though nothing would happen unless Patrick did. All the makings of an endless staring contest, but then . . .

"Patrick!" Kelly announced, answering his previous question with a delighted cry. He took Patrick by the shoulders, looked him up and down. Marveling at the sight of his best friend, Kelly then yanked roughly, pulling Patrick into a massive embrace.

Patrick's body went stiff. Playing possum as Kelly used his superior build to rock them back and forth in what felt like an extremely inappropriate slow dance. Kelly didn't seem to notice, and he rubbed his hands against Patrick's back, pulled away just in time to get his hands around Patrick's head.

Once again, Patrick remained still as could be, some primal instinct insisting his head was about to be ripped right clear from his shoulders. No worries, though. Kelly merely grinned, pressed his forehead against Patrick's, and let out a rapid, breathless rasp.

"Look at you, Patrick," Kelly whispered.

Kelly stepped back once more, gave Patrick yet another once-over. "Look at you! Look at you, you... look... aces!"

Patrick was trying to figure out which one of them was still dreaming when Kelly began to laugh. Slow and uncertain, as though trying it out for the first time. Truth be told, it was the first time Patrick had heard this particular sound coming from Kelly. It was pure, giddy, and, under different circumstances, it might have been contagious.

Time being, Patrick remained unable to even speak as Kelly brushed past him.

The laughter continued, rising and falling on the back of invisible waves, as Kelly reached out to touch the hallway walls. Fingertips exploring with light strokes, as though checking for wet paint, Kelly made his way to the stairs, where he broke into a sudden trot. Down, down, down he went, thunderous foot-falls rattling the house.

Patrick watched this mad dash, finally finding his voice: "You want anything, Kelly...? I could... cook up some eggs, I guess."

We've already done that, Patrick's angels reminded him.

Patrick took the stairs two at a time, leaped past the last five.

He ran into the kitchen.

Glanced left, then right; caught sight of Kelly's ass disappearing through the doorway to the den.

When Patrick caught up with him, Kelly was walking around the extensive, L-shaped couch, fingers stroking the brown leather, bare feet brushing along the gray carpet. Patrick watched from the doorway, debating whether to descend those four steps into the den. Kelly glided alongside the large glass table stationed between the couch and the flat-screen TV. He didn't bend down, didn't try touching this time; just moved his hands far above the transparent surface, as though preparing for the final act of a magic trick.

He paused. Cocked his head to the side, listening . . . "Huh."

"Hey, Kelly . . . ," Patrick ventured, heading down the steps. "I know I asked this a couple of whenevers ago, but . . . is everything all—"

"This . . . ," Kelly interrupted, trailed off momentarily before resurfacing. "This is, I mean this room. Here, right? This is where we had that Christmas party, way back when. . . ." Kelly glanced up, over to Patrick. "Right? My parents . . ." Kelly squinted. "My parents threw this kind of joint Christmas party, their friends in the kitchen, our friends in here. They let everyone get wasted, and, well . . . I mean, my parents were always drunks, they must have gotten . . ." Kelly's certainty seemed to be fading. "Wasn't this the place, Patrick? You, me, and Jenna stayed up past the dial, just talking, way back when, wasn't it?"

Despite knowing the story all too well, Patrick was having a hard time following. "Way back when, Kelly, I don't . . . I mean, that was just this past Christmas." Patrick walked over to a set of sliding glass doors leading out to the top of the driveway and innocuously drew the blinds. Long strips of plastic swayed in dissonant motion, rattled quietly against each other. "We're talking a few months here, if that, Kelly..."

Kelly's eyes widened, remembering something.... "Jenna."

"Well, you, me, and Jenna, sure—"

"Is Jenna still around?"

Patrick felt a bit more comfortable fielding this one. "She took off last night, remember?"

"Last night?"

"Last night, yes. Before today, if I'm not mistaken."

And now a lightbulb popped above Kelly's head. "Paper."

"What's ... what are you—"

"We get the paper, right?" Kelly climbed over the sofa, plodded toward Patrick. "The Verona Something-or-other, right?"

Patrick gave himself room to back up. "Yeah, *Verona Observer,* what's the big deal..."

Kelly didn't have too much vested in Patrick's sentence, and he took off once again. Up the four steps, and through the kitchen.

Patrick might have stayed put this time if he hadn't immediately sensed where this was all heading. Leaping into the kitchen, following his gut toward the front hallway, he saw Kelly at the far end, frantically undoing the brass locks on the front door.

"Kelly!" Patrick cried out, several seconds too late. The door was jerked open with wrenching sounds of protest from the unaccustomed paint job. "Nobody goes out through the front door!"

Oh, his angels nudged him as Kelly burst out the screen

door. *And there's the fact that he's running bare-ass naked out into the street at seven-thirty in the morning.*

Patrick turned back, rushed through the kitchen, catapulted himself over the steps leading down into the den. Hit the ground running, right arm reaching out and snatching a quilted blanket from the back of the couch. Legs pumping, Patrick smacked into the glass doorway, cutting through the plastic blinds in search of the lock, hands fumbling.

He got it, slid the door open, and tore through the blinds, hitting an immediate right.

Scattered twigs and acorns dug sharply into his bare feet, only a few wild steps taken down the sloping driveway before Patrick came to a scampering halt.

There, at the entrance to the street, stood Kelly.

Unfurled early edition held high over his head. Waving the ink back and forth, grinning like the first North Carolinian to actually win the Powerball. Unconcerned with his naked state, even as a few neighbors stepped out onto their lawns to watch the spectacle, coffee mugs trapped in a holding pattern just below confused lips.

"It's May!" he cried out, lifting his left leg and hopping around in a demented circle. "It's Thursday, May fifteenth! May fifteenth, two thousand motherfucking eight!" He paused, as though waiting for Patrick to react. When he got nothing, Kelly simply added: "AD!" before coming out with a long, booming laugh, not a shred of dignity as he returned to his outlandish jig.

And as a result, it was Patrick who noticed the car pulling up, not Kelly.

It was Patrick who felt his stomach turn at the sight of red and blue lights coming to life.

The halting whoop of a siren, almost undetectable beneath Kelly's hysterical peals of laughter.

It was Patrick who broke out of his trance, running toward Kelly as the patrol car pulled to the curb, and a pair of uniformed officers stepped out, already reaching for their cuffs.

All this, apparently, on the morning of May fifteenth, two thousand motherfucking eight.

2

As far as Patrick was concerned, there were three types of police officers: the kind who had better things to do, the kind who had nothing better to do, and the third bowl of porridge, which was always just right.

The two officers in Kelly's kitchen were of the first order. While both their features varied slightly—from age to eye color, build to facial hair—their attitude made them fraternal twins. It didn't matter that they had just started their shift, aftershave and deodorant still fresh under matching uniforms. It was of little importance that Patrick had shown them the utmost respect. Even with a naked Kelly McDermott, now thoroughly under wraps as he sat at the kitchen table, this pair of policemen was already watching the clock. Uninterested eyes floating about like overfed manatees; both had pulled out matching citation booklets, pens, and yet neither bothered putting one to the other. It was as though they hadn't even found the energy to agree on which one would be faking any interest in the situation.

And Patrick couldn't have been happier about it.

What would have ordinarily offended the slight sense of civic pride he had, Patrick now welcomed as a brilliant bit of luck. After all, these two had better things to do. A couple of little white lies, seasoned with a dash of big fat ones, and everything would turn out just fine.

"So." The mustached officer absently picked at his bristles. "You have a history of sleepwalking, Kelly?"

"I'm not sure..." Kelly's earlier excitement had abated, though none of it seemed to be out of respect for the situation. He remained with the paper clutched in his arms, blanket wrapped snugly around him. Tousled blond hair covering eyes that glanced over in Patrick's direction. "Do I have a history of sleepwalking?"

Officer Mustache turned to Patrick, raised an eyebrow.

"Well, there you have it, Officer..." Patrick did what he could not to take the officer's look and throw it in Kelly's face. "How's a guy going to know he's got a history of sleepwalking unless he's awake, am I right?"

"So does he, or doesn't he?"

"Not officially."

"Not officially," echoed the clean-shaven officer, eyes bowed slightly as though writing it down. He had remained with hat planted firmly on head, perhaps to detract from gray streaks infiltrating his sideburns. When he looked up, his eyes shot over toward Kelly. "And your parents are where?"

Kelly shrugged. "I don't know—"

"Hilton Head Island," Patrick interrupted.

"Hilton Head," Kelly repeated, nodding his head slowly.

"They're visiting a client," Patrick added. "Kelly's parents are lawyers."

"You seem a little out of it, Kelly..." Officer Mustache made his way around the table. "Eyes looking a little red there. You been doing any kind of drugs this morning, late last night?"

"No sir, Officer, sir," Kelly replied, appearing somewhat surprised at his own certainty.

"Seems like that's the only thing you *are* sure of."

"Yet, you don't even know where your parents are." Officer Sideburns rounded the other side of the table. "You sure you haven't been doing any drugs there, son?"

"I'm positive," Kelly affirmed, with a less-than-positive frown.

"He doesn't *do* drugs," Patrick volunteered, addressing all he could to Officer Sideburns. "Period. I mean, he's in great shape, just look at him..."

"We got a good enough look outside, thank you."

"If he's acting a little strange, it's because you woke him up," Patrick told them, all the while still wondering why Kelly was acting *beyond* strange. "I don't know if you know this, but waking him up in the middle of something like this can result in permanent brain damage. Some somnambulists have been known to die of shock."

Officer Mustache frowned. "Somnambulists?"

"Sleepwalkers."

"All sleepwalkers, or nonofficial ones like Kelly here?"

Officer Sideburns chuckled.

"Look, please..." Patrick felt circumstances tilting in an uncomfortable direction. Kelly's behavior was making attentive cops out of previously bored ones. Once interested in the situation, these two officers might actually get interested in their *jobs,* after which it was anyone's guess what they'd do to Kelly. Slap on the wrist or jail time, Patrick didn't feel like risking it. And so he reached into his treasure trove of bullshit and began handing out shiny gold coins. "Give Kelly a break, Officers. If he's not all that comfortable talking about his sleepwalking, it's only because he's never been diagnosed. And he's never been diagnosed because there's no telling what that might do to his career."

"Career?"

"I don't want to brag, but you're looking at the Buckeyes' starting quarterback come August." Patrick caught Kelly's confused expression out of the corner of his eye, charged ahead before the cops could notice. "Ohio State University, division one. Could've gone to Notre Dame, Michigan, Florida State, they were all clawing at each other for a piece of Kelly McDermott. Now, would either of you, given such an opportunity, want somnambulism as an official diagnosis? A disease that's been linked to vitamin D deficiency, hypoglycemia, and bone apoplexy?"

Officer Sideburns winced. "Bone apoplexy?"

"The worst kind of apoplexy," Patrick added, reminding himself to look up *apoplexy,* first chance he got. "The *worst* kind."

"Wait a second." Officer Mustache straightened, thumbs hooked onto his belt. "Did you say Kelly McDermott?"

Patrick swallowed. "Yeah."

"Kelly *McDermott?*"

"Yeah, we told you that when you brought him in—"

"Well, I'll be damned!" Officer Mustache smacked his citation book against his hand, followed up with the same against his partner's shoulder. "Richardson, this is Kelly McDermott! I read about him in the *Observer.* . . . I read about *you* in the

Observer, young man." Officer Mustache was focusing on Kelly once again. "Last month! They bumped Arizona to page two, for *high school football*. Talking about you being unstoppable. *Destiny's child*, that was the joke. . . . Remember that, Richardson?"

Officer Sideburns scratched his hat, sending it askew. "Well . . ."

"I *do* remember now!" Officer Mustache took a seat next to Kelly, who bobbed his head at a pacifying pace with everything he was told. "Yes. Yes, I remember you *had* applied to Ohio State, that's right! And you got in, well, that is *great*. Got the state finals this weekend, against . . ."

Patrick saw Kelly's eyes go blank at the sight of fingers snapping and decided to jump in. "Wilson. Going to play Wilson tomorrow."

"Going to *beat* Wilson tomorrow!" Officer Mustache laughed, stomping his foot and giving Kelly's neck a robust pinch. "I'm sorry, Kelly, we didn't know it was you. Did we, Richardson?"

"No, we didn't," Officer Sideburns agreed, growing bored once again.

Patrick masked his relief with a quick cough. "I'm sorry, anybody got the time?"

"Oh hell . . ." Officer Mustache checked his watch, forgot to share. "You boys should be getting to school pretty soon, shouldn't you?"

"Well . . ." Patrick smiled best he could. "Don't think Kelly can show up like this, now, can he?"

Officer Mustache shook the windows with his laughter, giving Kelly a few odd pats on the chest. "No, I don't suppose he could, now," he agreed, getting up and motioning Officer Sideburns toward the back door, laughter trailing behind him in giggly little bursts. He wiped a tear from his eye as Patrick opened the door, ushered them out onto the deck.

"Sorry about all this, Mr. McDermott," Officer Mustache called over his shoulder before turning to Patrick. "You keep an eye on him, son. Got a big life ahead of him."

"You bet," Patrick replied amicably.

"Shit." The officer grinned. "Time he gets to Ohio, he'll be playing *football* in his sleep!"

Another burst of satisfied laughter.

Patrick nodded, grinned widely, and shut the door.

Kept his pearly whites on display, cheeks straining, until he saw them safely around the corner. Patrick could almost hear his face creak back into neutral as he let out a shaky breath. Placed his arm against the door, and leaned his head against it. He closed his eyes, trying to get past what had just happened. It was over, done. Probably hadn't been more than five minutes, from the time the cops had caught Kelly dancing around outside . . .

Patrick opened his eyes, spun around.

Kelly's seat was empty.

"Kelly?" Patrick called out, voice cracking.

A muffled response came from nearby.

Patrick walked into the middle of the kitchen, gritty feet scraping against the floor.

The door to the walk-in pantry opened, and out came Kelly. The quilted blanket now wrapped around his waist, he held a box of coffee filters in one hand, a bag of Starbucks Italian Roast dangling triumphantly from the other.

"I *thought* I remembered my parents as big coffee drinkers," Kelly announced, pleased as a toddler with a block of wood. "I hope this coffee tastes as real as the rest of this feels.... Crazy, baby."

"Kelly ..." Patrick followed Kelly with his eyes, over to the coffeepot, where Kelly scooped up the plug, holding the cord in his fist like a dead black flower. "You don't drink coffee."

Kelly searched for an outlet. "You want some?"

"I don't drink coffee."

"Why the hell don't you drink coffee?"

"Because *you* don't, Kelly."

Kelly found an outlet, stuck the plug in. He paused, leaning against the counter, frowning. "And why the hell don't *I* drink coffee?"

"Because it's unhealthy." Kelly found himself repeating what Kelly had always told him. What Patrick, as a result, had always been proud to tell others. "Caffeine is addictive. It raises your heart rate, causes dehydration, which in turn can lead to gradual muscle damage. Not to mention that, as a stimulant, it keeps people from sleeping in ways that perhaps, you know ... we shouldn't be doing to ourselves...."

Kelly nodded thoughtfully. "This is all true. However, it does bring up an interesting question, doesn't it?"

"It does?" Patrick watched with disbelief as Kelly proceeded to prep the coffeemaker. Filling the pot, three scoops in the filter, smacking open the basket, plopping the filter in as he transferred water from pot to reservoir, all with the efficient speed of a lifelong coffee drinker.

"And that question is . . . ," Kelly continued, smacking the basket back into place and snapping the power on with a swift flick of his thumb. "What happens when dreamers drink coffee?"

Patrick desperately wanted to figure out what was happening to Kelly, only Kelly didn't seem to be giving him any *opportunity*, and so he entertained the question as best he could. "What do you mean?"

Kelly lifted himself up onto the counter. The ease with which he did it seemed to fill him with pleased astonishment, and he glanced down at his biceps. "Hey, check me out, I'm not half bad."

"Kelly, dreamers, what were you—"

"Shit, that smells good," Kelly said, leaning in close to smell the brewing coffee. He straightened, hands pressed against his thighs in a casual manner. "What I mean, Patrick, is what you yourself said. Coffee keeps you awake. That being the case, when we dream, and dream of drinking coffee, what then? I mean, it's been a while since I've dreamed. The shit they've got me on, side effects won't even let me dream, I still don't know how all this is happening but . . ."

Something caught his eye, and he turned to the row of windows behind him.

Patrick followed his gaze, tried to. Caught sight of a robin hopping around on the table outside. Chest an orange-rusty color, it cocked its head a few times with a 570 heartbeats-per-minute enthusiasm, let out a chirp.

Kelly raised his hand to the window. Caressed the spotless surface, as though patting the robin itself through some untold agreement with space and perspective.

Patrick leaned to his right, tried to catch Kelly's expression in the window's reflection.

Daylight. Too bright.

Though Kelly must have sensed it, and he turned back to Patrick with a sad smile.

At least, Patrick thought it was a sad smile. Seeing it on Kelly's face made him wonder. It was very much like trying to pick a professional acquaintance—the guy at Blockbuster, Waffle House, BP station—out of a lineup. Without the right environment, some people were simply unrecognizable. Members of the workaday world just walked on past each other on the streets, in parking lots and stores that weren't their own.

All like Kelly's displaced smile, suddenly gone as he continued to lecture. "Point is, to the best of my recollection, dreams elicit emotions. Right? You run into a monster, you're scared. Fall off a cliff, your stomach does a jig and the breath gets sucked right out of you. Kiss a girl, your heartbeat quickens. Hell . . . screw some pretty lady in your dreams, you *wake up* with a mess in your pants."

Patrick gave an awkward half nod.

"I don't mean you, Patrick," Kelly assured him, shadow of a smirk lost somewhere behind unrecognizable green eyes. "I mean everyone else." He leaped down from the counter and pointed in several directions at once. "Mugs?"

Without thinking, Patrick pointed to a cupboard in the far left corner.

Kelly jogged over, took down a coffee mug, and trotted back to the coffeemaker. "At any rate, if dreams have that kind of influence on our bodies, both sleeping and waking... well, then." Kelly dislodged the coffeepot and poured himself a cup. He turned to Patrick and held the mug under his own nose, eyes closed. Two deep inhalations, and his lids fluttered open; content and lazy, almost lecherous. "If we grant the premise, Patrick... what happens when we drink coffee in our dreams? Does our body treat it like a wet dream and act accordingly? Do we wake up? Or, being in a state of consciousness *within* the dream, does the caffeine affect *that* reality? Does all that roasted goodness, in fact, get further and further from waking us up, while sending us deeper and deeper into our dream?"

Kelly shrugged, took a deep breath. "Only one way to find out."

He raised the mug to his lips and took two large, scalding swallows. His eyes closed once again, cheeks imploding against his face, as though trying to suck out any rogue drops that had escaped his tongue. Eyes opened, rolled back momentarily in an eerie kind of ecstasy before righting themselves, lids wide, pupils dilated.

"Damn on a hot tin roof, that's good shit!" Kelly exclaimed, words peppered with pleasure-domed vowel sounds. "Oh! Damn, that is so—*Hell, yes!* Patrick, you've got to try some of this, amigo. It's like there's a party in my mouth and everyone tastes like the best damn coffee I've ever had!"

Patrick found the mug shoved under his nose, and his brain became one with his reflexes.

"No!" he cried out, swiping the coffee out of Kelly's hand, watching it fly across the kitchen.

Both of them watching it fly across the kitchen, through the doorway leading to the dining room. Soaring over the antique dining-room table, toward the glass cabinet filled with crystal plates and goblets, carrying with it fresh roasted coffee and the midflight certainty that some things simply can't be taken back.

It was with this understanding that Patrick barely flinched when the glass shattered. Glass doors to an antique cabinet housing a small fortune. The impact set off a chain reaction as the top shelf of finely polished mahogany collapsed, smashing down on the second shelf, smashing down on the bottom of the cabinet, obliterating all objects resting in between.

The world's most priceless sandwich.

Patrick found it in him to bring his hand to his mouth.

Two stray shards of glass broke away from the cabinet windows.

The afterthoughts of destruction.

Wind chimes, really.

Coffee dripping down onto the white carpet, and Patrick turned to Kelly.

Kelly did the same, only there wasn't the slightest bit of concern on his face. Less than concern, it was as though he actually had welcomed the destruction. As if it had proven some point. Kelly simply winked, went to get another mug, and poured himself another cup of coffee.

He took a sip, keeping a sly distance. "You sure you don't want any of this?"

Patrick shook his head. "You always said..."

"No, I understand...." Kelly brought the mug up to his lips. "I mean, good for everything I've ever told you, Patrick. It all sounds so wise, but..." Another sip. "Hell, this is just a dream, anyway. I'm thinking maybe wisdom's just not what's right for what little time we've got."

Patrick opened his mouth. A few seconds later, he spoke: "Sorry about the crystal."

Kelly gave the dining room little regard, shrugged. "Ah, well."

"Seriously, Kelly—"

"So, what are we doing today, Patrick?"

Patrick blinked. "We've got to go to school."

"School, eh?" Kelly walked over to the kitchen table, picked up the newspaper. "That's right, school's still in. That ought to be interesting...." He tucked the newspaper under his arm and gave Patrick a salute. "Guess I best get ready for school, then, huh?"

"Yeah," Patrick managed.

"All right." Kelly nodded.

He made his way past Patrick, down the hallway toward the front door. Found it was still open and closed it, not bothering to lock up. Then, without further ado, he plodded up the stairs.

Patrick took another look at the shattered remains of Kelly's family heirlooms.

Shattered glass and coffee stains soaking into the rug.

He heard Kelly rushing back down the stairs, saw him peek his head over the banister.

"Patrick!"

"Yeah?"

"We're taking the car to school, right?"

"Yeah."

Kelly's head bowed down in a strange act of humility. "Can I drive?"

Patrick squeezed his eyes shut, shook his head. "Yeah, you always . . . yeah, you can drive."

"Yeah!" Kelly proclaimed. His arm shot out from nowhere, raising the coffee toward a hanging chandelier. "See you in a few, Patrick!"

Once again, Kelly's footfalls shook the walls.

And Patrick was left in the kitchen.

He glanced over to the coffeemaker, saw the orange light staring at him.

The clock on the stove read a digital 8:15, and Patrick let himself get back to the basics.

Time to get ready for school.

Up above, second floor, the shower came to life.

Patrick strode to the coffeemaker and flipped the switch.

The orange light died out, and from somewhere upstairs, he heard Kelly singing.

#3

*P*atrick had simply assumed they were going to be late.

Even after Kelly stepped out of the shower, he remained in a state of cheerful disorientation. From his shoes to his keys, book bag and playbook, the entirety of Kelly's routine had to be retraced for him. He was like a large, dangerous child; even when Patrick managed to lead Kelly in the right direction, there was always another deviation to be dealt with. A brief couple of seconds sorting through his clothes, and Kelly had asked to be escorted to his father's closet. There he went about selecting a white dress shirt, black tie, and pants and a coat to match. They were nearly out the door when Patrick had to remind Kelly to get his cell phone. The two of them had bolted up the steps, Patrick leading his best friend through his own house, over to where his phone had been charging.

Kelly took one look at it, strode to the bathroom, and tossed it in the hamper.

"I got everyone I need, right here," he had said, winking. "Almost."

By the time they had finally made it out to the car, there was no doubt in Patrick's mind.

They were going to be late.

That was before Kelly jumped behind the wheel of his black Jaguar XK convertible, eyes glinting.

With wailing tires, Kelly backed out of the driveway and into the street. Hardly bothering to turn, he popped his back tires up onto the opposite curb, knocking over the neighbor's dark green rubber garbage can.

"Oops," Kelly said, as though mentioning the time to a passing stranger. With nothing more to contribute, he shifted into first and peeled out, flatlining his way toward the first intersection, where the stop sign was met without even an honorable mention. Speakers blaring, hip-hop station doing what it could to corrupt their young minds, Kelly took a sweeping right turn. He overshot his lane by a wide margin, suddenly nose to nose with a city bus speeding toward them.

Patrick's hands shot out, fingers sinking into the dashboard.

Strange what a luxury vehicle could accomplish, going eighty on thirty-five-mile-an-hour streets; with a casual nod, Kelly jerked the wheel, just enough to send them fishtailing back over to the right side of life, missing the bus by inches.

Ignoring Patrick's white-knuckled silence, Kelly revved the engine and offhandedly asked if they were headed in the right direction.

Patrick shook his head, pointed his thumb back behind them. "That way, Kelly."

"Oops," Kelly repeated, without an ounce of remorse or recognition.

He slammed on the brakes, sent the car skidding sideways. Came to a perpendicular halt in the road, Kelly's car taking its share out of both lanes, double yellow stripe bisecting his car nicely.

"Hey, Patrick." Kelly searched his surroundings with unhurried interest. "There a way to drop the top on this baby or what?"

A couple of cars screeched to a halt on either side of the Jaguar.

Patrick reached up above their heads, unhooked the handles.

He mashed down on a button between the two seats as the top began to yawn. Gears whirring, doing their best to please the rest of the world, already backed up in both directions. Morning commuters honked, pounded their fists against steering wheels, already rehearsing the story for coworkers, spouses, and drinking buddies.

All thanks to Kelly's sudden urge to have the top down.

"I make money for the money, 'cause money's got my back?" Kelly repeated radio-station lyrics, scoffing. "Can't believe I used to listen to this shit." He began fiddling with the knobs as the black top finally folded back into the car. "What's good around here, Patrick? What do *you* listen to?"

Choosing expedience, Patrick once again used his finger as the path of least resistance. Pressed 90.7, tuned right smack into some funk-minded jazz fusion.

The Charlie Hunter Trio, Patrick's angels marveled, calm as always. "Cueball Bobbin."

"Yeah!" Kelly grinned, fingers agreeing with high-hat cymbals. "If I had sunglasses, I'd put them on, this is *nice.*"

He twisted the wheel hard left and gave her all she had, back the way they came.

Hardly a second glance to the mess he'd made, blasting his way past trees, houses, all a blur.

Patrick winced as they tore past a parked patrol car, automatically sinking into his seat.

But in place of a siren, all that could be heard was a distant cry of a certain mustached officer: "YEAH, KELLY, STATE CHAAAAMPIOOON!"

Kelly laughed, threw his hands into the air.

Patrick felt that very air sandblasting his hair, violent whorls and eddies roaring in his ears all around him. Once again, no time to ask what was going on as another intersection loomed before them.

"*Left!*" Patrick yelled. "*Left, Kelly,* LEFT! MAKE A LEFT!"

Kelly's hands hit the wheel. A graceful downshifting arc sent them halfway onto the shoulder, gravel flying as Patrick began to wave his arms. Gasping for breath, hardly able to scream: "RIGHT, RIGHT TURN!"

"*Woo!*" Another stuntman's curve, and Kelly was loving it. "Guess it's like riding a bike, Patrick, all these years!"

Patrick twisted in his seat, desperately scanning for any damage they might have left behind.

One or two motorists stuck in gape mode, unsure of what they'd just seen.

Other than that, it appeared as though they had made a clean getaway.

Facing forward once more, Patrick saw the needle edging comfortably past seventy.

"Slow down, Kelly!"

"It's OK, Patrick!" Kelly cried out. "We're good!"

"We're going to get ourselves killed!"

"Not with you as my copilot!"

A slight dip in the road sent them sailing, tires slamming back down onto the asphalt with a jarring bounce. Patrick felt his teeth meet, two thunderbolt snaps keeping time with the music.

"Hey-oh!" Kelly called out, tailgating the car before him. He crossed over, hit the accelerator, and snaked his way out in front of the speeding Buick. With his mission now accomplished, Kelly kept his left foot planted on the floor. "All these close calls, Patrick, you think I would've shocked myself back awake by now!"

"You ARE awake!" Patrick roared over the clattering jazz drum, wondering if this is how old-timers in the fifties must have felt upon hearing that unbridled music, alien sounds signaling a dangerous new world, just over the horizon. "You are AWAKE, Kelly!"

"Then riddle me this!" Kelly gave a sly grin. He put a hand to his temple and mimed raising a pair of sunglasses up from his eyes. "Why haven't we hit a single red light on our way to school?"

The question reminded Patrick to give the road its due respect.

The road repaid him with a red light, some hundred yards away.

Some couple of seconds away.

"There!" Patrick yelled. "Red light, Kelly! Stop the car!"

"Uh-uh!" Kelly leaned forward, squinting. "I'm betting it's going to swerve first!"

"It doesn't swerve, it's a *red light*!"

"Green by the time I'm through with it!"

"KELLY!" Patrick screamed, knees curling up to meet his chest as the scenery folded around him. "FOR THE LOVE OF GOD, STOP THE CAR, THAT'S A RED..."

But Kelly's car had already made it through, blink of an eye.

A wink from some benevolent spirit, and rest assured, the light had most certainly turned green.

The rest of the ride unfolded in very much the exact same manner.

#4

*B*ill Montague stood before his homeroom class, looking out the nearest window.

Most of the classrooms at Wellspring Academy were on the ground floor, around four to a building. Each building was spaced out at varying distances, derisively referred to as compounds, and there generally wasn't much the windows had to offer: trees, birds, the occasional squirrel. A few of the rooms faced away from the surrounding forest, giving a view to the rest of the grounds. More buildings, unpaved gravel walkways cutting through lengthy strips of grass, already turning a coarse yellow from the heat wave. Not a lot to see out there, and yet this was how Bill Montague always began each morning.

On this particular morning, Patrick knew exactly what Bill was seeing.

Hustling past the window with Kelly in tow, he caught a glimpse of Bill observing his own private moment of silence. Arms behind his back, standing straight at five-eleven. A slight pitcher's mound rounding out his button-down short-sleeved shirt, blue and white stripes hanging over olive green cargo shorts. Gray hair pulled back into a thinning ponytail.

A casual observer might have dismissed him as a benign aging hippie.

Patrick knew better. "Let's move, Kelly."

Ever since Kelly had rocketed them into the parking lot and cut the engine, a quiet confusion had taken hold of his actions. Ignoring the hurried greetings from last-minute stragglers, he glanced around rapidly, eyes like incisors. A front-row skeptic searching for a flaw in the act of a master illusionist.

But Patrick's prompt seemed to bring him out of it; Kelly absently turned his shuffling into a light trot, and as a result, they coasted into homeroom at the very stroke of eight a.m.

Bill turned away from the window, eyes deceivingly indifferent behind clear aviator glasses. He glanced at the rest of the students, all seated around a group of rectangular foldout tables brought together in a giant horseshoe. His eyes went up to the clock. "Cutting it close there, Patrick, Kelly."

Patrick nodded, quickly inching around the table to secure a pair of empty chairs.

That's when he heard Bill's voice: "Kelly?"

Patrick turned. Saw Kelly waiting by the doorway, staring at his homeroom teacher.

"Is there a problem, Kelly?" Bill asked.

"No," Kelly said quietly. "No. It's good to see you, Bill."

Bill's lips gave nothing away, but his eyes granted a slight smile. "Nice duds, Kelly. Sit down."

Kelly glanced down at his suit and tie, then nodded. He made his way toward Patrick, mumbling a quiet *excuse me* for every student he passed. The two of them sat down, and Bill looked out the window once more, searching.

"A thought for you this morning," he told them, turning back to his flock. His hands met with two solid claps. "I know one or two of you have heard this one in my advanced chemistry class. Patrick..." Bill pointed in Patrick's direction, wearing a wide evangelist's grin. "My apologies, you're just going to have to ride this one out. As for the rest of you... I was once lucky enough to be golfing in Ireland."

The students all nodded, knowing Bill's penchant for good golf.

"I came to know a man by the name of James Finnegan. Golfed with him several times during my stay. And the man was amazing, a natural. Nobody would tell me how it was he never went pro, and I couldn't get a word out of him on the links. We'd go drinking afterward, and with the help of a couple of pints, he'd loosen up and turn talkative. The problem was, with the help of a couple of pints, he'd also turn incomprehensible. I mean, to me at least. His brogue was so thick, and he spoke so fast, that I literally had no idea what he was saying. The only reason I knew he was talking about golf was because everyone assured me that's all James Finnegan *ever* talked about. Here was this master, the greatest golfer you *never* heard of, and all his wisdom, his advice, *all* of it was lost to my ears...."

Bill pointed to his ears, just to bring the point home.

"But there were five words," Bill continued, "five words I always got. Five simple words that always shone through. *Are ya with me, laddie?* He'd interrupt himself every minute or so just to ask this question." Bill suddenly burst out with a litany of

Irish-sounding jabber. Slurred and over the top, brandishing a pantomime pint of Guinness in his fist, eyes askew before going lucid and saying: *"Are ya with me, laddie?"*

A few of the freshmen, sophomores gave him a laugh.

Even jaded seniors, juniors slipped him a smile.

Bill broke character with James Finnegan and shook his head, repeating the phrase once more: "*Are ya with me, laddie?* Every other minute he'd ask, and for fear of offending him, looking stupid, I'd nod my head, *oh, absolutely,* and let him go on with whatever it was he was saying. *Are ya with me, laddie... ?* The only five words from his mouth that I ever understood, and I never once took advantage of them."

Bill shrugged, stuffed his hands into two of the various pockets lining his shorts. "I could've learned a lot from ol' James Finnegan. But you all know where I'm going with this. Sure, don't be afraid to ask questions, don't be afraid to be the guy with his hand raised, we all know this. Not everyone's going to take the time to ask you if you're with them, so, of course, always be ready to step up without assistance. Though the most important lesson for you-all"—Bill leaned back against the chalkboard—"as members of this, I guess, *disorienting* existence we're stuck with... keep your eyes open at all times. Not just for those moments when you don't know Adam from Eve, but for those times when someone *else* might not be clear. When someone else might be seeking answers. Now, I'm a big fan of *mind your own business,* so use your better judgment. But don't forget that if you do always *mind your own business,* well, there will be several times at the end of your life when you will look back ... and regret not asking: *Are ya with me, laddie?*"

Bill smiled, pushed himself off the blackboard. He shot his hand in the air. "So let's have it. One freebie this morning, any question you want. Can't guarantee I'll have the answer, but anybody with a burning question gets to see how good it feels to let it out. Come on." Bill remained with his hand in the air. The younger students looked around nervously, while the older students looked around with their well-earned mixture of curiosity and disinterest.

Patrick saw Kelly raise his hand.

Bill begrudgingly lowered his arm, and sucked it up. "Well, I did say anybody, so ... what's on your mind, Kelly?"

And with all sincerity, Kelly asked: "Can you tell me what my class schedule is?"

The class division was once again clear in the ensuing laughter. Upperclassmen laughing at the perceived joke, underclassmen laughing because everyone else was. Kelly glanced around, curious, unflinching. Patrick thought he'd save his own flinching for whatever Bill had in store, as Bill was already padding out his retaliation with a cold stare. The laughter died real fast, trailed by a few tentative coughs.

Bill kept his eyes on Kelly for a full minute before bouncing once on his toes.

"No," Bill told Kelly. "I cannot tell you what your class schedule is, as I do not have a copy handy with me. However, this is a perfect example of what I was just saying. Patrick ..."

Patrick's head twitched. Unconsciously trying to stare at himself along with the rest of the classroom. He glanced around to cover for it, then took a breath. "Yeah, Bill?"

"Why is Kelly asking *me* for his schedule?" Bill asked, and it was clear now that he was taking this infraction with the same honesty as Kelly appeared to be displaying. "You're his best friend, you know his schedule cold. Obviously better than he does, at least. Why haven't *you* told him his schedule?"

Blindsided, Patrick reached for the first excuse he had: "He didn't ask."

"You really didn't see this coming?"

Patrick tried to get a better angle on the conversation, all thoughts failing him.

He gave up, and shook his head.

"Well, write his schedule down and give it to him," Bill instructed, plain and simple. "And next time, Patrick... antici-pate. *Are ya with me, laddie?*"

Patrick nodded reflexively, reaching into his bag for a pen.

Bill gave him one last squint. Another example in the making, before letting it go. "We've got some announcements," he declared, now peeking over his glasses at a xeroxed sheet of paper. "Let's get this day started already."

Patrick missed every announcement.

Finished up writing out Kelly's schedule just as homeroom wrapped up.

Slipped the sheet over to Kelly and told him to wait outside the door.

Patrick watched him leave, then approached Bill.

"What's on your mind, Patrick?" Bill asked, eyes focused on packing his green satchel.

Patrick kept his voice down. "I just wanted to talk to you about what Kelly asked."

"Uh-huh. I'm listening."

"It was . . . I just wanted to let you know that he was serious about that."

"I know."

"You do?"

"Gave him a serious answer, didn't I?" Bill paused to glance down at Patrick. He went back to packing his things, talking all the while. "Ever have one of those moments where someone asks you how old you are and for some damn reason or another, you have to actually think about it?"

"Can I ask you a favor, Bill?" Patrick found himself unconsciously pressing his palms together just below his chin. "Just this once?"

Bill slung his bag over his shoulder. "Of course, Patrick."

"Could you just . . ." Patrick struggled, words adrift. "Let it be known, to the other teachers, I mean . . . Let them know that Kelly's acting not himself, that he's acting weird? He woke up all strange this morning, and I just thought . . . If you could? So he doesn't get himself into any trouble."

Bill thought about it.

Patrick had expected such a reaction, though what came next was pure left field.

"You're a good friend, Patrick."

Before Patrick could summon the words, Bill went right

ahead. "Yeah, Kelly does seem to be a bit touched today. I'll put in a good word for him around the staff room. Wouldn't worry about him getting into too much trouble. Heard Ohio State finally won him over, so short of killing a man, doesn't look like this place is going to make much of a difference anymore."

Bill smiled, lips pressed together.

That's what regret sounds like, Patrick's angels whispered.

"You hear anything from OSU?" Bill asked.

"No . . . nothing yet."

Bill gave Patrick a smack on the shoulder. "Keep an eye on Kelly, best you can."

End of conversation, Bill's tan hiking boots were already taking him out the door.

Patrick caught his saxophone case staring at him from the table. He went over, picked it up, and shouldered his book bag. He stepped out the door, ready to guide Kelly in whatever way he could, and stopped short.

Kelly was gone.

Wandered away like a lost lamb.

Patrick glanced around in a slipstream of students. Bill's palm imprinted on his shoulder and final words floating in his head like alphabet soup.

Keep an eye on Kelly, best you can.

5

I t didn't start until after second period.

First period, Patrick had sat through an excruciating review session for his final in Medieval History. Not one of his strong suits, and time wasn't on his side that day. A watched kettle never boils. Same thing went for toasters and clocks. The seconds ticked off at the rate of one per minute, and Patrick's mind wandered further and further from his notes. Wondering if boiling a pot of water, *while* toasting bread and watching a clock, might actually make time go backward.

You're starting to sound like Kelly McDermott, his angels had admonished, slipping him notes beneath the teacher's steady drone. *The* new *Kelly McDermott.*

The New Kelly McDermott.

That was the term he had settled on.

Now trapped by the confines of everyday responsibilities, Patrick began what he could only describe as detoxification. No longer distracted by Kelly's bizarre behavior, he found he could no longer stop thinking about it. As time went by, he actually found himself sweating. His foot bounced nervously beneath his desk. Pen caps were chewed, notes became doodles, which soon enough became musical notation. He felt as though he was waiting for an inevitable explosion, eruption, some violent event just beyond his capacity to control.

Now that Patrick's angels had dubbed his friend the New Kelly McDermott, it was impossible to think of him as anything but. There was a new sheriff in town, but apart from that paranoid certainty, Patrick had little else to hold on to.

He was the first one out the door when class was dismissed. Ran fast as he could to Kelly's first-period class, bobbing and weaving between the rest of the students.

Patrick didn't know why he had expected Kelly to be waiting for him at the entrance. The rest of the students had already filed out, new ones rushing in like frigid air. He asked around, but nobody seemed to know where Kelly was. Patrick panicked, ran out to the parking lot to see if Kelly had simply jumped back into his car, itching for another chance at breaking the sound barrier.

The convertible was still there, and Patrick was going to be late for his next class.

Second period proved worse than the first, was asked to stay behind after a pen cap had popped out from between his nervous teeth and landed squarely in the teacher's herbal tea.

As a result, Patrick had already resigned himself to missing Kelly at the next juncture.

It was then, between classes, that people began approaching him. Each encounter with a different bent to it, a different inquiry into Kelly's behavior.

"What's up with Kelly? I ran into him between classes, and he was all happy to see me. Like he hadn't seen me in ages.

Like he even knew who I was to begin with; I don't think we've ever even *talked*."

"Hey, Pat, what's up with Kelly? I was just talking to him about Ohio State, and he *completely* blew it off. It's only been a couple of days, and it's like he didn't even care. It's like he didn't even know who I was, he looked right past me. *Weird*."

"I just saw Kelly in a suit and tie doing some kind of... I don't know, dance, with the ballet kids. Right in the hallway, he was grinning like I don't even *know*. What's *up* with him, anyway?"

Patrick had no answers, kept walking and talking as best he could. The grapevine continued to burn between third and fourth period. Some tendered stories about Kelly chatting it up with cliques outside his circle; talking music with the third-chair band kids, stopping to pick up some science geek's scattered notebooks. Others told of Kelly leading a full-class discussion on *cognito ergo sum* in their Philosophy 101 class, while further baffling accounts had Kelly demonstrating a flair for Spanish while seated in French 309.

That was the problem, ultimately.

While everyone could claim to know who Kelly McDermott was, not even a handful could claim to actually know anything *about* Kelly McDermott, who he *actually* was. And as a result, just about any interaction they had with him turned out to have the same diagnosis.

Kelly's been acting weird.

And the problem wasn't that Patrick disagreed with them.

He'd seen Kelly dance naked in the street, practically arrested, down two cups of coffee, turn stunt driver in his Jaguar

XK. There was no possible way to constructively argue with anyone's assessment of Kelly McDermott.

The problem, quite simply, was Patrick didn't have even the most remote explanation for it.

And so he bounced between comments like a clueless pinball. Fielding questions, comments, concerns, the go-to guy for all things Kelly. And for all his efforts, Patrick couldn't seem to find him anywhere.

Though one thing was for certain.

Kelly wasn't looking for Patrick.

By all accounts, Kelly was looking for Jenna.

Jenna sat on the bleachers with her knees together, toes pointed inward. She was fresh out of cheerleading practice. Only a small percentage of her was left to the imagination; her green and white skirt spanned from waist to mid-upper thigh, shorn halter top exposing her shoulders and flat stomach. Fine dark hair done up in small protruding pigtails.

Patrick remained standing, saxophone case by his feet, looking out over the carefully maintained grass. He found himself wishing he had a couple of stones to chuck. Wished this conversation were taking place elsewhere. The day had dragged on long enough for several school days, long enough for the rest of the school year.

Graduation, right around the corner.

Empty bleachers replaced with cooing friends and family.

Empty green replaced with folding chairs, caps and gowns.

"Strange thing about the jocks." Jenna put her elbows on

her knees, rested her chin on waiting hands. "They never eat lunch here. On the bleachers. This is their home, and yet the only people you see here are the mathematicians, chess club, bookworms. I wonder if it was them that noticed the lack of jocks, or the jocks that noticed this wasn't the place to be, come lunchtime."

"I don't know." Patrick pocketed his hands. "Never thought about it."

"Not that anyone comes out here that much anymore." Jenna wiped some sweat off her neck and sighed. "Too damn hot. Whole reason they moved the season was 'cause it was too damn hot in the fall, now it's too damn hot in the spring."

"I know."

"So what makes you think Kelly's going to find us here?"

"He's looking for you."

"Kelly takes his lunch with the football team."

"Usually, yeah."

"But today . . . ?"

Patrick wiped his palms on his jeans. "You're right. Nobody comes out here to eat anymore. I just wanted to get to you before he did."

Jenna let out a disbelieving chuff. "It's not like he's going around killing people."

"Less shocking, but no less strange."

"Probably nothing . . ." Jenna stood up. Bent down, scratched behind her left knee. "I remember once I spent an entire day positive I'd never heard the word *cat* before. I knew I had, of course. Didn't seem to do any good, though, all that knowing."

"This is more than that," Patrick said. "Or weren't you listening?"

"I was," Jenna assured him. "I guess I'm just having trouble imagining it."

"Imagining Kelly McDermott?"

"The *new* Kelly McDermott." Jenna smiled at Patrick. "What do you suppose that even means?"

Patrick never knew what to say to that smile. He only knew what he wanted to say, and that dog wouldn't hunt.

Instead, Patrick gazed across the football field. "I don't know."

Jenna joined him, pulled her hair back. "In a few more weeks, this place is going to be our last high school memory. They'll call us up one by one. Hand us our diploma. Bunch of us will probably send our caps flying in the air. Guess we'll all be *new* then, won't we? The new Patrick Saint?"

Patrick nodded. "The new Jenna Garamen."

"The new Kelly McDermott, perhaps?"

Patrick looked down at his sneakers. "As far as everyone else thinks, he's just acting strange. I wanted to talk to you, here in private, because I thought you should know it's more than that."

"Thank you." Jenna reached out, gave Patrick's shoulder a squeeze. "Thanks for telling me."

"It's OK." Patrick fumbled, reached down to pick up his case. "It's no problem."

"It is hot out here, though."

"Yeah."

"Come on." Jenna hopped down to a lower tier. Looked

up and extended her hand. "Let's go find the New Kelly McDermott."

Patrick took her hand, sweaty palms locking together.

He stepped down, felt her hand withdraw, said goodbye with his fingertips.

"Yuk," Jenna said, smiling.

She wiped her hand on the back of her skirt and skipped on down to the bottom.

Patrick tried to echo Jenna's sentiments, and cautiously followed her lead.

It was something he didn't like to think about.

Kelly and Jenna were together now. They had been for four years, and that was all that mattered. How it happened, the painful origins of an inevitable love affair, Patrick had safely tucked those memories away. Certain he wouldn't be opening that hope chest anytime again.

But then again, Patrick had never counted on the New Kelly McDermott.

Jenna and Patrick had been walking across the parking lot when history folded back on itself. Patrick heard Jenna's name, straight from Kelly's lips. He turned, a sluggish one-eighty, straight out of a bad dream. Dread sinking in, even at the ninety-degree mark, when he caught sight of Kelly standing at the other end. Patrick had almost forgotten the suit and tie; it gave Kelly a mythical quality, untouched by the scorching sun even as it warped the very air around him.

Kelly's eyes had already found their mark.

And as Patrick completed his turn, he saw Jenna staring back.

Eyes meeting across a proverbial room all dressed up as an asphalt wasteland.

Before Patrick could even think of closing his eyes, Kelly was already in front of her. Looking Jenna up and down with the same marvel he had bestowed on Patrick that morning. Of course, what was about to happen was a horse of a different color, and Patrick watched, helpless as Kelly sent his arms around Jenna and pressed his lips against hers.

It was no ordinary kiss. Kelly rocked her back in every last sense.

Even Patrick felt it, knew what this was. This was their first kiss all over again. All the excitement, discovery, all that Patrick had weathered was now back in full force. Worse than all that, it was real. Another building block, piece of the puzzle, the certainty that there was something happening here.

Eyes closed, even after their lips parted.

Jenna straightened, let out a shaky breath.

Patrick held on to his, petrified of what pathetic noise might escape if he let it have its way.

Too far, his angels lamented. *You've come too far to have this happen all over again.*

"Jenna," Kelly said, voice low. "Look at you."

"Wow, Kelly," Jenna replied, recovering somewhat. A single finger absently stroking her exposed stomach, almost getting caught in the belly-button ring with an indigo stone set in the middle. "I missed you, too."

"No, you have no idea," Kelly told her, grinning. Gave her a second, swifter kiss, stepped back. An artist admiring his own creation, and he began to laugh. "No, Jenna, you have no idea how much I missed..." Kelly turned to Patrick, gave the momentary impression that Patrick was about to receive a similar treat. Instead, Kelly sent his arms over both their shoulders, drew them close. "I missed the two of you so *much*."

The blast of a horn sent them all jumping away from each other.

A station wagon sat before them, engine purring impatiently, looking to get on with its day.

"Hey, come on, you two." Kelly linked his arms with theirs and led them farther into the parking lot. "Look at this, here we are. Together again. I swear, this day's been good to me as any that's ever actually happened."

Patrick kept a close watch on his steps, jostling against Kelly's exuberant strides. With Kelly in the middle, it was hard to gauge Jenna's reactions. The few times her face came into view from beyond Kelly's torso, all he could glimpse was a smile.

A wide smile, detailing every emotion that Patrick didn't seem to get out of the situation.

"So, Kelly..." Jenna broke free to face them as they kept walking. "Where are we going?"

"Well, the world is my oyster," Kelly replied.

"The world's always been your oyster," Jenna reminded him.

"We're going to his car," Patrick told her flatly.

"What makes you say that?" Kelly asked playfully.

"Because here we are," Patrick said, pointing to Kelly's Jag, top still down.

Kelly stopped, traced a finger over the paint job. "Well, I'll be damned, so we are."

This tepid admission of guilt was followed by the sound of wild cries and catcalls.

Idling in a lane several spaces over, Cody leaned on the horn of his enormous Ford pickup. It was one of those stylish models. Marketed as a useful aid in hauling five hundred tons' worth of construction supplies, driven by those without five hundred tons of construction supplies to haul. Though the handful of football players in the back of Cody's truck came pretty close. They gave the hydraulics a good workout, hopping up and down, basso voices calling out their star quarterback's name.

"Kel-ly! Kel-ly! Kel-ly!"

"Gonna stomp Wilson!" Cody roared out the open window. "FIGHT, FIGHT, OUTTA SIGHT! KILL, PANTHERS, KILL!"

The ensuing chorus of raucous cries was followed by cheers and applause from a number of passing students.

"Great." Kelly rolled his eyes. "These guys."

"Is it me, or has Cody been acting a little psychotic lately?" Jenna murmured, covering her mouth with her fist. "I mean, more so than usual?"

"Yo, Kelly!" Cody yelled, punching the steering wheel a few more times. *"You coming to lunch, motherfucker, or what?"*

Unabashed, Kelly threw his head back and laughed.

Patrick saw Cody's face smolder, wounded ego visible along his twitching jawline.

"Unbelievable . . ." Kelly shook his head, leaped into his car, and started her up. "Let's get the hell out of here before my brain collapses."

Jenna was more than happy to comply. She sat on the passenger door, and slid backward into the car. Legs up in the air, skirt hitched, revealing snug green underwear. With her head in Kelly's lap, she laughed and motioned for Patrick to join them.

The rest of the players in Cody's truck had grown silent, still struggling with Kelly's cold shoulder. In the front seat, Cody shouted Kelly's name, team spirit replaced with a demanding snarl.

For all the bullets Patrick had taken for Kelly that morning, he knew this wasn't a fight he wanted.

"Going once!" Kelly announced, revving the engine.

Patrick tossed his case into the car and dove in as Kelly pulled out and raced for the driveway.

"So where *are* we headed?" Jenna asked, sitting up.

"Patrick!" Kelly called out over his shoulder. "Can you get us to Long Street?"

Patrick nodded, scrambling for the safety belt.

Even with the school fading behind, he thought he heard Cody shouting after them one last time before Kelly really put the pedal down, and then they were gone.

#6

The funeral home's proprietor stood outside his place of business, watched as the three of them came to a stop across the street. They hopped out of the convertible with little reverence for the dead, and strode up to the pool hall.

Early-afternoon sun shone dully off large polymer windows that stretched across the front of the pool hall like a letterboxed film. Two of the windows were stenciled with large white letters against a green background, spelling out their destination:

ON THE RAIL

Kelly pushed hard against the wooden door, an easy swing inward. He walked through without the slightest hesitation. Patrick and Jenna let the door slam in their faces, unsure of whether to follow. There, in the center of the door, a small, hand-crafted plaque spelled out the house rules:

> NO UNDERAGE DRINKING.
> NO MISBEHAVIN'.
> NO DRINKS ON THE TABLES.
> NO FASCIST REGIMES.
> NO DISRESPECTING THE HELP.

Patrick and Jenna exchanged a look before the door swung open again.

"Are you two coming in?" Kelly asked. "Or am I going to have to take my game to the streets?"

Patrick decided it was best not to find out what that meant, and went ahead.

"Afternoon," the bartender greeted them with a friendly smile. He was somewhere in his midtwenties. Tall, thickset. Massive, even, though hardly out of shape. Brown skin light enough to allow for all sorts of racial presuppositions. Wide smile set for a welcome, eyes roguish enough to recognize the same sentiment in others. He scratched the back of his head with a pen, muscles bulging beneath a green jersey with nothing more than the word HERE printed on the front. "Welcome to On The Rail: rock-and-roll capital of the universe."

Patrick took a look around, searching for anything to back this up.

Sunlight filtered through the windows, stretching out over ten regulation-sized pool tables. Five on the left, laid out in horizontal dashes. Five on the right, four of them perpendicular to the rest. Brass chains hung down from the ceiling, dangling fluorescent lights over each table. Checkered tiles on the floor, alternating white and green. Green walls, white cracks at odd intervals. Foosball tables in the far left corner. Jukebox back by the men's room.

The place had a well-worn look to it.

Old as hell, but in it for the long haul.

Not another soul in sight apart from two barflies, reflecting over bottles of Miller Lite.

"Rock-and-roll capital of the world?" Jenna let out her pig-tails and shook her hair free.

"Yeah, that was a joke," the bartender announced. "Don't give me any shit, I'm stuck here till two a.m. Got to get my gig-gles any way I can, gosh-damn it."

"Gosh-damn right," Jenna agreed, stepping up to the bar and running her hands over the aging wood. "Gosh-damn right."

"Nice outfit." The bartender grinned.

Jenna bent sideways a little to look past her breasts, down to her skirt. "Yes, I'm a cheerleader."

"Didn't think it was my birthday."

"Don't give me any shit, I can leave anytime I want."

The bartender threw his head back and let loose with two succinct syllables: "Ha! Ha!"

It almost seemed sarcastic, but Patrick quickly realized that this was simply how he laughed.

"All right." The bartender pointed his pen at Patrick. "What do you want to drink?"

Patrick searched the room once more.

Spotted Kelly at a pool table, setting up a rack of balls.

"He can't help you," the bartender said with a dismissive grin. He backpedaled to a tall industrial-sized fridge with a glass door. Skimming past the rows of beers with his finger, he reached the bottom shelf and began rattling off all age-appropriate options. "I got some Kiwi or Strawberry Snapple, Snapple Diet Green Tea, Stewart's root beer, Stewart's Orange 'n Cream, water, Coca-Cola–"

"Iced tea," Jenna interrupted.

"Orange soda," Patrick added.

The bartender had their drinks before them in two shakes, and he pointed toward the back.

"Tell your boy over there it's four dollars per hour, per person."

"Thanks," Patrick managed, and wandered toward Kelly. His footsteps sounded exceptionally crisp against the unfinished floor. Green-felt tables watching as he approached his destination.

"How's your game, Patrick?" Kelly asked.

"Um..." Patrick placed his orange soda on the edge of the table. "I don't really play that—"

"Hey!" the bartender called out across the room. "Drinks off the table, son!"

Patrick mumbled a hasty apology and moved his drink to a nearby stool.

"Grab a stick," Kelly said, sucking back on a root beer. He smacked his lips. "Go on, Patrick, let's see what you've got."

Kelly jumped up onto a wooden riser, home to five chairs bolted into place. All with seats flipped up like wooden underbites. He flipped one down and settled in. Crossed his legs and motioned for Patrick to get going.

Patrick approached the nearest rack, not sure what he was looking for in a cue stick.

He picked one at random and returned to the table.

Jenna had parked herself on the chair next to Kelly. Legs crossed, diet iced tea resting against her knee. She was smiling broadly, enjoying her little stint as the pool shark's girl.

83

Royalty, Patrick's angels concluded with a quiet laugh. *All hail to the queen.*

Kelly kissed Jenna on the cheek and hopped down. "Want to lag for the break?"

"Do I want to *who* for the *what?*"

"Don't worry about it." Kelly pulled out a quarter. "We'll flip for it."

Patrick stared down at the balls. The few times he and Kelly had played pool, it had always been eight-ball. Eight-ball on crappy coin-operated tables. Now he found himself looking down at a diamond-shaped rack, one through nine, enough green between pockets to cover a cemetery.

"I don't even know what we're playing," Patrick said.

"Nine-ball."

"What's nine-ball?"

Kelly smacked the palm of his hand against his forehead. "My bad."

"Huh?"

"OK." Kelly leaned against the pool table, picked up a cube of blue chalk. He began to expertly file the tip of his cue, talking the whole time. "Nine-ball's about as simple as it gets. We got nine balls on the table, one through. Your object ball's always going to be the lowest one on the table."

"Object ball?"

"Meaning, you always have to hit the lowest ball on the table first. If the lowest ball is the one, you hit the one. If the lowest ball is the two, then go for the two. Generally, this means that the balls are pocketed in numbered order. You sink the three, then the four is the lowest ball, so you sink that. Sink the four, then you sink the five, all the way up to the nine ball."

Patrick glanced up at Jenna.

Chin resting on her palm, pinky trapped in the corner of a fascinated grin.

"Now, the nine ball is the only ball that wins the game," Kelly continued. "I could sink one through eight, miss the nine. Then you come along, drop the nine, and you win. Same thing goes at any point in the game. If the one is the lowest ball on the table, and it happens to be right next to the nine, which happens to be right next to a pocket... Well, you can hit the one to combo with the nine and win. You got it?"

Patrick did.

Thing of it was, Kelly's sudden knowledge of nine-ball seemed more irrational than any of the ignorance he'd displayed over the entire day. Patrick had understood every word. It was as clear as Kelly had been, and yet he found himself shaking his head.

"You want me to play a game on my own?" Kelly suggested. "Let you have a look?"

"I'll play you" came the bartender's voice.

The three of them turned their attention, saw the bartender leaning against the thirty-foot shuffleboard table dividing the space. Couple of empty beer bottles in his hand, paused en route to further duties. His perpetual grin wasn't challenging, wasn't demeaning. Just curious, looking for a way to kill time, and Kelly nodded. "Race to five?"

"Sounds good."

"Call it."

"Heads."

Kelly sent the quarter spinning.

Two minutes later, the thunderclap of Kelly's break sent a spectrum of colors across the green felt. Kelly stepped back and watched, waiting for the second law of physics to catch up. When the dust settled, the two and four balls had found their demise in two separate pockets. The rest were spread out nicely, enough to warrant an impressed nod from the bartender.

"Gosh-damn. Not bad, son."

" 'Preciate it," Kelly said with a respectful squint, and began to circumvent the table.

Patrick had taken his place up in the cheap seats, alongside Jenna. He sat, drink in one hand, cue stick resting against his shoulder, watching Kelly imagine the possibilities. The detached calm was a welcome relief for Patrick. It was one of Kelly's principal traits. Something to hang on to as the clock over the bar crawled past the one o'clock hour.

Then Kelly bent low over the table and sent the cue ball smacking against the one.

A shining streak of yellow, right into the corner pocket.

In four consecutive shots, Kelly rounded the table, putting the three, five, six, and seven to bed. He missed the eight by a hair, leaving the bartender to clean up the eight and nine. The pair of them paid their passing respects, reracked, and moved straight on to game two with Swiss-watch precision. Game two went by with the same speed and efficiency, Kelly moving in to secure the win with two consecutive bank shots on the eight and nine.

Three racks later and the count was 2–3, Kelly up by one game.

"My name's Casper," the bartender told Kelly, centering the balls for their next game. "Casper Noel."

"Kelly McDermott," Kelly said, extending his hand.

"Oh shit, son..." Casper eagerly enveloped Kelly's hand and shook it senseless. "Heard a lot about you, young man. Twenty-nine touchdowns, fifty-two hundred yards, sixty-eight completions. Gosh-damn, heard everyone was looking to get a piece of you. Where'd you settle on?"

"Ohio State, apparently."

"Congratulations. Let me tell you, they could use you."

"I'll take your word for it."

Casper leaned in and whispered something in Kelly's ear.

Kelly's eyes brightened, head nodded.

Casper headed over to the bar, checking in on the regulars.

Kelly made his way over to the seats, smiling. "Feels good to be playing again."

"You're playing good, Kelly." Jenna hopped down and gave him an embrace, kiss on the cheek. She gave his blond hair a tousle. "Got some skills there."

"Going to check out the jukebox. Anything you want to hear?"

Jenna shook her head and sent Kelly on his way.

"That's interesting," Patrick said sullenly. "*Got some skills.* That's your contribution?"

"Contribution to what?" Jenna asked, sipping her diet tea. "You saw him shooting."

"Shooting like he's been spending nights and weekends in here."

"How do you know he hasn't?"

"Because I'm with him every second of every day," Patrick whispered harshly. He glanced over to the jukebox, saw Kelly with his back to the room. "This isn't just Kelly acting strange. This isn't bizarre disorientation. All that was just Kelly not knowing his ear from his ass. But to suddenly walk up to a pool table and give this bar guy—"

"Casper."

"Casper, sure, for Kelly to beat him . . ." Patrick struggled with the words. "This is the first time today Kelly seems to know what he's doing. This is Kelly McDermott knowing what he's doing."

"Kelly's always known what he's doing."

"So have we."

"We've always known what we were doing?"

"We've always known who Kelly *was*."

"Hey, Patrick!" Kelly called out from the jukebox. "Got this guy here on the box. Herbie Hancock. The album is . . . *Head Hunters*. You want me to play a few from here, jazzman?"

"Uh . . . sure."

"What tracks?"

"First one's seven minutes long, it'll do."

Before Patrick could get back to his previous conversation, Casper approached the table toting a bottle of Pabst Blue Ribbon. "What instrument do you play?"

Patrick didn't immediately realize the question was his to field. "What?"

"Jazzman. What instrument do you play?"

"Sax."

"Alto?"

"Tenor."

"Damn." Casper jerked his head back with impressed surprise. "Small dude like you filling a tenor. I'm surprised I can't see your lungs through your shirt." Casper laughed heartily at his own joke as the jukebox kicked in. "You write your own music?"

"Yeah."

"Got any good songs done?"

" 'Round five hundred."

Casper waved a hand out, batting away at Patrick's claim. "You lie."

Patrick frowned. "No, it's true."

Casper pointed to Jenna. "That true?"

Jenna looked embarrassed. "I ... don't really know, Patrick never really–"

"Kelly!" Casper called over his shoulder. "Your boy here solid?"

"Pure titanium!" Kelly called out from the jukebox.

"Five hundred songs," Casper mused. "You got a problem with standards?"

Patrick shook his head. "I love them. But as far as playing goes, a musician should only do standards if he's performing for a crowd who's expecting them...."

"So where have you played around here?"

Patrick felt as though it was a trick question. "I play in the school band, at basketball games–"

"No, I mean where have you *played*."

"Uh . . . my room, really, is the only place–"

"Balls to that, son!" Casper actually looked upset at the thought of Patrick playing for an audience of zero. "Look, tomorrow night, after the game . . . you three should come over here after closing. I'm gonna have a little lock-in. Drink some bourbon, shoot some pool, just a select few. You guys come along, and Patrick . . . you and me are gonna jam."

Casper was displaying more faith in Patrick than he was used to hearing.

Before Patrick could accept, Kelly half sauntered, half danced his way up to Casper. One hand on his belt, the other raised alongside his head, palm out. He saw Casper extend the beer toward him, did a little half spin, and accepted.

"Keep it on the down low," Casper told him. "What do you drive?"

"Some kind of sports car." Kelly shrugged. "Convertible."

"Which one of your friends is going to be driving it later?"

Kelly reached into his pocket.

Patrick had turned his attention to Jenna, and he missed the silver glint of keys flying toward his head. Directly into his head, complete with a yellow flash of pain as the keys bounced from his temple and onto the floor. Everyone burst out in a bout of laughter overshadowed by concerned questions. Followed by amused swearing and further inquiries.

"I'm all right," Patrick said, shaking his head. "Ouch. I'm OK."

"That's right, hang tough." Kelly scooped up his keys and slapped them into Patrick's hand, turned to address the nearly empty room. "Here sits a brave individual. Somebody get this man a dragon to slay."

Kelly raised his beer and winked.

Patrick remained half crouched with his hand against his temple. The shock of blunt-force trauma forgotten as he witnessed Kelly with his head tilted back, eagerly taking down half his beer in three large swallows. On his periphery, Patrick saw Jenna wearing a less pained version of his own expression.

Kelly's selection of electronic funk/jazz kept on and on.

He removed the Pabst from his mouth with a satisfied smack. Kelly shook his head, wet lips smiling, elated eyes getting misty. "Oh yeah . . . It's been *too* long."

"When was the last time you had a drink, son?" Casper asked.

"Kelly doesn't drink," Patrick said, more as a footnote to his own thoughts.

"Oh really?" Casper gave a little fake laugh. Then, as though actually taking the time to consider Patrick's statement, he burst out with a loud, authentic cackle. "OK, then. Guess I'd better *not* go back to the bar and get Mr. McDermott another *not* beer, before he doesn't *not* finish this one. . . . Kelly?"

"Set 'em up, we'll be knocking 'em down." Kelly went in for another swallow, then paused. "Got a smoke for me, Casper?"

"Don't smoke. Wait, though . . ." Casper dug into his shorts and pulled out a pack of Camels. Tossed them onto the table. "Hank left those last night, help yourself. Got matches in there and everything." Casper turned and strode back to the bar, calling out: "Go 'head and break, Kelly!"

"Well, thank you, Hank," Kelly murmured, not a second's

meditation over who Hank might actually be. He picked up the pack of Camels, procured a smoke. With nothing more than the fingers on his right hand, he bent back the matchbook cover, guided a single match toward his thumb, and snapped a spark. The match flared up, and Kelly introduced it to his cigarette with two rapid puffs. He shook out the flame, took a deep drag, and released a plume of weightless smoke into the air.

"Yeah..." Kelly had another tug of his beer and set it down at Jenna's feet. He took a moment to stare at her legs. Reached out with a single finger and slowly traced from her knee down to her ankle. He looked up and smiled.

Jenna smiled back, genuinely touched, somehow.

Patrick waited until Kelly was at the far end of the table before leaning his head closer to Jenna.

"So here's Kelly," Patrick murmured. "Having a cigarette, pounding beers in a pool hall, on a school day during school hours, and listening to *jazz.*"

"Actually asking you what it was *you* wanted to hear," Jenna mused, turning to him with a raised eyebrow.

"Well, whatever." Patrick shrugged it off. "Is none of this even... you really don't have anything to say about all of this?"

"I'm not denying how strange it is."

"More than strange."

"I know it." Jenna glanced across the room, thinking. "I know this isn't... I know there's something happening here, but... here's the thing."

"What?"

"Seeing him here, now, like this... It just occurred to me. Have you ever actually seen Kelly McDermott happy before?"

Patrick blinked. He opened his mouth to a few seconds of static before forcing it out. "Sure."

"Like this. Actually happy?"

"Something's wrong with him. What difference does happy make?"

Jenna straightened her skirt, hesitated. "It's just nice that now at least one of us is."

"Hey, Patrick!"

Patrick turned, saw Kelly pointing the cue stick toward the waiting rack.

"Nine ball, on the break." Kelly grinned with fire in his eyes, smoke curling up from the cigarette lodged between his teeth. "Just you watch."

"He certainly seems happy," Patrick commented dully.

"And happy can't hurt, can it?" Jenna asked.

Kelly bent over and lined his sights up with the cue ball.

The clock on the wall read five past two as Kelly graced the table with another sledgehammer break.

Come five past four, all three of them were sitting in the principal's office.

#7

There had been a time when Wellspring Academy had gone by the name Pleasant Evergreen. Originally founded in the early fifties, it was one of the few southern schools that had desegregated in the days before *Brown v. Board of Education*. Built on the notion of individual students, individual needs, Pleasant Evergreen had always been considered the runt of the private-school litter. No grades, no real separation between academic and moral education, students were given evaluations, in contrast to the commonplace As, Bs, and Cs that were meant as an easy way to sum up educational abilities. Always short of funds, never short of contempt, the school had a track record of drawing jeers from both private and public educators.

They'd certainly never had a sports program worth talking about. Their soccer, baseball, and track fields occupied an all-purpose, poorly cultivated sprawl of sparse grass and arid, rocky soil. Their basketball court was built in an abandoned airplane hangar. No football to speak of. The game was considered too violent, equipment too expensive, student body too small to produce enough players who weren't too small.

Then, shortly before the new millennium, an anonymous donor dropped a million dollars on the school. Before word could get out, the administrators had hired a slew of contractors to build a state-of-the-art gym, complete with a weight room, swimming pool, and fully functioning locker rooms. A large portion of the surrounding forest was leveled, future site of their new soccer stadium. Two thousand seating capacity, complete with its own irrigation system for the summer months. It was then revealed that the donor's one caveat for the million was that every penny be spent on a better sports program for Pleasant Evergreen.

Shortly thereafter, Pleasant Evergreen changed its name.

As for what other changes came to be, the stories varied as memories of Pleasant Evergreen's past faded into the present of Wellspring Academy. While student evaluations remained, a secondary *point* system, easily transcribed into A through D, was added for the sake of securing slots in more prestigious, traditional universities. Teachers were still referred to by their first names, though titles were sneaking in through the cracks. Pleasant Evergreen was once helmed by a head teacher. Now Wellspring Academy was helmed by a principal.

Principal Matt Sedgwick, who had been there since Patrick had started.

The very principal who was now eyeing Patrick, Kelly, and Jenna from behind his desk.

"I'm a little surprised at this," Principal Sedgwick told them. His voice was soft, very much like the rest of his features. His eyes were blue, kind, and wavering. Middle age had imbued him with a head of thinning, semicurly gray hair. Tall as he was, a little over six feet, he moved with delicate motions, as though wary of disturbing the very air around him. "This is serious. You left campus without signing out. You ditched your classes, nobody had any idea where you were. . . . I know the year is ending and . . . Kelly, I understand everything has been finalized with Ohio State."

Patrick shifted his eyes. Looked past Jenna and over to Kelly, who nodded. "Yeah."

"Well, that doesn't mean you can just do whatever you like for the remainder of the year. The same goes for you, Patrick. And you, Jenna. I understand neither of you have heard from . . ." Sedgwick let it hang, waiting for them to fill in the blank.

"No," Jenna replied softly, hands in her lap.

"And Patrick?"

Patrick removed his finger from between his teeth, felt his nail tear. "No, Principal Sedgwick."

"It's Matt, please." Sedgwick went conciliatory, maintaining his softness. "And I'm sure you'll both get in, sometimes it takes a while. . . ." He turned to Kelly, trying to bring it all together. "You realize that just because you . . . Kelly, your friends may not . . . Look, we all hope for the best, for all of our students, but you can't just act . . . you're not done here, you–"

"*–can't just act as though your future's already waiting for you,*" Kelly said in perfect unison with Sedgwick. Perfect unison, as though mouthing the words from a favorite movie.

There was a quiet skip on the record as Patrick, Jenna, and Sedgwick did their best to wrap their heads around that moment. Patrick and Jenna, for their part, weren't able to get past it quite as fast as Sedgwick. Not that he let it slide.

Sedgwick's face took an instant turn for the worse. Stern and wounded, as though face to face with the dark side of nature, the incapacity to understand how some animals can bring themselves to eat their young.

"Kelly, I don't know what you think you're doing–"

"Maybe not," Kelly interrupted. He leaned back with his hands folded over his flat stomach, legs crossed. "But if we broke the rules, if *I* broke the rules, then this meeting must be about . . . I don't know, setting an example. Would you like to punish me now? Because we can do that if you like. If that's what you want."

"I want you to *understand* what you did."

"I know exactly what I did," Kelly said, just the facts. "I woke up both confused and happy to find myself sleeping in my room. Definitely confused, but certainly excited. I've been carrying it with me all day, and after a few hours at school, I thought I'd take it on the road."

Patrick had a choice between staring at the ground in hopes of lessening the impact of Kelly's impudence, or ogling him with the same appalled scrutiny as Sedgwick. Unable to help himself, he went for the latter. Stared past Jenna, who remained with her eyes downcast, even as Kelly kept right on: "I convinced Patrick and Jenna to go out with me to lunch. Instead, I took them to On The Rail, where I proceeded to play a few games of nine-ball. Have a few beers, a few smokes–"

"Wait, *beers?*"

"And smokes, with Patrick as my designated driver, so no harm done. I was in a hot race-to-five with the bartender, listening to some jazz, and enjoying this once-in-a-lifetime opportunity. Jenna wanted to change out of her cheerleading outfit, pick up her things, so I got Patrick to drive us back here. I understand exactly what I did, and now that I've done it, it's time to pay the piper. And I'm not sorry, sir. But I am certainly ready."

Sedgwick's Adam's apple worked in and out, popped the words out in terse bursts. "I don't think ... I don't appreciate the tone you're taking, you insolent ... You have to understand ... You really think this is the way we talk, we don't talk this way at Pleasant Evergreen—"

"Wellspring Academy, I thought."

"You can't just talk *that way!*"

"Talk what way?" Kelly asked, guilt free. "I told you the *truth.*"

"You did no such thing," Sedgwick snapped.

"Say what you will, sir, but I know what I know; That you beat me at the mart, I have your hand to show: If the skin were parchment, and the blows you gave were ink, your own handwriting would tell you what I think."

"What?"

"That's Shakespeare ... ," Kelly informed him. "And if I *had* lied to you, we wouldn't be having this conversation. That's all I'm saying."

"You were drinking *beer!*"

Patrick had seen the principal offended on several occasions; it was almost a matter of routine at Wellspring Academy; a politically correct holding pattern that had a particularly strong effect on most of the administrative staff. But this was more like rage, and he wasn't sure if Matt Sedgwick was equipped to handle such emotions.

"During school hours!" Sedgwick added, pale face flushing.

"I've *admitted* as much," Kelly insisted.

"Well…" Sedgwick stood from his seat, taking full advantage of his height. His voice became haughty, anger subsiding as though he remembered he had actual, binding authority over his students. "This just went from bad to worse, Kelly. And all of you are going to have to face some serious consequences—"

"All of us?" Kelly voiced what both Patrick and Jenna were thinking. "All of who? This was my mistake."

"And sometimes others suffer because of the mistakes we make," Sedgwick replied smugly. "Maybe this will teach you that."

"I *know* that." Kelly shot up from his seat. "But my mistakes aren't about to get them in trouble. *You* are. Just to prove a point that doesn't need proving!"

"You can sit down, Kelly."

"Or what, you gonna punish my *chair*?"

"That's it—"

The door to Sedgwick's office burst open, and Mike Redwood's voice beat his body across the threshold: "What the *hell* is going on?"

Kelly and the rest turned and saw the vice principal filling the doorway.

He stood a good couple inches below Matt Sedgwick, carried a good couple pounds extra around the face, torso, and stomach, but his sturdy foundation had helped him carry it well into middle age.

Patrick glanced back, caught Sedgwick frozen in apologetic terror.

"Wow..." Kelly blinked, as though battling a mirage. "Coach?"

"Kids?" Redwood motioned toward the door. "Would you step outside, please? I'd like to have a word with Matt, alone."

Patrick stood along with Jenna, let out a quiet breath.

"Outside the building, if you would," Redwood added gruffly, staring hard at Sedgwick. "It's going to get a little loud in here."

Jenna didn't miss a beat.

Seeing that Kelly was stuck in the moment, Patrick took hold of his arm and gently maneuvered him through the door. He reached back and closed it with a soft click.

Even as the three headed toward the exit, the shouts were already following them down the hallway. Commanding and laced with profanity, Redwood's diatribe appeared to be cutting right to the chase. Patrick glanced back one last time to assure himself that they really had escaped the lair of the white worm.

This time, his relieved sigh came out quite audibly as they left the administrative building.

Cody was waiting outside.

He, Zack, and a few others from the team, dressed in their practice clothes. Grass clippings and sweat stains covered them from head to toe. All leaning against the rail to the handicap ramp. It creaked menacingly as a couple of them thrust off, standing to attention at the sight of Kelly McDermott. A mixture of sluggish questions filled the air, only one emerging with any clarity.

"Everything all right in there, Kelly?"

"I don't know," Kelly replied truthfully.

"Coach is in there, straightening it out, though, right?" someone asked.

Kelly glanced back, unconcerned. "Seems so."

"Seems," Cody piped up, thick arms crossed over his chest. "Is my father in there, or not?"

"Yeah, he's in there."

"Yeah, we were out practicing a little, you know . . . how we always do." Cody's muscles twitched. He slowly ran his hand through his thick dark hair, a trait that seemed to run in the family. "Someone told us Sedgwick nabbed you guys. Took you to his office, so we sent in the marines." He clapped his hands, held out his palms. One of the players automatically tossed him the football. Cody trapped it between his palms with a loud smack. "Is this because you guys took off this afternoon?"

"We came back for Jenna's bag," Kelly told him. "And Sedgwick saw us, you're right."

"So this doesn't have anything to do with . . ." Cody let the rest go unspoken.

The rest of the team leaned forward, waiting.

Anticipate, Patrick's angels reminded him, and he shook his head on Kelly's behalf. "No."

"Oh..." Cody nodded, cradling the ball under his arm. "Just in case, you know... Edmund didn't learn his lesson, or maybe... someone else talked to Sedgwick."

"What are you guys talking about?" Jenna asked, stepping to Kelly's side.

"Football," Cody told her. "Nothing the jersey chasers need to worry about."

Jenna rolled her eyes. "Real nice."

"Ain't no rule book I've ever read that says I've got to *be* nice."

"Ain't no book you've ever read, *period.*"

"Kelly, you want to ask your bitch to take a walk?" Cody snapped, and launched the football.

Kelly's arm shot out in an arc, struck the football down in midflight. It bounced unevenly down the handicap ramp, between the legs of the players not fast enough to pick up the fumble.

"Maybe *you* ought to take a walk," Kelly suggested, unaffected by the sudden attack. "You look a little freaked out, might help to clear your head."

"What's your *fucking problem,* Kelly?"

"Hey, hold on, guys..." Patrick slid between the pair, felt the tension flowing like electricity. A quick inventory of everyone's face suggested the same spirit of a long-awaited mutiny. "Come on, Cody. I was there, Sedgwick was just trying to lay down the law. Same as he tried two years ago, remember that? And remember who had the final say? This is no different, nobody's got *anything* to worry about. All right?" Patrick looked from one to the other. "Kelly, Cody, all right?"

"Who cares?" Kelly said abruptly, if not a little on the cheerful side. "We're getting out of here."

Jenna didn't hesitate.

Kelly took her by the hand and led her away.

"I've heard things about you, Kelly!" Cody called after him.

Kelly kept right on walking, his figure growing small as he walked across the campus.

"I've heard a few things," Cody told Patrick. "Heard Kelly's not acting himself."

Patrick found himself in unfriendly waters. A full-length brigade of pure muscle. Silent eyes daring him to speak.

"Got a big game tomorrow," Cody reminded him. "I'll be fucked if I'm going to lose it."

Patrick took two steps back. "You won't."

"Better not."

There was no sense holding his ground. No sense talking reason to Cody. He liked to win, almost as much as he hated to lose; it was who he was.

And Patrick was nothing without Kelly by his side.

He didn't need his angels to remind him of that.

8

*P*atrick and Jenna sat out on the back deck, silent for the time being.

Even with the sun ceding to the evening sky, the temperature was still floating around a humid eighty. Trees gasped for breath, leaves limp. Clouds above put in an appearance for purely decorative purposes. Even the sound of passing cars gave the impression of tires sluicing through damp marshlands rather than over parched roadways.

Patrick sighed, maybe because of the heat.

He picked up his iced tea, took a sip. Ignoring the stream of condensation dripping into his lap, he pressed the glass against his head. Closed his eyes, relaxing maybe. Thinking about Kelly. Only now Kelly wasn't around. It had been two hours since he had driven off without so much as a hint of where he was going, leaving Patrick alone with Jenna. Both keeping their thoughts to themselves, and Patrick didn't mind the chance it presented.

It's a hot and cold running kind of life, Patrick's angels consoled him. *Every day, something new.*

And in that spirit, Jenna surprised him as the first to open talks to the inevitable.

"I guess maybe it's just the fascination that has me right

now," Jenna said. She was sitting behind Patrick and to his right. Her voice sounded deep and boundless in the thick heat. "I like psychology. The acting, cheerleading, all that nonsense, it's always been extracurricular, and I've never really liked it, you know?"

Patrick nodded.

"I've always tried to see it as an experiment. I guess that's what I've told myself. Just like what I've told myself for most of today.... You ever read *The Man Who Mistook His Wife for a Hat*?"

"No."

"Hmm."

"It was the pool," Patrick told her. He rubbed the glass over his brow. Set it down, and spread the water over the rest of his face. "It was just...how did he play that well? It's not the things he's forgotten, it's all the things he can suddenly *do*. Smoking, drinking. Kelly doesn't *drink*. Never has. How is it he suddenly starts, and how is it that when he does, he handles it like a full-blown alcoholic? Give a nondrinker two beers and they're already slurring their words. Give Kelly a six-pack and *he's* soberly quoting Shakespeare to the principal."

" 'Say what you will, sir, but I know what I know,' " Jenna recalled. She dragged her chair around the table, over to where Patrick was sitting. Her cheerleading outfit had been traded for cutoffs and a thin light-blue T-shirt. She leaned forward, elbows on her knees. "That's from *The Comedy of Errors*."

"I know."

"I was in that last year, over at the Playhouse."

"That's how I recognized the line."

"I thought you guys..." Jenna sat up, pleasantly surprised. "Kelly had practice and a game that weekend."

"Eh." Patrick waved his hand in the air, trying to paddle past the subject. "I snuck away, managed to catch the opening."

"You should've told me. Come up afterward, something like that."

"I wasn't with Kelly, so..." Patrick left it at that, hustled back to his original point. "So what do you think? About Kelly, how does that *happen* to someone?"

"It is possible," Jenna said. "You've heard of Andy Kaufman, right?"

"Comedian, they made a movie about him. Jim Carrey, right?"

"Well, as far as *comedian*, yes and no...He was more of a performance artist."

"What's that mean?"

"It means he liked to fuck with people."

Patrick smiled nervously. "OK."

"Maybe that's a bad introduction, though. Andy Kaufman was a gentle soul. He was caring, soft-spoken, he never swore. He was a vegetarian, practiced Zen Buddhism. Didn't smoke, didn't *drink*. He slept around a lot, but come Christmas Eve, you'd never be able to find him because he would be busy going through a list of every woman he ever slept with, calling them up, and, in all sincerity, wishing them a merry Christmas."

Patrick couldn't help but be charmed. "Cool."

"Then there was Tony Clifton."

"Who's Tony Clifton?"

"Tony Clifton was a character Andy Kaufman created. Tony was a Vegas lounge singer, the world's worst performer. He was crass, couldn't sing, made tasteless jokes, and generally left his audience feeling worse than when they came in. Andy would put on this ridiculous pink tuxedo. He'd put on a fake nose, mustache, hideous wig, and dark sunglasses. And he'd become Tony Clifton. Nobody ever saw him put on the outfit, nobody ever saw him take it off. Andy always insisted that Tony Clifton was another person entirely, and he played it to the hilt. Anytime Andy went on the town as Tony Clifton, he'd swear, treat people like crap, smoke, and order sixteen-ounce porterhouse steaks."

"But . . ." Patrick sat up. "That's just acting, right?"

"He'd order an entire fifth of Jack Daniel's and pound the whole thing. And it made him drunk, sure, but consider who was really drinking it. Andy Kaufman, beneath all that makeup and costume, a man who never touched the hard stuff. Who should have passed out drunk after just *one* drink."

"Or two."

"That's right."

Patrick sighed. He stood up, wandered over to a wooden bench built along the entire edge of the deck. He looked out past the yard. Into the thicket of trees, catching sight of white streetlights. A train whistle let out a nearly extinct plea from some miles away.

He stuffed his hands in his pockets. "That doesn't explain anything."

"It's not supposed to explain." Jenna stood up, walked over

to where he was standing. "It's supposed to...I don't know, give us a clue. People are capable of these things."

"What things? Andy Kaufman was an actor—"

"Performance artist."

"Performance artist, he had an *excuse*."

"So?"

Patrick threw his hands up. "So I want to know *why* Kelly is suddenly in a...I don't know, whatever it is that allows him...Does he even know he's...?"

"Patrick..." Jenna lowered her voice. Put her hand gently on his shoulder. "Calm down."

"I *am* calm," Patrick snapped. "And if I weren't, I'd still have every right to not be. What I'd like to know is why you're talking about performance artists, when it really has nothing to do with the reality of... Aren't you even *concerned*?"

"Hold it..." Jenna withdrew her hand, taking back all sentiment along with it. "Are you saying I don't care about what's happening to Kelly?"

"Well, you and the New Kelly McDermott get to relive first love all over again. It seems to be working out pretty well for you."

Patrick felt those final words doing their best to scramble back down his throat, but it was too late. He stared at Jenna, hemorrhaging all prior defiance. Train whistle giving it one last go in the purple distance.

Jenna's eyes didn't hint at any real offense.

If they had, maybe Patrick could've found it in him to keep right on hammering. Instead, he saw confusion, concern.

Ambushed, uncertain, it was a checklist of his entire day, now written across Jenna's face. It was nothing short of what he'd been asking for, only this wasn't because of Kelly.

Jenna was looking at him as though this were the New Patrick Saint.

Patrick swallowed what felt like sandpaper. "Jenna, I'm sorry—"

"No." Jenna raised her hand, cutting him off. "No, you don't get to apologize. Now that you've said what you have to, I get to air my own laundry, thanks."

"Jenna—"

"Maybe this isn't all that bad for me." Jenna folded her arms. Southern accent shaping her vowels, a sure sign she wasn't about to be cut off. "You say you don't know what's going on, you ask for my opinion. I give it to you, and you get all in my face because I didn't let you know how I *feel* about it. Well, sorry if I haven't actually decided yet, Patrick. But you clearly have. So why don't you tell me; why are *you* so concerned?"

Patrick knew hesitation would put him at a disadvantage. But there wasn't any way around it, he was already at a loss. His angels whispering in a frenzy of overlapping words. Fragments of ideas from all directions. Hardly a chance to understand one when another cut in, weaving in and out. Hopeless as trying to follow a single thread through an immense woven tapestry.

Nothing to do but step back, and view the whole pattern.

"Because," Patrick said, aware that his face had given his ineptitude away. "Because it is frightening." He grasped for something further.

"Because he's asking me my opinion," Patrick said. "Because he's *encouraging* me to do things instead of *telling* me to do them. Because he's standing up for me . . . Because he's just letting me be."

"Yeah."

"And it feels so . . ."

Jenna nodded. "Dangerous."

"Undesirable," Patrick concluded, quietly.

It was getting dark.

Hard to read Jenna's expression, though her voice seemed to accept what she'd heard: "I know."

Patrick nodded. "Can we not fight anymore?"

"I don't know." Jenna remained with her arms folded, torso swinging lightly from side to side. "We've never actually fought before . . . ever, I think. Is that possible?"

"When you think about it, I guess. We've never really been alone together."

"No, I guess we haven't."

"First fight . . . ," Patrick agreed. "First time alone."

"We were alone on the bleachers today."

"Twice in one day is even more impressive."

"Another unexpected side effect of the New Kelly Mc-Dermott."

Patrick let out a tired laugh. He wasn't sure what to add, very much conscious that this was as long as he'd ever managed to keep his eyes trained on Jenna's. Which must have gone for her as well, another first. Definitely not appropriate to comment on, but the secret was well worth keeping to himself.

"So you saw me in *The Comedy of Errors*?" Jenna ventured.

"I was sitting at the back."

"Who did I play?" Jenna asked slyly.

"The Courtesan."

"I know, right?" Jenna laughed, embarrassed. "Get the cheerleader to play the whore, isn't that always the case?"

"When you put it like that, I feel kind of bad telling you how good you were."

Jenna looked down. "I wanted to play Luciana."

"Hey." Patrick bent his knees, tried to catch a glimpse of her face. "Next time."

Jenna lifted her head. "Next time."

The familiar roar of an engine put an end to their conversation.

Patrick glanced over his shoulder and saw a pair of headlights flood the driveway.

They cut out, along with the engine.

"Well, he found his way back," Patrick commented. "That's something, right?"

"You should ask Kelly."

"What?"

"Just ask...," Jenna said, filling their remaining seconds with fast words. "You want to know what's going on with him, you might as well do it now."

Patrick wrung his hands together, turned toward the driveway. "Every time I've tried, he's just..."

"Moving too fast?" Jenna suggested.

"Hasn't given me much of an opportunity."

"They say there's no time like the present."

"I could've told them that."

"I've got your back." Jenna laid a hand on Patrick's shoulder. "This is us now."

No time for Patrick to relish the sound of that last statement.

Kelly was already bounding up the path connecting the driveway to the deck. Ignoring the steps, he leaped up onto the attached bench and triumphantly stretched his arms out. Each hand clutching a hanger. Each hanger displaying what might as well have been twenty-dollar bills all sewn together.

Patrick's mouth refused to open, brain demanding more time to get past what his eyes were seeing.

On the right, a slender red evening gown hanging by a pair of lace straps.

On the left, a perfectly ironed burgundy shirt covered by a perfectly tailored black jacket. Underneath, a pair of pants peeked out, swaying lazily.

It didn't take a fashion designer to appreciate how scandalously expensive they were.

"Kelly." Patrick already knew it was going to be the wrong question, but there was just no stopping curiosity. "What is that?"

"Armani," Kelly replied, hopping off the bench. "The dress: Versace."

"I don't get it."

"Just asked the guy what was best . . ." Kelly shoved the suit into Patrick's chest. "And I did the rest."

"Kelly, I don't know..."

"Sorry, the dress is spoken for," Kelly informed him, handing the second hanger over to Jenna. "This is for you. And *both of you*"—he jumped back, pointing at the pair—"get on into the house and change. We've got a seven-thirty reservation at Spiro's, so I'd like to be out of here at seven-twenty. If either of you want me, I'll be in the shower."

Kelly winked and bolted for the back door.

The outdoor lights came on, spotlight on Patrick and Jenna. Holding on to their new threads as though they'd just been handed a child in a wicker basket.

Music began to blare from the open window to Kelly's room.

Patrick glanced up and cleared his throat.

"Kelly," he managed weakly, finally forcing the question out. "What is going on?"

"OK..." Jenna nodded, watching along as they saw Kelly jumping on his bed, stripping off his clothes. "That's a good start, Patrick."

Patrick nodded, neck still craned. "You still got my back?"

"Believe it or not."

"Well..." Patrick threw the suit over his shoulder. "Doing anything for dinner?"

Jenna did the same, didn't answer.

And if it weren't for the mosquitoes, the two of them might have stayed that way, staring up at Kelly's window, well into the night.

#9

Her name tag read *Savannah*. A few raven strands of hair had freed themselves from her thick ponytail, the signs of a busy evening. The only signs of a busy evening; her wide smile, set in red lips against dark skin; the willing sparkle of her eyes as she stood at the podium; the rest of her was taking it all in stride. Looking over the floor plan, doing what she could not to triple-set any of her waiters.

When she looked up, her enormous hazel-brown eyes overtook Patrick, and all previous delusions collapsed under her gaze. His new suit had managed to fool him for a while. That slick burgundy shirt, sharp black pants, black jacket that inauspiciously gave the impression of wide, well-developed shoulders; for a while there, Patrick had actually felt a strange sense of improvement.

But as he followed Savannah across the restaurant, Jenna and Kelly leading the way, Patrick began to sense the make-believe. He began to shrink in his suit. A loose shoelace came undone, whipped against his lower shin. Every table they passed was occupied by well-dressed couples, families, people who belonged. Stray splinters of conversation lodged in his ears, everyone far too comfortable. Patrons far too at ease, the hostess far too beautiful and accommodating. Their table was far too elegant, forks far too numerous. Napkins folded into a geometric improbability. Thirty-foot-high ceilings crisscrossed with industrial vents and water pipes painted a soothing, dark copper hue. Even the babble of conversation rang with an exclusive lilt, politely hinting that perhaps Patrick would be more comfortable sitting at the children's table.

Patrick took his seat, accepted his menu with a quiet nod.

He glanced over at Jenna as she picked up her menu.

The red dress looked perfect on her.

Maybe because she was *made for it,* his angels muttered. *Maybe because everything looks perfect on her.*

The waiter came up and introduced himself.

Timothy. Spiky blond hair, white shirt, black apron.

Kelly stepped up to bat, producing the wine list.

"It's been a good day," he told the waiter. "We're looking to celebrate."

"Good to hear, sir . . ." The waiter held his hands behind his back, at the ready. "Anything to drink?"

"Got a favorite bottle of red wine?"

The waiter hesitated.

"I'm not talking about something you think we can afford," Kelly assured him. "I mean, pick your favorite bottle of red wine. Even if you've never tried it, just heard about it. Hell, you could lie to me and pick the most expensive one you've got. Life is an illusion, and I'm looking to be deceived for as long as I'm here. . . ."

The waiter thought he'd give it a shot.

He pointed to the bottom of the list. "I'd have to recommend the Beau Vigne Cabernet 2003."

"Then that's what we'll have. . . ." Kelly slipped a hundred-dollar bill into the wine list and snapped it shut. "With our meal . . . Time being, we'd like your most expensive bottle of champagne . . . It's all right if it's not your favorite, we'll take it anyway."

"That would be the Veuve Clicquot Ponsardin Brut Yellow Label," the waiter told them, all concern swept beneath a broad grin as he collected his bribe.

"Excellent." Kelly smiled. "Have it at the table in two minutes and Ben Franklin gets a playmate, catch my drift?"

The waiter practically sprinted for the bar.

Patrick felt himself grow back into his suit, but only for the time being.

"So, Kelly . . ." Jenna picked up her menu, casual as can be. "You want to tell us what this is all about?"

"Oh, I don't know." Kelly reached for his glass of water. Took a sip and crunched on the ice. He stared into the candle, flame reflecting off blue eyes. "There was this man I met once. Name of Bond. James Bond."

Patrick rolled his eyes. "OK, Kelly."

"I know, believe me," Kelly assured them. "He was used to it. Got that same reaction his whole life. He was a detective. Used to be a detective for the LAPD. Way back when, in the nineties. When I met him, brother was long gone from that scene. This was in Louisville, Kentucky. I was working in a bakery."

Jenna snorted in midsip, sent water and ice back into her glass. "Did you say bakery?"

Patrick heard a burst of enchanted laughter at a nearby table. It seemed everyone was having their moments that night.

"Bakery, that's right . . ." Kelly smiled, still staring at the candle. Marveling almost. "I was working at a bakery."

"In Louisville," Patrick added. "Kentucky."

"Home of the man himself, Mr. Muhammad Ali." Kelly frowned. "At least, I think it was Kentucky. Can't really remember the year . . . or the place, I must have been young still. I remember Bond was turning fifty, that was the occasion."

"Detective James Bond," Patrick added. He undid the top button of his shirt. "And you were working at a bakery."

"Can't imagine you working in a bakery," Jenna said.

"Well, it's not exactly what you'd think," Kelly told her. Told the center of the table, reached up to run his hands through his hair, as though remembering he had any to speak of. "Don't get me wrong. It ain't easy. It's a hundred-mile-per-hour job, especially if it's one of those more-than-bakery places. The kind with a full menu, a restaurant-bakery. You're constantly working in those places, between orders for lunch, or breakfast. You've got orders to take care of, special orders like cake for birthdays, anniversaries. Making brownies, cookies, muffins, all the crap that goes in those glass display cases."

The waiter, Timothy, arrived with the champagne.

Three glasses.

He cradled the bottle in both hands, showed off the orangy yellow label for Kelly's approval.

Kelly nodded without looking. "Truth be told, you don't need any real experience to work in most kitchens. Not at the level I was. Most times, it's just someone telling you what to do anyway. So I found myself working at this bakery in Louisville, and anyway, there was Detective James Bond. Ex-detective James Bond, I can't ... quite remember what he was doing there."

A muted pop signaled the flow of champagne.

Three glasses, poured all around.

"Would you like to hear the specials this evening?" Timothy asked.

"We are *dying* to hear the specials," Kelly assured him.

"Excellent," Timothy cooed, before launching into a calm, rehearsed litany. "Tonight we have a very special salad of crab apples and Roquefort tossed with baby greens, fresh cracked pepper, and a sweet-and-sour lemon vinaigrette. Our soup is a cold sweet potato, served with a three-berry garnish. And the catch tonight is tilapia—"

"*—Sauteed in butter and olive oil, served with fresh tomato ceviche and basil-roasted jicama,*" Kelly concluded, finishing off in perfect unison with Timothy.

Neither one of them appeared to notice what was happening until the silence that followed.

Patrick and Jenna shared a glance, then cautiously eyed Kelly, who wore the same confused look.

With his tip on the line, the waiter broke out of his amazed silence with an impressed smile. "Well, that's some talent you've got there."

"Must've read the specials on the chalkboard," Kelly said with bewildered modesty.

"We don't have a chalkboard," Timothy informed him. He turned to Patrick and Jenna. "I'll give you a bit of time to look over the menu. Whenever you're ready, I'll come on over and . . . see if I can guess your orders."

Timothy left the champagne in an ice bucket nestled on a metal stand.

Patrick tried to push through any further distractions. "So what's this detective James Bond got to do with us?"

"How about a toast first?" Kelly said, raising his glass.

"No," Patrick insisted. "I want to hear this."

Kelly paused, glass in midair.

Jenna did the same, put her glass down and withdrew her hand.

"Well . . ." Kelly put down his glass, folded his hands in his lap. "Point is, Mr. Bond and I ended up going to dinner together. Well, he treated me, truth be told. Being nice, I suppose; that was also the day I got fired, but that's neither here nor there. I asked him the same question, what the occasion was. He told me that he was simply trying to enjoy one last night before everything changed for him. I thought this was a bit on the strange side, but he made it pretty simple. He said he'd done the same thing when his wife was about to divorce him. He'd go out to top-tier restaurants, order the best cigars. As though he knew that, pretty soon, he wouldn't be able to enjoy anything anymore. Told me of another time, when he was on the road through the southern states. Tracking down a group of kids who had burned their school to the ground, back in ninety-nine."

"I remember hearing about those kids," Jenna said. "Back when I was, like, nine."

"Me too," Patrick said, frowning. "It happened, I don't know, maybe a day before Columbine. . . . There *was* a detective named Bond involved."

"I don't remember all the details . . . ," Kelly told them. "But Bond was working against his department's orders. After a huge mishap in New Orleans, Bond got mixed up with a con man and his girlfriend. He needed to get them down to Key West, and on the way, he did the same thing. Had a feeling it was all about to end for him. Badly, it seemed, and so he treated these strangers to a glorious meal at a high-end Italian restaurant. Went all out, charged it without a second thought, he was just that certain that it would be the last meal he'd be able to enjoy in a good long while."

Patrick reached out and toyed with a miniature saltshaker. "That's some story, Kelly."

Kelly squeezed his eyes shut, squeezed the bridge of his nose. "I think that's how it was. That's how I think I remember it, at least."

"And all this happened in Louisville," Patrick concluded.

"Yes."

"And when was this?"

"I'm not sure . . ." Kelly picked up his champagne glass. He stared at the bubbles, sighed. "Time's been kind of strange for a while now."

"A while how?" Patrick asked.

"Can we toast, please?"

"Kelly, you've never been to Louisville," Patrick said. He glanced over at Jenna, who had once again been trapped in an amazed smile. "Jenna, has Kelly ever been—"

"Well, I haven't *yet*," Kelly said, rolling his eyes. "Not as far as you know."

"Jenna?" Patrick prompted.

"Kelly." Jenna raised her glass. "I'd like to make a toast, but there's something you have to tell me first."

Kelly obliged, raised his glass.

"Where do you think you are?" Jenna asked, holding out her bubbly. "Could you tell me that?"

"Well, shit, you could've just asked," Kelly told them nonchalantly. His sunburned face seemed unconcerned, eyes sad and happy, contradictions awaiting that first sip of champagne. "The fact that you haven't bothered to ask only made me more certain as the day went on."

"More certain of what?" Patrick asked.

Jenna leaned close to Kelly. "Kelly, where do you think we are?"

"I'm in a mental institution."

For a few moments, Patrick let it slide as nothing more than a metaphor. He'd always been told the world was a crazy place, after all. You'd have to be insane to be sane, there were endless examples, perhaps Kelly was simply coming out and admitting he was as concerned with his future as the rest of them were.

"I am in a mental institution," Kelly repeated, and now there was no doubt he meant it. Bobbing his head silently, as though marveling at the notion, he added: "And I'm sound asleep. Sound asleep, and having the best dream... the only dream I've had in many, many years."

Jenna's glass remained in her hand, wasn't ready to toast.

Patrick didn't even reach for his. "What do you mean by *years?*"

"Guys...," Kelly said. "I know none of you are really here. I know that this place, these people, even myself, that this isn't here. Because this, right here, is round about twenty years ago, as far as my life is concerned. I'm closing in on forty years old, and we're going to have this toast because I'm positive, any minute now, I'm going to wake up."

Beat.

Patrick couldn't remember a single point in his life when his mind had rang so empty. Nothing to say, nothing to do. Not a single dispute or contradiction available, because there was no arguing with the impossible. He simply let Kelly's revelation go unchecked as his glass gravitated toward the center of the table of its own accord.

"Also," Kelly added as he leaned forward, "I'm getting the tuna tartare for my starter, so maybe you all ought to try something else, and that way we can all share."

Their champagne flutes met with an uplifting clink.

And Patrick's brain began to thaw, just enough to set a lone angel free and whisper an equally senseless lament: *Should've called dibs on the tartare, loser.*

10

The three of them closed the restaurant.

Their bill came out to a number reserved for class-action settlements.

Kelly slapped down his credit card without a peep.

Signed with a flourish, adding a tip that would most likely clear the waiter of all student loans.

Patrick hadn't gone beyond his first glass of champagne, and he drove them all back to Kelly's, whereupon the liquor cabinet was raided, stereo plugged in, and night sky filled with the drunken laughter of two wasted teenagers.

Or to believe Kelly, one wasted teenage girl, and one wasted middle-aged man in a teenager's body.

Patrick sat at the same table as his friends, drinking lemonade and watching Kelly light up another cigarette. Jenna was pouring two shots of Chivas Regal, giggling uncontrollably. A good portion of Scotch fell onto the table, through the cracks, and onto the deck. The whole table was a mess of such mishaps. A sticky battlefield, covered with all the bottles they could get their hands on, determined to sample each and every one before even considering the evening over.

Patrick had given up hope on serious discussion of Kelly's delusion for a while now.

Jenna had gotten tipsy halfway through the bottle of champagne and simply granted the premise. After that, the subject had been all but forgotten, until the big hand had snuck its way past midnight.

"OK, future boy!" Jenna snorted, sliding a glass over to Kelly. Both her straps had slid from her shoulders, breasts in serious danger of announcing their presence. "Here's what I want to know.... In the future, what happens to me? Who do I become?"

Kelly blew a plume of smoke into the air, grinning with drunk abandon. "No idea, baby."

"Liar!" Jenna raised her glass. "You're just trying to protect the future from us changing it! Otherwise, if we know too much, we'll destroy our own destiny, right? Like in the movies."

"Except . . . !" Kelly reached for his glass. "This isn't really the past.... Patrick?"

Patrick picked up on his cue without much enthusiasm. "This isn't the past. Kelly's in the future, dreaming about the past." He caught Jenna doing her best to focus, swaying slightly with drink in hand. "What he's saying, Jenna, is that this isn't really happening. You and I aren't really here. We're all in the future, running around in Kelly's happy little dream."

Jenna turned to face Kelly, drink sloshing around. "I am your dream woman, is that it?"

"Have to drink to that."

Kelly and Jenna hadn't actually toasted in over an hour, and they downed their drinks.

"So, OK, future boy . . ." Jenna puckered her face, shook her head with a horselike flap of her lips. "You don't have any excuses, then. What am I in the future?"

"I told you, I don't know."

"So you're from the future...." Patrick shifted in his seat, stretching. "And you can't tell us anything about it?"

"I just can't tell you *everything*...," Kelly countered. "To be fair, most things. One of those things happens to be what happens to Jenna, what happens to you, Patrick...."

"That's mighty convenient there, Kelly."

"What do you want from me!" Kelly stood, reached over the table, searching for a bottle to sample. "Guys, I can't remember anything."

"Well, that's normal," Jenna assured him, mocking the comforting tone of a guidance counselor. "It's been twenty years, Kelly."

"No, I'll be honest about this," Kelly conceded, picking up a bottle of Beefeater. "I don't even remember most of *my* life. I don't remember what I've done, where I've been. I can't even remember what I'm doing in that goddamn nuthouse. I mean, maybe it's the drugs they've shot me up with, but all I've got left are moments, anecdotes, things I know I've grown to like—"

"Like six-hundred-dollar dinners!" Jenna testified, waving her arms in the air.

"Hey, I *wish* there had been more of those." Kelly poured them each a hefty amount of gin. "But what can I say, all I know is that I'm giving us the royal treatment. Once I fall asleep tonight, I'm just going to wake up back in that goddamn room, which, honestly, I can't even remember what it looks like."

"Even though that's where you are right now," Patrick said with a withering look. "Dreaming all this, twenty years from now."

"Doesn't the memory prove it? You've all had dreams. You wake up on an island. You find yourself running up a set of crumbling steps, some awful creature ripping at your heels. You're in bed, going at it with a girl you once knew, only she's still the same age as she was fifteen years ago, and what information do you have? Are there ever any hints, or answers to your questions? What am I doing here, where did I come from? If we could remember them, we'd wake up from our dreams the moment they started, because we'd be *too certain they were dreams.*"

The CD had run through its tracks, came to a stop with a depressed whirl.

Kelly took advantage of the gaping silence to make his way over to the stereo. He bent down, pressed Play. From out in the darkness, a dog barked. Kelly waved in that direction as though letting it know that, yes, he was getting to that. He skipped ahead a few tracks, settled on the one he wanted.

With this fresh injection of music, Kelly closed his eyes, listening to the gravelly voice of Tom Waits. Droplets of piano coupling with lush violins. He followed along without mouthing the words, holding his finger up when it was time for them to listen.

" 'If I exorcise my devils, well my angels may leave too,' " he sang along, off-key and uncaring. " 'When they leave they're so hard to find.' "

"Are you really going to go?" Jenna asked. Suddenly somber, though far from sober. Her eyes were sad, taking Kelly in for all he was worth. "When you fall asleep, that's it? Good-bye, Kelly?"

"Let me tell you guys something. . . ." Kelly remained standing, glass of gin at the ready. "I don't remember much about Kelly McDermott, but my impression is that he was a loser. Maybe not in any way that people think about losers. He was apparently worshipped, feared, successful, but . . . What can I say, a loser can be all those things and more if they got no heart. . . . And if any of this were real, if I were really here, I'd tell you to kick Kelly to the curb. . . ."

Kelly sauntered over to his chair and plopped himself down.

"Fuck Kelly McDermott," he concluded, looking into his glass. "I'm going to miss you guys come tomorrow."

Jenna set her glass down and wrapped her arms around Kelly.

"Miss you, too," she mumbled, rubbing her face against his neck.

Patrick didn't avert his eyes in time, and their lips joined together in a wet exchange. He watched them tumble into each other, mouths searching, eyes closed. The music played on, the night quietly accepting their union. Patrick's stomach turned a few times, deciding between pain and guilty wishes for his tongue in place of Kelly's.

Not that it mattered.

Jenna straddled Kelly's lap, and the pair continued to kiss.

Maybe Kelly's right, Patrick's angels said, did what they could to pat him on the back. *Least as far as they're concerned, you don't even exist right now.*

Patrick ordered his legs to lift him from the chair.

He turned and walked toward the door, secretly hoping one of them would notice.

Ask him to stay awhile.

It wasn't until he was halfway through the kitchen that he realized it wasn't going to happen.

Patrick counted the steps leading up to the hallway, into the guest room.

Didn't bother to brush his teeth. He didn't wash his face, take off his clothes. Just spread himself over the bed, shoes hanging over the edge. He reached under the pillow and pulled out the envelope. Turned it over in his hands, eyelids drooping.

Fell asleep with the Ohio State coat of arms nestled in the corner of his mouth.

Woke up in the same position. So flawless, it felt as though time had failed to pass. All at once, it was light outside. The cheap plastic clock on the night table read seven-thirty. Patrick rolled his eyes around, unsure if he should bother getting up.

He did, of course, peeling the envelope from his face. He sat up and stared at it, as he had several times since fishing it from the mailbox in late January.

January, February, March, April, May. Patrick's angels rattled off the months. *Just how long do you plan to keep this nonsense up?*

He didn't answer, just went through the same tired routine: opened the flap, pulled out the letter, and unfolded it. His eyes scanned the words *Dear Patrick Saint,* tracing each letter, holding off the moment when he would need to look at the following words . . .

Congratulations on your acceptance...

With quick motions, Patrick refolded the letter, slipping it back into the envelope and under the pillow in one smooth motion. He stood up, cleared his throat, and glanced around to make sure no one had seen.

Nobody had, and then he remembered Kelly McDermott.

Patrick took a few tentative steps toward the bathroom.

Once again, he decided to poke his head into Kelly's room.

The place was an absolute mess; empty liquor bottles, desk dragged halfway along the wall, several feet from where it should have been. Clothes scattered every which way.

Jenna lay sleeping in Kelly's bed. The comforter wrapped itself around her naked body like candy-cane stripes, snug between her legs.

Patrick traced the contours from her toes up past her calf, thigh...lowered his eyes before he could get any farther. He stood at the threshold, listening to her snore. Imagining how comfortable her body must feel.

He turned and made his way down the steps.

Counted each one, shuffling his way into the kitchen.

Patrick looked around. Kelly's pants lay abandoned in the middle of the floor. To the left, he caught sight of the disaster area that was once a collection of priceless crystal. He sighed, cold light of day coming in through the windows. Reached up and picked at the corner of his eye, trying to remove the crusty evidence that he had, in fact, managed to sleep.

Paused in the middle of it, frowning.

He opened the back door and stepped outside.

Kelly was seated at the table, facing the forest.

Perfectly still, modest enough to remember his boxer shorts this time.

Patrick surveyed the damage, marveling at the vast army of bottles. Half of them turned over due to reasons Patrick preferred not to think of. The morning had an actual chill to it, for once. Gray clouds filled the skies. Crickets replaced with the fresh chatter of birds.

Patrick circled around, Kelly's face slowly coming into view.

His eyes open, glassy.

Dead, Patrick's angels warned, just seconds before Kelly's eyes shifted.

Looked up at Patrick with a pleading exhaustion.

"Hey," Patrick managed.

"Patrick . . . ," Kelly croaked, reaching for a lit cigarette and taking a drag.

He's still smoking! Patrick's angels screamed. *Still smoking.*

"Sleep well?" Patrick asked, batting away the real questions.

"Patrick . . ." Kelly's eyes begged for a way out of what he was about to say.

Patrick frantically tried to meet his wish halfway, but there was no stopping it.

"It's still today," Kelly told him. He looked down at his hands, then back up. "Patrick, I'm still here. And it's still today."

Friday. May sixteenth, two thousand and eight, Patrick's angels clarified. *Makes sense to us, Patrick.*

What's your excuse?

TODAY II

11

"A thought for you this morning...," Bill Montague began, looking away from the window and addressing his homeroom class. "Henry David Thoreau once wrote 'Beware of all enterprises that require new clothes.' "

Patrick thought it might be mere imagination, but for a moment, Bill's eyes lighted on him. On him and the Armani suit, a knockout ensemble even in this wrinkled state. He glanced around to see if anyone else had caught on.

Nobody had, and Bill continued. "I had a friend once, name of Addison. Addison was a man who lived as best he could, following another one of Thoreau's famous tenets: 'Simplify, simplify.' He was a white T-shirt-and-jeans kind of guy. One-pair-of-shoes kind of guy. One-jacket kind of guy. He had very few actual *possessions*. He liked food and cigars, rum and fireworks, he always told me, because they were gloriously temporary.

"One day, Addison went in for a job interview. Bought himself a suit, and fastened the tags out of sight with safety pins, hoping to return it after he was done. Thing was, he got the job. And what he didn't realize is that, generally, the suit that gets you the job is the suit you wear on the job. But a job's not a lunch hour, it's nine to five, five days a week. So Addison had to buy himself a few more suits. Spend a little extra on dry cleaning. Cutting his own hair wasn't doing the trick anymore, neither was shaving with an electric razor. To cover his new expenses, he worked all he could to get a promotion. Which he got, followed by a new briefcase for work. Followed by better suits, more suits, because now he had to look the part of a manager. He even had to buy 'casual' clothes, the things he was expected to wear when not wearing... well, what he was expected to wear.

"And it didn't end with clothes. New apartment, which began as a lease and ended up as a mortgage. New furniture, decorations for when he had company over. Had to hire a maid service once a week to keep the place up to code, it kept on and on..."

Bill stopped then, glanced up at the clock.

Saw that the time was getting away from him, and wrapped things up. "Not to say that he isn't a very successful man. But every now and then he comes down to visit. We go fishing together, and damned if he doesn't always have something he's got to buy before we head out to the mountains."

Bill didn't add anything more.

He glanced at the empty seat next to Patrick, then shook his head. Reached over to a nearby table and picked up that morning's business.

"Some quick announcements, then you-all can get on out of here...." Bill flicked the first item on his list. "For the prom... the school has requested that all students park in the Marriott garage. I know it ain't free, but that's where the security we've hired is going to be concentrated, so help us out if you could.

"Item two. As you all know, we've hired out a fleet of buses for any students who want a ride out to Charlotte tonight for the game. Lots of seats, not enough to go around; be sure and sign up by the end of lunch if you don't want to waste your own gas. Buses leave at five. Game starts at eight. That's all I know on *that* subject.

"And item three. We'd like to remind you not to leave campus without signing out. I don't care if you're heading to a sporting-goods store to buy me a new set of clubs, *everybody must sign out.*" He folded the paper in half and stared directly at Patrick, and the empty seat next to him. "Remember, we know where you live."

Patrick averted his eyes, pretended to search his pockets for a pen.

"All right," Bill concluded. "You-all can go. Have a good day, and"—the students were already rising from their seats, heading for the door—"don't forget to study for those finals next week!"

Patrick made a valiant effort to collect his things as fast as he could.

"Don't kid yourself, Patrick...," Bill advised, standing by the door. The rest of his homeroom filed past, and with the last student, he closed the door and leaned against it. "I think we ought to talk."

Patrick didn't bother feigning innocence. He let his saxophone case fall to the floor with a loud thud. Took off his satchel and deliberately dangled it over the table before releasing it. It dropped on the table like a flaccid body bag.

"Feeling a little haughty today, Patrick?" Bill asked.

Patrick watched him walk toward the center of the room.

"I don't blame you," Bill said, coming off as more of an

insult than anything. "Principal Sedgwick told me what happened. You and Kelly are in the clear, so it's not as if *I* can get you into any trouble.... Where *is* Kelly McDermott?"

Patrick gave Bill a hard stare. "He's sick today."

"You're pissing me off, Patrick."

Patrick considered getting a little pissed himself, though he knew straightaway he wouldn't be able to match Bill Montague's steely indignation.

"You know, I did what you asked," Bill said. "I told the staff yesterday to lay off Kelly. That I thought he was acting a bit strange. That maybe he was a little rattled. Headed off to Ohio State, new start, lots of pressure, especially with this game tonight. God help me, I actually used *the game* as a way to keep Kelly safe."

"What do you mean, keep Kelly safe?"

"Seemed to me you were trying to protect him. From what, I don't know. I was just doing you a favor. I wonder now why I bothered. Seems to me Kelly knows he can do whatever he wants as long as Redwood is there to bail him out."

"It wasn't *like* that. Kelly wasn't trying to get *out* of being punished yesterday. I actually think he was a little surprised when Redwood intervened. I'm as confused as you are...."

Bill waited for Patrick to finish.

Patrick glanced down, wishing he'd found the time to change that morning. Trying to find a way around this conversation. Trying to find a way around an explanation.

Bill's face softened all at once. "Patrick, where's Kelly?"

"I don't know."

"Did you see him this morning?"

"Yes..." Patrick wouldn't allow himself to divulge the details, skipped straight to the crux. "He got into his car and took off. I used his father's car, drove here with Jenna."

"Do you know where he went?" Bill glanced over to the door's small rectangular window and saw a collection of faces waiting to start their first class. He waved them off. "Patrick, do you know what's wrong with Kelly McDermott?"

"No."

Bill crossed his arms.

Patrick prepared himself for another verbal assault.

Instead, Bill dropped all questions, along with his arms. "All right."

"What do you mean *all right*?"

"I mean all right, as in *here's the deal....*" Bill turned his back to the door, as though there might be spies taking an interest in his proposal. "I can hold off the staff, Principal Sedgwick, for a while. Until lunch. But once they've got a little free time on their hands, I'm going to have to give some answers. So I want you at my place right at the start of lunch."

"Uh...I thought you weren't supposed to have people in your—"

"Just knock on the door." Bill walked backward toward the entrance. "If Kelly isn't here by then, I'm going to need some answers. And if you want to help Kelly, you'd better supply some."

Patrick felt his mouth go dry. "You said Kelly was in the clear around here."

"Sedgwick is looking for a reason to bring Redwood down a

peg. . . ." He reached back and turned the handle. "And Redwood's looking for a scapegoat. My advice . . . Don't give them one."

The waiting students began to file in, and Patrick wearily fought against the current, struggling with each step toward the exit.

Patrick, Jenna, and Kelly all shared a free period on Fridays.

Both Patrick and Jenna convened at their normal spot, outside the main counselor's office, second period, at ten-twenty. Jenna had been the first to arrive. Patrick found her sagging against the wall, head tilted to the side, resting on the sign-out sheet. Good as asleep, no telling what was going on behind her sunglasses.

"Jenna . . ."

Her stance didn't change, mouth opening just enough to croak. "Yeah."

"Hey, Jenna."

"Have I died?"

"No." Patrick scribbled his name on the sign-out sheet. "I've got to stop by my house. You feel up to coming with me?"

Jenna nodded.

"You going to sign out?"

Jenna pointed limply to the slot right above Patrick's name.

Patrick took a closer look at the mess Jenna had left there. "I didn't know you spelled your name with three wavy lines. I always thought it was just two."

Jenna moaned and followed Patrick to the car. "Aren't we going to wait for Kelly?"

"He got held up. Told us to catch him later."

"Why are we going to your house?"

"I wanted to talk to you . . . ," Patrick said cheerfully, hoping to throw Jenna off the scent. He opened the door to the borrowed SUV and helped her in. "See if we can't get you a cup of coffee."

"I don't drink coffee," Jenna mumbled.

"You also don't drink alcohol, best of my recollection." Patrick closed the door and went around to the front seat. By the time he started the car, Jenna was curled up against the window. Sunglasses askew, fast asleep.

She remained unconscious for the entire ride, hardly stirring.

Patrick pulled up to his house, parked out front. Careful not to wake Jenna, he slipped out of the car and tiptoed his way to the mailbox. A quick peek inside revealed nothing. He glanced around, hoping to catch sight of the mail truck.

Nothing but empty lawns showing off their perfect haircuts.

Patrick knocked on the passenger's-side window. Jenna's tongue and upper lip were splayed along the glass, the orifice of a giant squid caught in a mad scientist's shark tank. Patrick knocked again, harder. Jenna's face peeled back, leaving behind a dripping work of art. The door opened, and Jenna leaned out, seat belt saving her from an ugly fall. Her sunglasses slid off her nose, into the gutter. She wiped her face off with the inside of her arm.

"I'm so disgusting," Jenna apologized, eyelashes half-glued together.

Patrick took her by the hand, led her up the slight incline to his house.

Minute though it was, the change in elevation had an adverse effect on Jenna. By the time they'd made it through the front door, she had her hand over her mouth. Wide eyes forecasting an unfortunate accident that sent her running up the stairs. Patrick barreled after her, yelling *"end of the hall, end of the hall."* Whether she heard or not turned out to make no difference. He saw the strands of Jenna's hair stream into his room, and made it through the door just in time to see Jenna on her knees, firing a poorly aimed stream of vomit in and around a small teal wastebasket.

Patrick leaped to her side, gathering her hair out from the path of destruction. A little too late, sadly. Some of the puke had already bonded with a couple of unfortunate tangles, not to mention the goodly amount that had soaked into the carpet and spattered along the nearby bookshelf.

All over your little brother's books, Patrick's angels admonished. *The curators aren't going to like that.*

He waited patiently as Jenna's convulsions subsided. With shuddering breath, she reached out a blind hand, clutching the front of Patrick's jacket.

"You're not going to pull me in there, are you?" Patrick asked.

Jenna shook her head.

"Hang on..." With his hand still holding Jenna's hair, he stretched his other arm out, grasping for a tissue box. He managed to knock it down, pull out a few sheets. He handed them to Jenna, and she accepted with a trembling hand.

Wiped the corners of her mouth clean.

"Oh man..." She raised her head, eyes watering with white gone red. "I am so *sorry.*"

"Never mind," Patrick reassured her. "Come on and lie down."

They made their way over to the bottom bunk. Patrick kept Jenna's hair away from her neck, holding on to it as if it were a vomit-soaked leash. She sat down, then slowly sank onto her side. Patrick got down next to her, on his knees, keeping a handle on her hair. Keeping the space between them at an awkward minimum.

"I'm going to drip barf all over your bed," she moaned apologetically.

"It's not my bed," Patrick told her, reaching for her hand and guiding it to his. "Hold on to that for a second."

Still on his knees, Patrick shuffled to the tissue box. Shuffled back, and reached out to relieve Jenna of her duties. Their hands met with a tiny shock. Patrick sucked in his breath through his teeth and began wiping Jenna's hair with multiple sheets of double-ply.

At the far wall, Miles Davis remained frozen in time, trumpet blaring at Birdland.

Jenna's eyes moved around the room. "I don't think I've been in here for years."

"You and Kelly usually take the guest bedroom," Patrick said. Worried about the connotations, he added: "Whenever my parents are out of town."

"So it's been years."

"Yup."

"You sure?"

"Sure as I can be..."

"It's just that..." Jenna coughed, clearing her throat of

residual waste. "It hasn't changed. I remember thinking how young this room looked even back when we were freshmen. All the kiddie books, models..."

"My parents never bought us our own separate toys," Patrick explained, giving her hair a second go-through. "We shared everything, so these were also my brother's."

"Oh God..." Jenna sat up suddenly, strands falling out of Patrick's hand. "I'm sorry, Patrick, I didn't mean..."

"Don't worry about it...." Patrick gave a cardboard smile. "It was a long time ago. I was eight at the time, so I kept everything. But since they were also his, I wasn't allowed to get rid of anything once I got older.... Couldn't even switch rooms. Mom and Dad do need their separate offices."

Jenna looked down at her knees, still uncertain of her absolution. "I guess your parents never got over it."

"No, they did.... It's more like they never did anything about it." Patrick motioned with his head. "You should've seen the look on their faces when I put that poster up.... Didn't say anything, though. They never do."

"Ugh," Jenna groaned. She sunk back onto the bed.

"You OK?"

"The power of suggestion," Jenna laughed dryly. "Kelly actually had me believing tomorrow would never come."

"You mean today," Patrick corrected.

"I mean whatever it was Kelly believed."

"Yeah, about that..."

Sensing a change in tone, Jenna lifted her eyes.

Patrick coughed. "You know how when you woke up this morning, and Kelly was gone?"

She nodded.

"And you know how I told you that when I saw Kelly, he had seemed completely fine? That he had wanted to get to school early, and talk to Coach Redwood? And that's why you and I went on our own, because Kelly said he'd see us there?"

Jenna's eyes narrowed suspiciously. "Yeah?"

"It's a bit more the opposite of everything I just said."

"Oh?" Jenna rose once more, brushed at a few damp tendrils resting on her neck. "And what *is* the opposite of... all that?"

Patrick sighed. "Kelly was already awake when I woke up. I don't think he actually slept the whole night. When he saw me, he freaked out and started rambling, threw on a pair of pants that were... in the kitchen, got in his car, and just..." Patrick raised his arm, palm flat, and sent it forward.

Capped it off with a small wave.

"So, you don't know where Kelly *is*?"

"No."

"You mean we've lost him. Like some kid at the fair?"

"Yeah."

"And to top it off, he *still* thinks he's dreaming?"

"No..." Patrick hesitated. "He's past all that now, he's... moved on."

"Moved on *where*?"

"Well, from what I gather..." Patrick stood up, moved to the dresser. He backtracked and did what he could to postpone all revelations. "So, the first thing he said to me was *It's still today. Patrick, I'm still here, and it's still today.* After that, he kind of went on automatic. Kept repeating... *It's actually happened. It's not a dream. I'm back. I really am back. It's 2008...*" Patrick tensed up, knowing full well that Jenna wasn't an idiot. "And well, that's what Kelly's... decided, I guess."

No longer concerned with hair or hangover, Jenna lowered her head. Let it hang limply for a few seconds. Then, taking a deep breath, she curled back up and sighed. "Let me see if I got this straight.... Kelly no longer believes he is in an institution. Twenty years from now. Dreaming all this up. Instead, it turns out that Kelly *was* in an institution, only now, rather than *dreaming* he's here with all of us, he's actually, physically *traveled twenty years back through time....* Time travel. Please tell me I completely misunderstood, Patrick."

"No, that's it exactly."

Jenna's face remained deadpan. "Neat."

Patrick was about to follow up when he heard his mother call out his name.

It wasn't her voice that surprised the pair as much as its unexpected proximity to them. Halfway up the stairs, judging from the sound of it. Footsteps closing the distance. Jenna shot Patrick a look, unsure what passed for proper etiquette in Patrick's house. Patrick stared right back, panicked. Unsure what kind of face to put on, or how to signal: *I don't know, Kelly's the only damn person who's ever been in this room, so there's no telling if it's because nobody else ever comes in here, or if maybe Kelly's the only other person allowed in here, allowed to sleep in the lower bunk, because he simply came along at just the right time.*

"Patrick?" his mother's voice called out from the top of the stairs.

"Yeah," Patrick managed. "I'm in here."

The affirmation forced Jenna to her feet. Almost immediately she was swaying against the winds in her brain, and had to steady herself against the bedpost. She managed to get it together and, working fast, ironed out her clothes with erratic strokes before striding over to Miles Davis for a closer, more casual look.

Patrick's mother appeared in the doorway. She set her black leather satchel down, raised her right arm, and brought her hand to rest against the doorjamb. A pair of matching pumps gave her an extra two inches, tan-colored suit tailored to aid the same illusion. Hair up in a bun, showing off her agile features, slender neck.

She surveyed the scene with courtroom eyes. "Patrick, what are you doing home?"

"Free period," Patrick replied, taking the stand. "It's Friday."

Patrick's mother sniffed. "Where's Kelly?"

"He's at school."

"I hope I'm not interrupting anything."

"Nope." Patrick motioned over toward Jenna. "Nothing."

"Hello, Jenna."

Jenna nodded, always polite. "Hello, Mrs. Saint."

"How are you?"

"I'm well, thank you."

"Mmm." Patrick's mother nodded. "Still working at Foot Locker?"

"Yes ma'am."

"Patrick, what's that smell?"

Patrick saw Jenna's mouth open, and he hastily stepped forward. "I'm sorry, I wasn't feeling well. I just got real nauseous all of a sudden, and I couldn't make it to the bathroom...." Patrick motioned with his head to the wastebasket. "I'm sorry."

Patrick's mother glanced down. The discolored spot on the rug glared up at her. She looked over at Jenna, sorted through the contradictory evidence in her hair, wrinkled clothes, and bloodshot eyes. With pursed lips, she turned back to her son. "Didn't get any on your suit."

"Well..." Patrick brushed at his pants with both hands, unsure what she was asking him to explain.

"Because it *is* a nice suit."

"Kelly got it for me."

"And you didn't get vomit on it, so that's good.... Everywhere but the suit, it seems."

"I'm going to clean it up...."

"Patrick, you've got a letter here...." She reached down and removed a sealed envelope from her bag. Raised it as she would a summons. "I haven't opened it yet."

Through the locomotive rush of blood to his head, Patrick heard Jenna gasp: "Is it from Ohio State?"

"No," Patrick's mother replied curtly, eyes trained on her son. "It's not."

The trap was set, and Patrick had to fight against a lifetime of desire to keep from walking into it. He stared at the envelope waving lazily in his mother's hand. Searching for clues. Thickness, postmark, return address, anything that might give it away without having to ask.

What's inside was decided upon days, maybe weeks ago, his angels marveled. *And look at the time it's taken,* is still taking, *to get to you.*

"Starlight," Patrick said out loud.

His mother frowned, halted the hypnotic coaxing of the white envelope. But her recovery was instantaneous. "Well." She lowered her arm and slid the letter back into the confines of her bag. "I just stopped in to pick up a change for this afternoon. I prefer blue for depositions. Maybe we should just wait for your father to get home. . . ."

"Mrs. Saint," Jenna spoke up, reaching for the wastebasket. "I can clean up here, if you need a moment with your son—"

"Don't touch that," Patrick's mother snapped.

Jenna's hand froze, inches from the rim.

"Thank you, but I'll take care of it," she continued, smoothing over her outburst with a genial nod. "Patrick and I will discuss this later, with his father. When he gets home. Tonight."

Patrick nodded.

Jenna took a step back.

"You two should get going," Patrick's mother suggested. "These next few days are the important ones."

Jenna and Patrick made a silent exit, eyes lowered as they passed his mother. She stood at the top of the stairs as they went down. Stood at the bottom as they cut through the living room. Stood at the front door as they glanced back over their shoulders, keeping watch from an always-indefinable distance.

12

"What was that about, back there?"

"Nothing..." Patrick slowed to a stop, waited for the light to turn green. "Nothing important."

Jenna stroked the armrest absently. "Wasn't from Ohio State."

"Huh?"

"I thought OSU was the only school you hadn't gotten into."

Patrick squinted up at the stoplight, images of his acceptance letter dancing in his head.

"I feel better, Patrick. . . . I feel a bit better now that I . . ." Jenna groaned, remembering just what it was that was bringing her out of her stupor. "I'm sorry about puking in the wastebasket like that."

"Not too many ways a person can puke in a wastebasket; you did fine."

"Are you mad?" Jenna asked, leaning forward a bit, trying to get a read on Patrick. "Are you mad at me, Patrick?"

"I'm not mad."

"What was that letter about?"

"I'm not mad," Patrick repeated, pressing on the accelerator as the light turned green.

"Your mom doesn't like me hanging out with you."

"Believe me, my mom's got no problem with you hanging out with *me*."

"Oh." Jenna looked down, folded her hands together. "Just with Kelly, I guess."

Patrick didn't answer.

"I'm not stupid, Patrick."

"I know . . ." He flipped his turn signal, slowing down for the entrance to Wellspring Academy. "I know you're not stupid. I'd just rather not . . . I'd rather focus on Kelly right now."

"What do you suggest?" Jenna asked, looking out to the passing forest lining the winding driveway. "I mean, what do you think we can even do?"

"Keep him from getting worse."

"I don't know if he's really gotten *worse*."

"Oh . . ." The driveway opened up to the gulf of white lines and parked cars. Patrick focused his attention on finding their spot, kept his heart from sinking any further. "I kind of *thought* you liked him better this way."

"That's not what I meant."

"You *don't* like him better this way?"

Jenna didn't answer.

Patrick found their space and slid in. Turned off the engine and waited.

"It's funny," Jenna sighed, bringing her hands up to cover her face. "This is the second time you've brought this up."

"No, I haven't."

"Yes, you have." Jenna dropped her hands, and Patrick was

amazed to find a smile hiding beneath it all. "You brought it up yesterday, at Kelly's house. Right before he showed up with your suit and my dress."

"Another banner moment for the New Kelly McDermott," Patrick muttered.

"You were upset because I was enjoying myself just a *little* too much. You're jealous of Kelly."

"I've *always* been jealous of Kelly," Patrick informed her, a little surprised to hear it come out so blatantly. Surprised, but unabashed. It was a bit like taking his own shot at vomiting, a welcome purge. "When it comes to you, I've always been jealous."

Patrick glanced over, found Jenna staring at him, confused.

"Surprised?" he asked.

"No," she replied. Her abrupt honesty seemed to startle her, mouth open as though looking for a way to backtrack into familiar territory. Instead, she forged ahead. "No. But it's just not the kind of thing you're supposed to ... It's conceited, to imply that you'd be ... that you—"

"I was upset, last night, because you weren't *concerned* enough," Patrick interrupted, talking fast to keep her from taking it any further, because Jenna was not a stupid girl. Just polite, but both of them seemed to be in short supply of manners, and something had to stop Patrick's heart from migrating to his sleeve. "Jealousy is a passing emotion, meaningless. I wasn't upset that you were enjoying yourself with Kelly. I'm *glad* you were. But it's all fun and games until someone loses an eye, and now we've got a time-traveling Kelly McDermott out there somewhere, probably scouring the countryside for the nearest wormhole, and we've got no way of bringing him back to earth!"

"Uh, Patrick . . ."

In his mad rush to paint the perfect doomsday scenario, Patrick hadn't noticed that Jenna was no longer paying attention to him. Her eyes were focused straight ahead. Neck urging her head forward, and that concerned expression he'd been searching for had finally made its appearance. Patrick shifted in his seat, looked through the windshield, and slowly grew to understand why.

He did not immediately recognize Kelly McDermott. A bit of a mind-bender, as what he saw should have been Kelly McDermott at his most recognizable. Freshly showered, blond hair lightly tousled. In place of his father's suit were a pair of blue jeans and a casual white-collared shirt, topped off with his team's letter jacket, green and white colors, with the WA badge stitched onto the shoulder.

He stood in front of the car with a wide, confident grin.

Book bag slung over one shoulder, football nestled in his right arm.

It was Kelly, all right.

Perhaps a little too *Kelly,* Patrick's angels observed.

"So much for scouring the countryside looking for wormholes," Jenna added, getting out of the car.

Patrick followed, approaching Kelly with a reserved nod. "Hey, Kelly."

"What's up, Pat?" Kelly reached out and playfully smacked Patrick's shoulder.

"Not much, not much..." Patrick watched Kelly put an arm around his girlfriend's waist, draw her close with a gruff kiss on the cheek. Jenna smiled nervously and slipped Patrick an urgent look. He couldn't decipher its meaning, went ahead and asked, "How are you feeling, Kelly?"

"Feeling good," Kelly said, nodding his head to some invisible beat. "Better than ever."

"Good."

Kelly continued to nod, grinning widely.

Jenna let out a breathy laugh, nodded along.

Without realizing it, Patrick had also fallen into their head-bobbing ritual, and he had to make a conscious effort to knock it off. "A little hot for the jacket, isn't it, Kelly?"

"Huh... I hadn't really noticed."

"Oh." Patrick held off for a moment, then dipped his shoulder playfully. "I guess the earth is probably, like, a hundred degrees warmer in the future, huh? This must be like Anchorage for you, right?"

"Ha!" Kelly held his hands up in mock surrender. "You got me, Pat. Hey, look, I'm sorry I've been acting like such a freak, guys."

"What?"

"Seriously, I've just had a lot on my mind. Big game coming up. Gotta beat Wilson tonight, right?" Kelly palmed the football and hoisted it above his head. "STATE CHAMPIONSHIP, BABY!"

A wave of cheers and hollers arose from every which direction. Students en route to class held their fists in the air as they walked by. In the distance, someone began to chant *Fight, fight, outta sight,* gaining a little momentum from others before the excitement faded into isolated pockets of applause.

"So, babe..." Jenna bumped Kelly with her hip. "You sure you OK?"

"Yeah," Kelly insisted, giving her another kiss on the cheek. "It's all good, baby. I'm back in the saddle. You got nothing to worry about."

"I wasn't really—"

"KEL-LY!"

Zack trotted up to them, hand held over his eyes, casting a shadow over his pie-pan face. Sweat poured down his neck. An archipelago of damp blobs dotted his UNC jersey, light blue turning gray beneath his armpits. "What up, Kelly?"

"What up!" Kelly hooted. He took Zack's hand and shared a quick man-hug. Two bumps on the back, before falling to a safe distance. "What's going on?"

"Ain't you hot in that jacket, man?"

"Guess I'm just superstitious. Gotta beat Wilson tonight, right?" Kelly looked as though he was about to repeat his previous grandstanding. Instead, he took off his jacket and held it out for Patrick to take.

Patrick stared at the jacket as though Kelly had just offered him a dinosaur bone.

Reaching up slowly, he took it off Kelly's hands.

"That's right," Zack agreed, ignoring Patrick. "Speaking of which, we got some plays we want you to take a look at before class." He sent a fat thumb over his shoulder. Cody and a few others were waiting at the edge of the parking lot, enjoying a couple of laughs.

"Yeah, man," Kelly grinned, giving his book bag a pat. "Got my playbook and everything."

"All right, man. Let's do it."

"Let's do it!" Kelly turned to Patrick and Jenna. "I'll see you guys later, cool?"

He sauntered away without waiting for a reply.

The smell of vinyl drifted up from the letter jacket still hanging in Patrick's arms. He watched Kelly jog over to the football team. All previous acrimony had apparently been laid to rest, high fives and man-hugs all around. The sight left Patrick feeling empty. The last guest to leave the party, wondering where the evening had gone.

"You all right, Patrick?" Jenna asked. Her almond eyes were following the same scene. Hair a stiff mess of gnarled brambles.

"Yeah."

"It's kind of like volunteering at a suicide hotline, and having someone call to tell you what's happening on their favorite show."

"That's Kelly for you."

"A little *too* Kelly, if you ask me."

Patrick sniffed. "What?"

"Doesn't matter," Jenna said dismissively. She kicked at an imaginary rock and watched it skip across the parking lot, all signs of Kelly now gone. "Say goodbye to the New Kelly McDermott."

"Yeah."

"Thanks for letting me puke in your wastebasket," Jenna said, smiling warmly. "I'm going to hit the showers. I'll see you in class."

Jenna gave his shoulder a squeeze and headed off for the locker rooms.

Patrick was left standing next to Kelly's car. Wearing the suit Kelly had bought for him. Holding on to Kelly's letter jacket, a single sleeve brushing against the ground like an elephant trunk.

13

His mind kept going back to the jacket.

The jacket and the football.

It was the first day of presentations in their Modern Psychology class. A welcome day for anyone who wasn't scheduled to present their final project. It was just a matter of showing up and feigning interest. Some doodled, others stared into space. Finishing homework for other classes was a big favorite. It was the homestretch, and everyone was working for the weekend.

From his seat, Patrick watched Kelly slouch in his desk, situated one row down, one row over. Going the extra mile to ignore everything around him. There was the football, resting atop his books. Kelly kept his hand planted on it, scrutinizing the white stitching as though peering into a crystal ball.

And then there was the jacket.

Patrick kept going back to the football and the jacket, unable to shake the eerie settlement reached between Jenna and his angels.

A little too *Kelly.*

It was halfway through the fifth presentation that Kelly sat up in his chair. Cautiously alert, he leaned forward, propped up with both hands on the football.

Patrick glanced up, surprised to find Edmund standing before the class.

Not that Edmund wasn't supposed to be there. He was the only freshman in the class, given special permission to join as the only freshman in advanced calculus and trigonometry. Still, that wasn't what accounted for this perplexing reaction. It had only been two days since Kelly had duct-taped Edmund to the flagpole, photographed him naked from the waist down. Seemed like another life–*another Kelly*, his angels whispered– but Patrick *knew* it had only been a couple of days.

In that short period, Edmund had withered. Patrick wasn't sure if that fully captured what he was seeing. Edmund was no less a skinny little shrimp than he had been two days before. It was more of a fading quality. Not unlike the bleached pastels of old photographs or a barely noticeable scar. His eyes were distant. Staring straight ahead, voice a hollow monotone.

Edmund was *lessening*, somehow.

Patrick could see Kelly straining to hear, now tilting his ear toward the front.

"This is where Carl Jung's notion of the collective unconscious comes into play...," Edmund was explaining, unaware that two people up from nobody were now listening. "The simplified notion that our inner thoughts manifest themselves in direct relation to the world outside our minds. Like when you're thinking of a person and two seconds later they call you..."

Edmund's voice dropped a little.

For a moment, Patrick was convinced that Edmund was about to vanish right before the entire classroom.

The substitute teacher, a round woman with a frizzy French braid, prompted him to speak up.

"...to the speed of light!" Edmund's voice rose sharply before regulating itself. "When they shot the cesium photon at the wall, their readings detected residue from the collision appearing a trillionth of a second before the actual collision itself. In essence, it traveled back in time."

Patrick saw Kelly's hand twitch, rise slightly from the football.

"Possible, of course, because a cesium photon has no mass." Edmund's eyes shifted over to Kelly, and the slow chant of his nowhere voice was disrupted. He began to fidget, rock lightly from side to side. "As do... same as thoughts, which have no mass... and, if thoughts do travel, which there are... have been studies... with little bearing but... if thoughts could travel to light speed... Then maybe they can go backward, too, so... When your friend calls you, the thought could very, might... very well travel back two seconds and occur to you right before your friend..." Edmund swallowed. "Right before your friend actually calls."

Kelly's hand shot up.

Edmund tensed, knees pressed together. Nails digging into his palms.

The substitute half stood from her seat, frowning as though she'd forgotten what a raised hand meant. She pointed at Kelly, referring to him as *you.*

"So is it possible, then, for a person to travel back through time?" Kelly asked.

The class sprung to life, chuckling derisively at the perceived joke.

Going on the same assumption, the substitute rolled her eyes.

Edmund's discomfort swelled, grew into a malignant fear.

"No, it . . ." His voice cracked. "The theory of relativity won't allow for it."

"Why?"

Kelly's question set the classroom on another roar. It wasn't a question of what the joke actually *was*, only that this simply *had* to be a joke. The few sympathetic souls who kept quiet did it for the same reasons, but their solidarity was lost on Edmund. His petrified degeneration only fed the fire. A warbling kind of noise escaped his lips as he bolted for the door.

Directly on his heels was Kelly McDermott.

The football rolled off the desk, and continued its wobbly journey across the floor.

Looks like Kelly forgot who he was there for a second, Patrick's angels said.

Before the football had come to rest at the substitute's feet, Patrick was already out the door. Heading after Kelly McDermott, who was heading after Edmund.

And all of them, Patrick determined, were going to have to stop meeting like this.

The final stretch took them practically right back to where they had started.

Edmund was a runner, greased lightning. Agile, too, he led

them on a wild chase that spanned half the campus. Rounding buildings, changing direction with nimble irregularity, the scrawny freshman turned the school into an obstacle course for army cadets. He weaved between cars in the parking lot, shot up the stairs to the science building, cut through the science building, out the back doors, wasn't halfway down the wheelchair ramp when he leaped the railing, landing on his feet and tearing in the opposite direction.

If it weren't for the lock on the basement door to the main building, he might have even made it. From his distant third place, Patrick saw him dart toward the door, arms outstretched. Planning to cut past the snack machines, no doubt, and beeline through the new music room they'd never finished building, and out the emergency exit.

Patrick didn't hear the impact. He was too far, and it came off looking like a gag from a silent movie. Edmund had simply bounced off the door upon impact and fallen back. From ninety degrees to zero, the needle on a sound board after the music dies.

By the time Patrick reached them, Edmund had scrambled to his feet in a series of crablike motions. Unable to run any farther, he held his arm out, the last line of defense.

"Leave me alone," he managed.

"What are you running for?" Kelly tried to take a few steps closer. "You all right, Edmund?"

"I'm warning you...," Edmund gasped, eyes of a cornered animal preparing itself for a last resort. "Stay away from me."

Classes were slowly being let out, students beginning to fill the outdoor passageway. One or two looked over. Not enough for an audience, but that kind of fever spread faster than most.

Patrick looked across a wide stretch of grass between the compounds and saw Principal Sedgwick, watching them with a disapproving stare. He stood with his arms by his sides, shoulders tense. The undecided stance of someone witness to a beating, telling himself that, any second now, he would intervene.

He began to walk over, mouth moving in a silent rehearsal.

Kelly didn't notice, still doing what he could to reason with Edmund. "I'm sorry about what happened in there," he assured him. "I didn't mean to embarrass you like that, I really am interested in your theory."

"You've done enough!" Edmund cried out, the very specter of Kelly's benevolence serving only to infuriate him. "You've done enough, you've *proved your point*!"

"What are you—"

"I've done *everything* you asked!" Edmund insisted, voice rising. "I haven't told a *soul*!"

Patrick could actually see the hair on Kelly's neck stand up, nearly translucent follicles pointing north. He saw Kelly bend closer and whisper something, and for a moment, the fear left Edmund's face; eyes focused as though managing a complex set of equations.

Patrick found himself tensing, secretly hoping that a page was about to turn.

And he was filled with honest disappointment as rage came rushing back to Edmund's cheeks. "This is a test...," Edmund seethed, shaking his head. Fists clenched.

"No, Edmund, not a test—"

"That's *all* this is! You told me, you said not to tell anyone, *not even you!*"

The stares were multiplying, on the verge of becoming a crowd.

"OK, guys." Principal Sedgwick stepped in. He remained to the side, doing what he could to address Edmund while keeping a stern eye on Kelly. "Edmund, what's going on here?"

Edmund took one more step back before turning on his heels and running like hell.

Kelly looked as though he was about to give chase when something stopped him. Sedgwick had marked him with a cold stare, but Patrick sensed this wasn't what had Kelly stuck in his own shoes.

And it appeared as though Sedgwick was of the same mind. He could tell that Kelly wasn't the least bit interested in whatever judgment he had settled on, and that stung. Gave him more reason for offense than whatever infraction he thought he'd just witnessed.

"Kelly..." Principal Sedgwick cleared his throat, doing his best to assert his presence. "I'm getting pretty tired of all this—"

"Something's going to happen," Kelly interrupted, speaking in a perfect monotone. Addressing no one, just gazing after Edmund with a glassy revelation. "Oh my God."

Sedgwick frowned. "Kelly?"

Patrick put a hand on Kelly's shoulder. "Kelly?"

Kelly turned to Patrick with lucid trepidation. "Something bad is going to happen, Patrick."

The certainty with which he said it sent a cold finger down Patrick's spine. "What's going to happen?"

"What are you talking about, Kelly?" Sedgwick asked, insisting that he still existed.

"I don't remember," Kelly told Patrick. Dread replaced with outright dismay as he added the one thing he seemed absolutely sure of: "Soon."

Patrick watched as Kelly turned, trancelike, and walked away. He was about to follow when he was blocked by Principal Sedgwick.

"Hold it right there," he ordered. "I'm glad we've got this chance to speak."

Patrick didn't think Sedgwick was glad about anything. "What is it?"

"I'm not the only one who's noticed Kelly's disruptive behavior around our community," Sedgwick told him, pink face a mask of forced consideration. "He's got a lot of people worried."

"He's all right," Patrick told him.

"Even though something bad is about to happen." Sedgwick's eyes glimmered with pleased accusation, pleased at having the upper hand. "Something soon, I presume?"

Patrick decided to ignore the question. "I'm going to go and talk with Bill."

"He seems to have taken Kelly's side these past few days."

"So now it's about sides . . ." Patrick took the urge to spit in Sedgwick's face, channeled it into a contemptuous sneer. "That's some community you've got here, Principal Sedgwick.

Close your eyes, and it's just like another warm day in seventeenth-century Salem."

Sedgwick returned the glare. "Watch it."

"I'm going to talk to Bill." Patrick moved to shoulder his satchel. Remembering that he'd left it in his previous class, he skipped the dramatics and simply walked away.

Immediately cleansed of all posturing as Kelly's words returned to stake their claim.

Something bad is going to happen, his angels said. *Looks like we've got a genie and no bottle here.*

So much for the triumphant return of the Old Kelly McDermott.

#14

B·ill lived in a trailer near the edge of the old soccer field.

This was Patrick's first time there. His first time even using the dirt road, an uphill climb of fifty yards or so that cut through the forest and opened up to a small gravel tableau. An uneven relic of Wellspring Academy's humble beginnings, once used for game-day parking. All that remained from those less prosperous times was Bill's trailer. Situated at the far end, perched on a series of industrial cinder blocks.

From what Patrick understood, Bill had lived there for years. It doubled as Bill's office. There had been a time when he would take meetings there with his students, but that had stopped right before Patrick had been assigned to his home-room. Part of a new policy protecting the school from any kind of liability. As a result, Bill was stuck holding conferences any-where on school grounds that he could.

The gravel crunched soundly under Patrick's shoes as he made his way over.

He hopped the wooden steps up to the front door, opened the screen, and knocked.

From a distance, Patrick heard someone calling his name.

Across the way, on the edge of the old soccer field, Bill waved him over. He was standing next to what appeared to be a giant upright caterpillar. As Patrick trudged across the parking lot, he realized it was actually a set of golf clubs. Bill was already teeing up by the time Patrick made it to his side. Lining up with a driver and focusing on the ball. He took another look at the abandoned expanse of mangy grass scarred with rocky patches of clay-colored dirt.

Patrick gave him room, saw Bill pull back and swing.

The pair of them watched the ball sail up into the sky.

It disappeared in the midday glare, reappearing at the far end of the field as a distant hailstone.

"Look at that," Bill commented as brush swallowed his ball. "*And* I sliced it too far."

"Yeah."

"Know anything about golf, Patrick?"

"No ..." Without thinking, he added: "Do you?"

"Ha!" Bill reached into a bulging pocket, dropped another ball on the ground. "Good one."

"Sorry."

"I deserved it." Bill sheathed his club, pulled out another. "Saw that Kelly's back."

"Yeah."

"Don't you think it's a little hot for that jacket?"

"Superstition, Kelly said."

"Never understood that kind of paraphernalia." Bill readied himself for another swing. "Like students who wear their college across their sweaters. If they can't remember that kind of thing on their own, they shouldn't be allowed on campus." He swung, followed the trajectory. No analysis this time, just a question as he continued to stare out into the forest. "How did you and Kelly end up becoming friends?"

Up to that point, Patrick hadn't even realized they were having a conversation. It wasn't the easiest thing for him to do, give in to any kind of communication. Awareness had always stood in the way. Exchanges between people made him suspicious; he regarded the practice as a little dirty. Shameful, a strange form of adultery. Fabricated peace between periods of never-ending conflict.

The exception to the rule had always been Kelly.

Though starting the day before, Jenna had joined in.

And now, it appeared, Bill of all people had made an impression.

"I guess we met in the hospital."

Bill looked a little surprised. "Buddies since the beginning, really?"

"No, it was... When I was eight, I was in a car accident. I was carpooling back from school with my brother and two other kids when there was a head-on collision with a cab. Even that, I had to take people's word for. Last thing I remember was standing with my brother outside the school, waiting for our ride. Then I woke up in the hospital.... I was the only survivor. More than that, I'd scraped clean with nothing but a mild concussion."

"Was this how your brother died?"

Patrick hadn't remembered mentioning his brother. It hadn't even occurred to him that Bill would know he once had one. "Yeah. On impact, so thank God for that, I guess. Anyway, I came to in observation, and Kelly was lying in the bed next to me."

"Huh..." Bill's face was respectfully free of opinion, though his eyes had softened somewhat. "What was he in for?"

"He was in the cab that hit us."

Bill straightened, as though Patrick had just told him that Kelly had actually died in that accident.

"That's right..." Patrick nodded. "His parents were out of town doing the pharmaceutical circuit, and his aunt had picked him up. She and the driver were killed. Kelly was the only survivor.... Nothing but a mild concussion."

"Stands to reason you two became friends."

"With a little help from my parents. They kind of appropriated him. Hired his services as my new little brother. He never really warmed to the idea. My parents worship him, and he goes along with it, like celebrities when they get fawned over by random fans. I guess he kind of just let it happen. I kind of let it happen. Thinking about it these days, all that's happened, it feels as though that was only a cause for our relationship.... No real *reason*, though."

Bill nodded once. "So is Kelly all right now?"

"You mean from the accident?"

"I mean with the memory lapses, erratic behavior, falling off the face of the earth."

"You don't like Kelly very much, do you?"

"Well..." He pulled out another golf ball, let it drop at his feet. "He's never struck me as cruel, stupid, or unruly.... You know, this school used to be a lot different. Back when we were still Pleasant Evergreen. This place was built on some very revolutionary ideas, some very good ones. Desegregation, specialized attention. When we took that money, though, put every last dime into sports, things changed."

"I thought the donor said the money had to be spent on sports."

"That is what they say...." Bill turned sideways, bent his knees, and lined up his club. "Once we had the gym and the new stadium, we had to keep them maintained. We had to attract more athletes, invest in our future alums to cover our bases. We added the supplemental grading system to help students get into the bigger universities. Meanwhile, we're still using secondhand books, our science labs are still waiting for upgrades they've needed since day one." Bill swung a little too hard, the frustrated result sending the ball at an ungainly forty-five-degree angle. "But Redwood calls the shots. It's all about the sports now. If we win this state championship, we stand to ... I can't even bring myself to say it. And it's not that Redwood doesn't think he's doing good. It's no different from half the people that came out of the sixties . . . bit by bit, doing good has spiraled into something else."

"Beware of all enterprises that require new clothes."

Another ball was readied. "I guess when I look at Kelly, I see what this place has become."

"You seem to be taking quite an interest in him now."

"I like the new Kelly McDermott." Bill smiled, smacking the ball out into the trees.

The sun crawled across the sky, burning the ground beneath their feet.

"I think Kelly's..." Patrick didn't want to get into detail, but he felt as though he needed to sound it out. "I think he's trying to be all right."

"You know"—Bill plunked down another ball and turned to face Patrick—"once a change has occurred... once you've gone too far, once the world is no longer the one it was yesterday... it's very hard to go back. Most people kind of get the idea and try to make the present match up as best it can. But it's just an excuse."

"For what?"

"To keep from going forward." Bill's face looked sadly resigned. He ran a hand over his head, down past his gray ponytail. "I like the new Kelly McDermott, but I don't know how welcome he is around here. We're just not ready..."

Patrick didn't know what to say.

He didn't think there was anything *to* say.

"It's like we're all just waiting for tomorrow," Bill murmured, taking his position alongside the golf ball. Patrick gave him his space, wiping off sweat with his priceless Armani jacket. The pair of them kept quiet as Bill continued to rocket those miniature comets over the desolate field. As lunchtime drew to a close, they made their way across to collect the ones they could find.

15

It wasn't much more than Zack and a few members of the football team who saw how it started. They would say, later, that it began with Kelly. With Kelly laughing at Cody, unapologetically laughing *at* him. Around a dozen students had seen the simple argument escalate to an incomprehensible shouting match over that freshman geek with all the upper-level math and science classes. By the time the first unsuccessful punch was thrown, the crowd count stood at around fifty.

That was when Patrick had happened upon the scene, making it around fifty-one.

He cut into the crowd, bursting through the membrane to find Kelly and Cody rolling around on the ground, between grass and gravel. Close body blows, arms a tangle as they continued to shout through clenched teeth.

"What did you do?!"

"Fuck you!"

"Tell me!"

"I'll *kill* you, you fucking—"

"What did you *do* to him?!"

Patrick was frantically seeking a chance to intervene when Coach Redwood shoved his way past the cheering students and yanked Kelly off of his only son and heir. Cody vaulted to his feet. He charged once more, under the impression that his father might actually continue to hold on to Kelly, allowing Cody to pound some respect into the insurgent McDermott.

Apparently, even Redwood had his limits in public. Grabbing hold of Kelly's jacket with one arm, he launched out his free hand. It was spot on, fingers wrapping around his son's arm in an iron grip. He swung Cody, sent him flying backward.

"Cody, you stay back!" he barked, pointing. "Stay *back*!"

"You tell me what happened!" Kelly yelled, struggling to break loose.

"You shut up!" Redwood ordered. "Shut up!"

"He started it!" Cody fumed. His face was smudged with dirt, a bit of blood crusted around his ear. "I didn't–"

"I won't have this!" Redwood shoved Kelly away, then grabbed him again. He dragged him toward Cody, whom he collected in his other hand. "Not when we've got state tonight! You two want to kill each other afterward, fine! Move it!"

Shoving Kelly through the wall of students while dragging his son behind, Redwood made off with the two. A few people kept watch as the coach headed off toward the proverbial woodshed. Most, however, turned to Patrick as the crowd dispersed. Not seeking any answers, because few people ever talked to him. Though their faces displayed no shortage of questions.

And he knew it wouldn't be long before someone was going to want some answers.

But Patrick wasn't one for being proactive. He spent the last few minutes of lunch wandering the campus, looking around unenthusiastically. Searching for answers the same way he had always pretended to search for people at school dances, anything to keep from actually having to dance. Students floated past him, every now and then engaging him in a question-and-answer routine that was growing tired.

So tired that Patrick eventually snapped: "He's a time traveler, OK?"

The sophomore girl who stood before him took a moment to digest this information. Her bright yellow dress lifted gently in the breeze, exposing sandals and green painted toenails. For a moment, Patrick was certain she would simply walk away, disgusted with his disregard for her genuine concern over Kelly McDermott.

But her expression remained benign as the daisies in her tangled sandy hair.

"Well...," she mused, smiling sweetly with deeply stoned eyes. "No cure for that."

"No," Patrick agreed, a little angry at how absolutely right this little hippie girl was. "No, there's no cure for time travel. Nothing to be done."

"So what are you going to do?" she asked.

"Didn't you just hear me?" Patrick replied, laughing nervously at the opportunity to actually have this conversation with *someone.* "Nothing to be done."

"Yeah, but you can still . . . you know, help him."

"Help him?"

"No cure for cancer, either."

"No."

"So you accept it, right? And then you find ways to live with it. Work around the rest of the world."

It was almost fitting, this advice from someone renting a summer home outside reality. "You really think that works?"

"Works for my mom and me," the girl said with a funny little sigh.

Patrick held back the sympathetic wince, swallowed. "I'm sorry."

"About what?"

"Your mom . . . the cancer and everything."

Patrick was taken aback by her sudden laughter. "My mom doesn't have *cancer.* . . ."

She giggled, snorted, and absently brushed a finger along his collar, then wandered away.

Son of a bitch, though, Patrick's angels marveled as the bell rang, signaling the end of lunch hour. *Even without all that tragedy, the pothead's got a point.*

Patrick didn't know how he knew Kelly would be sitting on the bleachers. Or he told himself he didn't know. Now that he had finally decided on a course of action, Patrick's angels were taking every opportunity to demonstrate the dangers of flirting with Kelly's madness. Their babbling voices did all they could to shove his face in it, the tight grip of a master's hand forcing his dog to see just what he'd done to the living-room rug.

Kelly doesn't remember.

He's going back to the scene of the crime without even realizing it.

It's been far too long for him, twenty years.

"Shut up," Patrick told them, ascending the aluminum seats.

Kelly was sitting second row from the top. White threads like loose nerves hanging from the shoulder seam of his letter jacket. His eyes were closed. A distressed scowl did away with any illusions of narcolepsy or transcendental meditation. Shallow breaths, hands resting on either knee. Fingers tapping out Morse-code nonsense.

Patrick stood by his side, wondering if Kelly even knew he was there. He raised his hand in an unseen greeting. "Hey."

Kelly opened his eyes. He didn't acknowledge Patrick, just breathed in. Eyes gazing upon the stadium, the hollowed remains of an aluminum tortoise.

"Um..." Patrick wasn't sure if people actually said things like what he was about to ask. The occasion had never come up, and the fact was almost depressing enough to keep him from trying. "Do you... want to talk about it?"

"If I do, it won't be what you want to hear," Kelly said. His words were steeped with defeat, uncharacteristic of both the old and new Kelly McDermott. "I know what's expected of me, now."

Patrick took the space next to Kelly, sitting on his own hands.

"Now that I'm actually here, it's so strange...." Kelly scratched his nose. "It's so strange. I'm here, physically here, and yet... I can't come back. I tried. Tried talking shit with my teammates, grinning like an idiot. Taking crap from Sedgwick. Listening to that cream-puff talk about community and togetherness, while he stands around, just looking for a problem to make him feel like he's in control. And Redwood, that big renegade asshole. I hate fuckers who just want to win. Who can't live without that validation, a goddamn proof of purchase."

Kelly shook his head, clenched his fists, and released. "I hate bullies. I hate them, Patrick, and this is who I've got to be now. And I can't."

"You were..." Patrick tried to stop himself from going along with it, but he couldn't help it. "You were never really a bully."

"Yeah?" Kelly scoffed, disgusted. "Then what was I?"

"You...just were, I guess."

"I tried so hard today. To be whatever that was, to keep from..." Kelly looked at Patrick with beseeching eyes. "This is really happening, Patrick....I know you don't believe me. I can hardly believe it myself. Maybe I'm still back there in that institution, maybe none of this is real. But I don't think so. In fact, I don't even know what to think. I don't know what I'm doing here, how this is even possible...." Kelly paused, nodding with enough momentum to get his body rocking. Psyching himself into a decision. "But now I have to know. I have to figure this out, Patrick."

"Because something bad is going to happen?" Patrick said.

"Do you at least believe me about that?"

Patrick didn't answer. Not because he didn't believe. He did, in fact, feel that Kelly was very right about this. Even worse, he was certain this wasn't just some prediction with fair odds in its favor. This was more than neutral pessimism, because there was always something horrible looking to sink its teeth into any life unfortunate enough to wander too close.

Something bad was going to happen, something with far-reaching consequences.

Patrick believed it, but he didn't want to. He didn't want to break from what he knew to be true and authentic. Didn't want to waltz into the void with Kelly McDermott, and he couldn't bring himself to answer.

"Because if you *do* believe me," Kelly told him, "then you need to help me. Whether or not you believe that the Kelly McDermott sitting here is not the Kelly you once knew."

"Then I need you to listen to me," Patrick insisted, standing up to face Kelly. "It doesn't matter whether you came from twenty years in the future or five minutes from now. Nobody likes who they are, you understand?"

"I like who I am just fine."

"Well, you're a teenager now," Patrick informed him. "And the only thing that matters is who you're supposed to be. I want to figure out what's going on as much as you, but *until we do* . . . You need to stick to script. Keep it as loose as you like, but you have a responsibility to the present."

"Meaning?"

"At the very least, you have to play in that game tonight." Patrick leaned close. "And you have to win."

Kelly stared up at him with a blank expression.

For a moment, Patrick thought his lecture had turned him catatonic.

He was about to wave a hand in front of his eyes, contemplated a crack across the face, when Kelly finally spoke: "Jenna can't know."

Patrick stiffened. "Can't know what?"

"Jenna does not get involved in this," Kelly ordered.

"You can't just keep Jenna out of this."

"When it comes to this, I can do a whole lot of whatever I please," Kelly said. "You want me to march in rank and file, fine. But if something bad is going to happen, if I'm so determined to wreak havoc on the present, as you've so kindly pointed out—"

"Kelly—"

"*If* that is the case, I don't want Jenna to end up hurt or *dead*!"

"Oh!" Patrick raised his arms high. "And I guess it's all right if that's how *I* end up."

"Something tells me that we just might deserve it, Patrick."

Patrick lowered his arms, slowly.

From behind him, he could hear the sound of the flag whipping briskly in a sudden, unexpected gust of wind.

Kelly rose from his seat, nose to nose with Patrick.

"Tell me what happened to Edmund."

16

*K*elly and Patrick parked outside, looking up at the gray two-story house.

The clock read 3:15.

"This the right address?" Kelly asked, looking out the window.

"Yeah, this is it."

The two of them sat for a while, waiting.

Outside, trees lining the sidewalks of Unity Park sheltered them with a forgiving blanket of shade.

"What if he's got some kind of after-school thing?" Patrick asked.

"I don't think he does."

"The game starts at eight."

"Fuck the game..."

"I know it's hard trying to"–Patrick had to fight how ludicrous it sounded–"to live in the present, be this person you're not. Anymore. But we still don't know what any of this means. We don't know why this is happening. Do we even know why we're *here*?"

"Because something bad is going to happen," Kelly said grimly. "And Edmund's the key."

"Oh, and you know this *how*?"

"I don't *know* anything."

"Yeah, you and I should start a club."

"And the rest of the world can join." Kelly sighed as he glanced out the window, over to Edmund's house. "Tell me, Patrick... How often do you hear of a tragedy *anyone* saw coming?"

Patrick didn't answer, innately aware of where this was going. Silent with misgivings and still unable to come to terms with a Kelly McDermott who would even touch upon such an issue.

"It's always after the fact, isn't it?" Kelly turned back to Patrick. "Nobody sees it coming, but after the fact, oh sure; should've seen it coming. I know we can't predict the future. And I know I can't *remember* it, I know that I don't *know*. But I can *feel* it."

Patrick briefly thought of all the prophets throughout history.

It wasn't about knowing, it never had been.

"And even you have to admit, Patrick, the writing is on the wall," Kelly said. "How surprised would you be–honestly surprised, if something horrible happened to Edmund. The boy's carrying around a world of hurt, he's unhinged, maybe desperate–"

As Kelly spoke, Patrick thought back to that day out on the field. Edmund had switched from hysterical tears to single-minded fury in the span of a few simple heartbeats. Bound against the flagpole, cords in his neck bulging, swearing his revenge.

I'll kill you all.

"Wait, what are you saying?" Patrick interrupted. "You're saying Eddie's a psychopath?"

Patrick was unprepared for Kelly's palm, hardly even saw it. It smacked against his arm with enough force to throw him back against the passenger door. His head bounced off the window with the hollow sound of knuckles against an empty bottle.

"Don't call him that," Kelly snapped, furious. He grabbed hold of Patrick's arm, dug in tight. "He's not a psychopath. Edmund is a depressed, lonely boy. He's barely hanging on, and now he's being blackmailed with a potentially humiliating photograph in the possession of someone who I consider to be, if I may be so bold, an *actual* psychopath."

Patrick could feel himself beginning to bruise under Kelly's angry grip. "Kelly—"

"I don't *know* if something bad is going to happen to Edmund, but I *should. Both* of us should. Because we *helped* do this to him."

Kelly released Patrick from his grip and sunk back into his seat, scowling at the odometer.

Patrick slowly reached up and rubbed his arm, in shock.

"This could all mean nothing," Kelly said, voice flat. "And maybe it's all windmills in my mind. But even if I *am* jumping at shadows . . . It doesn't mean we don't owe him . . . If we can help Edmund, fix this mess we've made. What we did to that poor kid . . ."

Kelly trailed off, and at the sight of his unapologetic lament,

Patrick was instantly contaminated by it. Channeling the vile self-loathing like a lightning rod. His arm throbbed, as though everything that Kelly felt had been mainlined into him, a near overdose that forced him to look away. An elderly couple shuffled past the car, trying to make out Patrick's face.

"Are you disappointed in me?" Patrick asked. "That I could do something like that to another person?"

"Surprised, I guess...I was just so positive you were the good one."

Patrick almost choked on Kelly's words.

"It's all right." Kelly put an arm around Patrick's shoulder. Looked him right in the eye, a steely commitment rendered in bright blue. "It's all right if you don't believe me. You don't have to for us to make this right. And we are. We're going to fix this."

"Right now, looks like." Patrick motioned past Kelly.

Edmund was walking up to his house. Shoulders slumped beneath a blue book bag, eyes fixed on the concrete. Out of his pocket came a set of keys. He paused before the limestone steps leading up to the porch, a rumpled figurine in the shadow of an unwelcoming dollhouse.

"Think he's going to listen to us?" Patrick asked.

Kelly's only response was to open the door.

The two of them made their way across the street, silently, like a couple of G-men. Unable to shake off damp images of Edmund's pleading eyes, they held off for as long as they could. It wasn't until they'd made it to the walkway that Kelly finally spoke.

"Please don't run, Edmund."

And to Patrick's surprise, he didn't.

From the top of the steps, Edmund turned around and faced them. Unafraid. He disengaged his book bag and let it slide down his arm. Wrapped one of the straps around his hand and made a fist.

That's a weapon you're looking at, Patrick's angels warned. *You know where he lives now.*

As if to respect this declaration of war, Kelly stepped forward with his arms outstretched.

Palms open.

Patrick remained as he was.

"I know what I did now," Kelly said. "Patrick told me."

Edmund stood his ground.

"I don't know why I would do something like that," Kelly continued. "I wish I could say it's all in the past, but here we are. You don't have to accept my apology. You don't have to accept either of our apologies right now. But, right now, I *do* need you to listen to me. And I need you to believe me."

When Edmund spoke, it was nothing short of a dare. "Why should I?"

"Because I can help you," Kelly told him. His conciliatory tone shifted to that of negotiation. "If you want to make this mercantile, that's good enough for me. You don't believe I'm sorry, then you'd better believe I can get you out of this.... Long as you're willing to help me."

"So, I saw you and Cody fighting today," Edmund informed him.

"I thought you seemed a bit more comfortable with me than you did this afternoon."

"I've got two bricks in my book bag...." His face compressed with a trembling, now very familiar rage. "That's why I feel more comfortable talking to you."

"You do what you have to do."

"I'm really sick of you assholes...." The profanity faltered somewhat, as though Edmund were experimenting with it for the first time, though his fury was no less succinct. "I wish you'd *killed* Cody today."

"Help me out, and neither one of us will have to, Edmund."

Edmund relented a little, his grip around the strap loosening. "What do you need?"

"It's complicated."

"You've got three seconds."

"I'm from the future," Kelly said plainly. "Twenty years in the future, and I need you to tell me how the hell that's even possible."

Perhaps the statement was too outrageous to warrant a reaction. In the seconds that followed, that certainly seemed the case. Not a peep from Edmund. Not even a whisper of an emotion on his face. Even the birds had ceased their teatime gossip to swallow what Kelly had just announced.

Without so much as the bat of an eyelash, Edmund turned around.

Walked across the porch and unlocked the front door.

Unaware he'd even been holding his breath, Patrick let it out, heart sinking.

"Well?" Edmund walked back to the edge of the porch. He slung his bag over his shoulder, looked down on them with a superior impatience. "You guys coming or not?"

The birds went back to their business, and Edmund motioned for them to follow.

Just as Kelly was wrapping up his story, Edmund's mother came in with a tray of brownies and lemonade.

"Is this OK for you?" She stood at the entrance to Edmund's room, shoulders practically filling the entire width of the doorway. Not that she was excessively fat, just thick. An opera singer's body, dressed in hospital scrubs, name tag reading *Rachel-Ann*. Blond hair pulled back, accentuating the spherical dimensions of her face. A set of plucked eyebrows rested high on her forehead, large doe eyes sparkling with the desire to please. Her lips were moist with red lipstick, parted in a hopeful, servicing smile. "Eddie doesn't get much company."

"Mom." Edmund's voice dropped low. His cheeks went red, jaw contorting as he twisted in his chair, knees banging uncomfortably against the side of his wide antique desk. *"Please..."*

Rachel-Ann paused in the middle of the room, genuinely confused by her son's sudden desperation. "What's wrong, Eddie?"

Patrick saw Edmund's expression turn from embarrassed to plain miserable, words caught in his throat. It appeared as though Edmund never got *any* company, to the point where his mother had no idea how to behave in front of teenagers, and Edmund had no way of explaining just how awful things were already going.

"Looks good," Kelly piped up from his seat on the brown carpeted floor. He flashed a broad smile. "Brownies and lemonade are the only thing I eat some days."

"Oh, aren't you sweet?" she cooed, Georgia accent thickening. She moved toward Edmund, who quickly removed a series of papers from his desk to make room for the tray. There must have been an entire pan's worth of brownies there, though it didn't stop her from letting them know: "If y'all want any more, just go ahead and ask.... I'm Rachel-Ann, by the way."

Edmund ushered her to the door. Rachel-Ann was attempting to compliment Patrick's suit when Edmund managed to get his mother over the threshold and gently close the door on her.

He leaned against the wall, waiting for someone to make fun.

"Well?" Kelly asked.

"She's just trying to be nice," Edmund said defensively.

Patrick, half-stretched out on the bed, decided against smiling.

"I wasn't talking about your mother," Kelly assured. "I was talking about time travel."

"Right, OK..." Edmund moved back to his chair, keeping a suspicious eye on Kelly all the while. He sat and swiveled to face them, holding on to the armrests as though preparing for takeoff. "Time travel...This raises a couple of questions."

"Actually, I have one first," Kelly said, raising his hand.

Edmund nodded, still monitoring every move they made.

"Are you just going to let everything I told you slide? I kind of figured this was going to end before it even got started, but you're really going to accept it all? Just like that?"

For a moment, Edmund's face sagged with a recognizable dread. As though, at any moment, the closet door would open to reveal the entire football team, clutching their sides with uncontrollable, vicious laughter.

Patrick was already preparing for Edmund to go for that bag of bricks.

"I don't have to believe you," Edmund concluded. His fear was gone for the moment, replaced with a superior hostility. "Whether you're completely insane or not doesn't interest me. Very little about you interests me. I'm out for myself here, and if you want to know about time travel, I'll tell you everything I know.... Which, I might add, is considerable."

"So is it even *possible* for a person to travel back in time?" Patrick asked, eager as Edmund to get the ball rolling, get it all over with.

"No," Edmund replied.

Well, that was easy enough, Patrick's angels said, smirking.

"OK, then." Kelly looked at his watch. "So, same time, next week?"

"It's not possible, first of all, for a *person* to travel back through time," Edmund specified. "Remember the cesium photon I was talking about in class? They shot it, light speed, against a wall—and the residue showed up a billionth of a second before they actually fired the shot. Now, whether you see it as traveling into the future or in the past, that's just a matter of perspective, I suppose."

"So why can't a person do the same?"

"Far as traveling at the speed of light, the theory is that the body wouldn't be able to handle it."

"So that's it?" Patrick asked.

"That would be it if you were a *person*."

Kelly pointed at Patrick. "I think *person* is the word that best sums Patrick up. Me too, for that matter. Am I wrong?"

"Not about Patrick. But take a look at yourself, Kelly. You say you're...," Edmund trailed off, as though worried about even entertaining the notion. But there was a part of him that seemed to be gaining momentum, secretly enjoying the attention, the apparent respect. "You say you're from twenty years in the future? Well, I don't see a thirty-eight-year-old mental patient sitting here. If you've traveled back through time, then where, exactly, are *you*?"

"Go on."

"It's no wonder you thought you were dreaming...." Edmund plucked a brownie from the tray, then quickly returned it. "Maybe if you'd woken up to find yourself in the past, and *still in your thirty-eight-year-old body*, then time travel would have come fairly easy. Not to mention how much easier it would've been to convince us that you were the future Kelly McDermott." Edmund's eyes narrowed. "But this is the body of the young Kelly McDermott, with the older Kelly trapped somewhere inside."

Patrick sat up, began to scoot forward. "What are you saying?"

"I'm saying, for lack of a better word, it was Kelly's *soul* that traveled back through time."

Kelly frowned. "You don't strike me as the kind who believes in souls."

Edmund straightened slightly. "What's that supposed to mean?"

Patrick glanced at Kelly, who calmly repeated: "You don't strike me as the kind who believes in souls."

"Oh?" Edmund glanced between the two, eyes ricocheting madly. "What do I strike you as, then?"

"Clinical," Kelly replied. His voice never turned defensive or condescending. "Intelligent, empirical. Practical, Edmund."

"Well, I *am*, and despite what you and Patrick may think, there's nothing wrong with that."

"Despite what *I* may think?" Patrick's sympathies for Edmund took a quick vacation, and he stood up from the bed, looking down at Edmund with incredulous eyes. "So you're some kind of deep, unapproachable mystery, but you get to figure me for some idiot piece of shit."

Edmund cringed slightly. "You don't know what it's like."

"What makes you so sure?"

"Because you've got Kelly to make sure that never has to happen." Edmund began to shake, eyes going dark. "That you don't end up duct-taped to *some flagpole, while everyone else stands around laughing!*"

The realization of Patrick's involvement with the rest of the team came rushing back. But with the weight of guilt, something else; a dark uncertainty kneading at his heart, making a bed and settling in. Edmund had arisen from his seat, taken the few steps necessary to come face to face with Patrick, and in Patrick's own soul, there were suddenly no second guesses.

Kelly's right about Edmund, his angels insisted. *You can just feel it.*

Kelly came up from behind and collared Patrick, jerking him back, out from the path of a right hook that was never thrown. Patrick landed on the bed, welcomed by a choir of shrieking springs.

Kelly sent a finger in Patrick's direction. "Calm down, we're his guests." He then turned to face Edmund, who now appeared unable to account for Kelly's behavior. "Edmund, I'm sorry for what happened, and you're right about every last bit of it. But please believe me when I say... that I could *really* use a brownie. Right now."

Edmund stepped back, face blank. He glanced from Kelly, down to Patrick, then back to Kelly. His intelligent, empirical, practical mind amazed at an actual display of the new Kelly McDermott at work. He reached back, picked up a brownie, and handed it to Kelly.

Kelly accepted it with a nod, then nonchalantly returned to his seat on the floor. He took a bite out of the brownie, chewing thoughtfully. Swallowed, then nodded in Edmund's direction. "You say, for lack of a better word, that my *soul* has traveled back in time.... Do you believe in souls?"

"I don't . . . ," Edmund managed, retreating to his chair. He glanced over at Patrick, as though contemplating an apology.

It didn't come, but Kelly wasn't looking for one. "If not souls, what *do* you believe?"

"Contrary to what you might think . . . ," Edmund began before correcting himself, cautious now. "I'm not against imagination. I believe there is a scientific version of a soul, one we haven't discovered yet. Call it essence, life force, morphic fields. Much in the same way that I believe thoughts can travel through time due to their lack of mass, it is possible that someone's 'soul' could travel back in time."

In the silence that followed, Patrick could feel the fence begin to mend.

Kelly stood up and walked over to a bookcase. He kicked his feet out with each step as though trying to shake off invisible sand. Or taking the time to assure himself that he was in possession of an actual body.

"So if Kelly's soul is here," Patrick began, throwing his own caution to the wind, "what's going on with Kelly's body in the future?"

Edmund eyed his bookshelves. "Guess we'll find out twenty years from now."

"Edmund . . ." Kelly was absently moving a finger along several books. He kept his back turned, voice low, tentative. "If it really is possible to travel back through time, then . . . is it also possible to change events, the very course of history?"

Edmund squinted, as though deliberating whether or not to

complicate things. "If you want to look at time as a straight line, then probably not." Edmund deliberated some more, then rubbed his eyes. "For example, say you travel back to 1865 and warn President Lincoln that if he goes to see *Our American Cousin,* John Wilkes Booth is going to kill him. Your plan succeeds, but it raises a serious problem. Now that the assassination of Lincoln never happened, how could you have ever known of it in the first place? And if you couldn't have known it, how could you then stop it?"

"Paradox," Patrick volunteered. "You could even cease to exist."

"That's what's known as *the grandfather paradox.* But Kelly's got enormous gaps in his memory. He remembers who you are, where his parents keep their coffee. He remembers *things.* Those *things* he can't remember can easily be written off as simple memory loss from the fact that all this, in his mind, happened twenty years ago. What he doesn't remember are *events.* In fact, he's *been* changing events since he first woke up to find himself here. But there's no real paradox as far as Kelly goes, because he doesn't know what he's changed. He can't remember what he did instead of going to the pool hall, for example. It's almost acting like a safeguard, freezing memory in order to assure that his essence can continue to exist."

"Then again," Patrick stepped in, getting caught up in the conceptual swell, "maybe Kelly doesn't remember anything because he's accidentally changed so much that now none of those things have ever happened."

"Then again," Edmund shot back, not ready to cede to

Patrick just yet, "his memory loss could always be one gigantic side effect of time travel."

"There is that, yes."

"Not to mention that *things* versus *events* can get kind of tricky," Edmund added.

"Tricky how?" Patrick asked.

"Suppose Kelly's been masquerading as a superhero all the time we've known him. . . ."

Patrick couldn't help but laugh at the thought of Kelly as a superhero.

Edmund looked hurt, before realizing it wasn't a bad bit of comedy. Unused to the notion of *laughing with*, he allowed himself a nervous titter before continuing. "Yes, crazy, but that makes it an excellent example. At night, Kelly dresses up as Batman and roams the streets as a vigilante. It is severely counterintuitive behavior, and yet it happens regularly. Nightly, even."

"I'm loving it," Kelly encouraged him.

"What could've been considered an event is a common enough occurrence to become a fact. Something he should easily remember upon traveling back in time. And yet, upon opening his closet and finding black tights and a cape, he could easily dismiss it as a Halloween costume he once wore."

"Why?" Patrick asked.

"Because during the day, there was always a part of Kelly that rationalized it as perfectly normal. It would be necessary for engaging in such an extremely improper fashion. He's rationalized it, you see. In his head, he's told himself it's OK. It becomes nothing to him. As a result, when he comes back in time, that whole part of his life is erased along with everything else."

"Is that actually possible?"

"Just how many of your sins keep you up at night?" Edmund charged with an admonishing look. He then turned to Kelly, not entirely prepared to let him off the hook. "You could have any number of skeletons floating about in your closet that you haven't even begun to touch upon."

"Yes, but *what if*?" Kelly insisted.

Patrick glanced up, surprised at the urgency in his voice.

"I mean, what if I did know something?" Kelly specified. Patrick could hear the added informality tacked onto the question, covering for his deeper concerns. "Even if I didn't know for certain, even if by accident, are you saying I couldn't change it?"

Edmund didn't catch the undertones and strode across the room, face grim. "Linear is just an objective view of time, and I've never really been a fan." He unceremoniously moved Kelly aside and began to search the bookcase. "Every time we're faced with a decision—two roads diverging in a yellow wood, and all that—we assume that the choice we make severs that second, or third, path. That we then move on along the only existing time line."

Edmund unsheathed a thick paperback and handed it to Kelly. "In the short story 'The Garden of Forking Paths,' Borges suggests that the only way to truly tell the story of humanity is to incorporate every possible path every person could possibly take."

Kelly tossed the book over to Patrick.

On the cover, a man with thick lips and dark, slicked hair regarded Patrick with an unimpressed, yet critical eye. Judging from the clothes and texture of the black-and-white photograph, it looked to be a portrait from the midforties.

Or possibly yesterday! Patrick's angels announced gleefully. *Who the hell even knows anymore?*

When Patrick looked up, he was surprised to find that Edmund had pulled a rather large, semiportable chalkboard from behind his desk.

"You have a chalkboard in your room?" Patrick asked, unable to keep from sounding incredulous.

Before Edmund could even begin to recede back into his awkward shell, Kelly held up his hand. "Don't listen to him. Show us what you have to show us."

Edmund nodded, drew a straight line. "To go to the store, or not to go to the store." Edmund drew two diagonal lines diverging from the straight line, labeled one of them *a* and the other *b*. "These are your decisions. Say you go to the store, here on line *a*..." Edmund sent two more lines angling out from line *a*. "Then you have to decide whether or not to stop for a hot dog. But say you stay home, here on line *b*..." Edmund moved to line *b*, drew another set of splintering lines. "Whether to watch the game, or go for a walk..." Edmund then repeated the process several times over, with each new line getting its own helping of *what if*s. "The bifurcations go on and on and on."

"Like the branches of a tree," Patrick observed.

"No."

"OK, I'm going to shut up now."

And somehow, Edmund smiled. "Don't blame yourself, Patrick."

It was a hell of a thing for Patrick to see him smile, to know such a thing was possible.

"Say we start with our original two decisions." Edmund erased everything but the original line and its two options. He pointed to decision *a* and *b*. "To go to the store, not to go to the store. But say, later on, you have specific plans for dinner. If neither of these two paths interferes with that, then they both bend to meet back at that future point." He drew a line from *a* tilting downward, and a line from *b* tilting upward. The final result was the original time line, topped off with a diamond shape. "And once again, the same goes for all those other lines. When viewed close up, the whole thing looks more like a chaotic honeycomb than anything. In fact . . ." He tapped the chalk against his lips. "This could attest to why you remember certain things from far in the future. The ripples of certain changes in the present might die out before they can affect certain future events."

"But if I suspected something was going to happen, could I change it?" Kelly asked warily.

He didn't sleep last night, Patrick's angels reminded him. *It's still today, remember?*

"Maybe . . . ," Edmund speculated. "While you may be looking at a line and a diamond on this chalkboard, the overview is far more complex. Complex, and far more dense. Compact." He pointed with his chalk to the space inside the diamond. "This, right here, isn't empty. It can't be, there's no such thing as empty as far as I'm concerned. This space is filled with more of those branches and diamonds. It's all so compact that, essentially, all these scattered points are touching each other at once. We only see one path because that's all perception will allow. And we can't effect change, because the body can't physically do it." Edmund shrugged. "But apparently—"

"—*you're nothing but soul, Kelly*," Kelly finished off in unison with Edmund.

"OK." Patrick raised his hand, used to this by now. "How do you explain that, Professor?"

Edmund stared blankly at Kelly.

Kelly gave him a guilty look.

Three knocks on the door, followed by the voice of Edmund's mother.

Kelly, Patrick, and Edmund shot from their positions and snatched up a few brownies.

The door opened and Rachel-Ann stuck her head in, grinning at the sight of her boys.

"Don't forget the garbage, honey."

Patrick caught Kelly's eye, tapped his wrist.

Kelly nodded, and the three of them made their way down the stairs, through the kitchen, and out the back door. Rachel-Ann showered them with goodbyes, enthusiastic offers to bag the leftover brownies. Edmund, once again, was forced to put another door between himself and his mother. He trudged down the crumbling brick steps, came to a stop before the plastic garbage can, and paused.

"You know, it's got me to thinking..." Edmund grabbed on

to the handle and began to wheel the receptacle out from behind the house. Patrick and Kelly walked alongside, carrying blue recycling bins filled with empty Deer Park bottles and neatly folded Hamburger Helper boxes. The heat wasn't all that bad in the shade of Unity Park, and the three of them strolled in amiable unison, stretching the moment.

"I met this guy once..." Edmund swatted at a mosquito, kept on rolling. "Over there, in the park. His name was Lucky, and I think he was kind of drunk. But as my mom was so kind to point out, I so rarely have anyone around to talk to–"

"OK there." Kelly gave Edmund a slight nudge. "Let's get back to Lucky."

Edmund nodded. "Well, we were talking about this very subject. Time travel and all that. Destiny versus chance, free will and... Well, he told me about a theory he had called *the common thread.*"

"What's that?" Kelly asked with a lazy curiosity.

"He thought that amongst all those cross sections and bifurcations, there is a single thread that follows a path forward in time, yet passes through nearly infinite outcomes at one point or another."

"Huh?"

"Start at the beginning, and then go forward," Edmund explained. "Picking paths at random, the only rule being that you have to go forward. Imagine it as a very crooked, highlighted path. It was his idea that this one path could never be strayed from. Think of it as passing through that one line where you decide to go for the store. During that time, if you happen to coincide with the common thread, there would be no decisions. That one portion of time is immutable. All paths that led there get locked in."

"Is it possible?"

"It's *philosophy*." Edmund rolled his eyes a little, as though the very notion was right up there with Bigfoot and flying ponies. He came to a stop at the edge of the driveway and placed his elbow on the garbage can, leaning against it. "Besides, he insisted that with so many different options happening so often, the odds of the common thread affecting you for more than a split second are nearly infinitesimal."

Kelly wiped his forehead. "But it could happen for a longer period."

"Conceivably . . ." Edmund's face drained of all emotion, as though realizing this time spent with Patrick and Kelly was about to end, despite all that talk of eternity. "It'd be sad to be stuck with that, wouldn't it? Nothing changes, and you're finally . . . all alone, absolutely helpless?"

Kelly shook his head. "I don't think anybody's helpless."

Edmund kicked at a stray acorn. "But we are alone."

"I'm going to fix this, Edmund."

Edmund sniffed abruptly, raised his head. There was no trace of what precious humor or life he'd shown during conversation. His eyes weren't sad, weren't angry. The only thing that shone through was a crippling acceptance, a defeated urge to save face in the presence of an ultimately impossible promise.

"Do whatever you like, Kelly." Edmund shrugged. "You can't change a damn thing."

Edmund presented them with a dignified nod, turned, and walked away.

Patrick watched him disappear around the back of his house. He turned to Kelly, found him staring in the same direction, absently scratching the back of his head.

"You did your best," Patrick said, unsure of what that even meant.

"We're just getting started," Kelly informed him, nodding with a slow certainty.

"And we had a deal."

Kelly took a look around, a barely audible sigh bringing him back to the sights and sounds of the everyday. Afternoon sunlight cut through the trees, a brief history of time shared by all. Kelly tilted his head up toward the branches. He nodded once more, as though acting on silent orders from the shallow rustle of leaves, and turned to Patrick.

"We had a deal," Kelly agreed, pulling out his car keys. "It's game time."

17

*J*enna had been waiting for them, sitting on the curb in her cheerleading outfit.

Kelly parked in the street, pulled the brake.

Patrick leaped out, playbook tucked under his arm. The proud memories of Edmund's smile began in the presence of Jenna's wounded scowl. "Jenna...What are, uh...what are you doing here?"

"I want a lollypop!" she cried, voice shrill.

Kelly and Patrick exchanged a look, almost lost in the early evening.

"I got lost," Jenna continued to whine sarcastically. "I got lost on my way to Candyland, and no one will help me find my *daddy*!"

"Uh..."

"I got a ride from someone!" She jumped to her feet, pigtails bouncing. "After you two left school without me. After an entire hungover day without seeing you!"

"I'm sorry, baby," Kelly said earnestly. Slipping back into his poorly researched role as the old Kelly McDermott. He popped the trunk, removed a large bag with his football equipment in it. "Pat and I had some things to take care of. You know how it goes."

"How it *goes*? You disappear this morning, show up again acting like nothing's wrong. You get into a fight with Cody, then disappear again, and now you're here talking about how it *goes*? What could that *possibly* mean anymore?"

"Maybe this should wait until after the game," Patrick intervened begrudgingly. Growing a little tired of being Kelly's public defender. Certainly losing his touch. "I mean...you know, state championship and all."

"The game, huh?" Jenna put her hands on her hips, the classic starting position for any cheer. Patrick almost expected more sarcasm, maybe an ironic tirade in the form of a saccharine chant. Instead, she just laid out a hypothetical. "It's third and eight on the fifty-yard line. Wellspring's trailing by one with thirty seconds left in the second half. Wilson's caught on to your running game, and Cody's asking for a deep fade, left. Do *you* call it, *Kelly*?"

Kelly didn't answer.

Patrick had to resist the urge to peek into the playbook.

Jenna caught him eyeballing it, and rolled her own. "Yeah, you two are a pair of regular, all-American, USDA-approved football stars. You want to tell me what's going on, Kelly?"

"I've got to get dressed," Kelly said, heading up the driveway.

Jenna didn't like that, and the two of them argued their way along the driveway, up the stairs, and across the deck without a second glance at the destructive results of the previous night's romp.

By the time they entered the house, Patrick found it was becoming nearly unbearable. He hung back in the kitchen.

Watched them head along the downstairs hallway and up the stairs, flared passions sufficiently apparent in each thudding footstep.

Patrick groaned and retreated to the den.

He could still hear the stomping of feet, trace exactly where they were, almost what they were doing. Their voices poured through the air vents, filtered through minuscule cracks in the ceiling and floors. Taking charge of his life via remote control, Patrick turned on the TV, pumped up the volume, and clicked over to BET J.

There wasn't much time to enjoy it.

"You can't even get dressed without my help!" Jenna was spewing, hopping down the steps, arms in the air. Kelly followed her down, dressed in full football regalia. "You tried to wrap your shoulder pads around your legs!"

"So I'm a little fuzzy on details!" Kelly took the bag he was carrying, now filled with his street clothes, and tossed it at Patrick. "Has it ever occurred to you that *I* might be hungover?"

"No!"

"There is no such thing, Jenna!" Kelly put up his hand in a dismissive block. "There is no such thing as the *New Kelly McDermott.*"

"Well, that's too bad...," Jenna said, arms crossed. "Because I'm breaking up with the Old Kelly McDermott. I'm dumping him for the new one, because I like the New Kelly McDermott *better!*"

"There is a scrappy minority that seems to believe the same thing," Patrick offered, switching sides without even realizing it.

"You want me to win this game or not?" Kelly snapped.

Patrick closed his mouth.

Jenna glanced between the two of them, just another suspicion to add to her list.

And with an impending conflict of interest about to explode in his face, Patrick did what he had always considered to be an airtight retreat in times of distress. Excused himself to the bathroom with no real need to go. Just headed through the kitchen and up the stairs, covering his ears as their voices began to collide once more.

Patrick dropped the toilet cover, sat down with a hefty grunt.

Closed his eyes, hung his head. The flotsam and jetsam of the past day and a half whirled in the darkness. Patrick felt he could fall asleep right there, like a victim in shock. His head began to buzz in rhythmic bursts. On again, off again. He thought about popping an aspirin when the buzzing simply stopped.

Undoubtedly, the most precise headache he'd ever experienced.

The buzzing started up again, and Patrick opened his eyes.

Lifting his head, he realized that this wasn't simply in his head.

Just pretty damn close.

He reached out, grabbed hold of the white wicker laundry basket, pulled it between his legs. The entire basket was vibrating. Patrick tore off the lid. Peered into the pile of sweat-encrusted clothes and began to rummage violently like a rogue bear.

When his hand finally wrapped around it, Patrick didn't make the immediate connection. The buzzing tumor was removed, and all at once, he remembered. That first morning. Kelly taking his fully charged cell phone and dropping it in there without a second thought.

Patrick flipped it open as the buzzing stopped.

15 MISSED CALLS.

Thumbing the arrow pad, he navigated to the call-history menu.

Scanned the list, landing on the last three missed calls.

His heart skipped a beat, and he thumbed his way to voice mail. He skipped every message up to the one that had him praying.

"Kelly, it's Mom . . ."

Patrick leaned back against the toilet tank, recognizing the tone. One that might have passed for concern had it been any-body else's mother. Patrick knew better.

"Your principal called us today. He didn't realize we were out of town, but I told him we were glad he did. Call us back, we'd like to have a talk with you."

"Love you, too, Mom," Patrick muttered on Kelly's behalf.

The next message was from Kelly's father. One that might have passed for concern had it been anyone else's father. Patrick knew better.

"Well, Kelly, we've cut our stay short for you. We'll be arriving

on the 7240 on American. It should land at four p.m. Don't know if we'll make it in time to see your game. We still want to talk to you."

Patrick had an urge to bolt from the ceramic throne. He would, in a moment, but there was the matter of that last message. Never mind that he had a good idea what it would be, what was about to happen. He stayed glued to his seat, phone bolted to his ear.

"Hey, Kelly. We were hoping you'd be there, help us with our luggage. If you feel like calling back one of these days, you can tell us when your game starts. We're about a block away, guess we'll see you or we won't."

There it was, another nice little disaster.

"To erase this message, press nine. To save, press seven. To replay—"

A high-pitched scream found its way from downstairs and under the door.

Patrick was almost sure that message wouldn't need replaying.

First, there was the matter of the bottles outside.

Kelly's parents walking around the back, wheeling their black rectangular carry-ons behind them. Maybe even getting past the steps, halfway across the deck before coming to a full stop. Unprepared to find the green iron-mesh table converted into a wet bar. Taking in the exodus of their entire liquor cabinet. Caps and corks lying on the ground like spent ammunition; a couple of bottles lying on their sides, passed out as though they'd had a bit too much of themselves.

Patrick missed all of that, still checking Kelly's messages at that point.

When the scream hit, he tossed the cell phone back in the laundry basket. Slammed the cover back on, an automatic attempt to undo what was about to happen. Patrick was out of the bathroom and down the stairs in three seconds flat, bursting into the kitchen to find Kelly's mother rooted to the spot. Trembling in her tan-colored power suit. Hands pressed against her face, horrified scream still frozen on glossy lips as she stared across the kitchen. Past the second set of kitchen doors, through which the remains of their once-great collection of crystalware lay shattered across the decimated cabinet, table, and coffee-stained rug.

From down in the den, Patrick could hear an argument in full swing, the booming voice of Kelly's father, repeating demands for an explanation without breath or pause.

Kelly's mother let out a wounded squeak, just getting warmed up herself.

Patrick smelled the usual cocktail of beer and white wine on her breath.

"Mrs. McDermott, just to let you know, *that* was entirely my fault," he began. His words came out fast and measured, without the slightest thought as to whether there was anything that could save them now. "Kelly was making some coffee and he offered me some. I overreacted, I guess, and I slapped it out of his hands, a little hard, I guess, and it just went..." Patrick held out his arms stiffly in the direction of the dining room, an artist unveiling his worst piece of work to date.

With a few choking exhales, Kelly's mother found her voice. "And you've been *drinking*!"

Patrick remembered the table of debauchery and prepared to launch ahead with another explanation. He didn't get beyond the words *We were just* when Kelly's father barked from the other room, demanding that Kelly's mother get in there *right now!*

"Kelly, what is going *on*?!" she cried out, stalking toward the den.

Patrick saw her descend the steps. A despairing knot wrapped itself around Patrick's stomach, pulled him against his will toward the sound of hollered accusations. He was already certain of what would be waiting there.

What he found instead was Kelly's father, inexplicably on the defensive. An older version of Kelly McDermott in a pinstripe suit. Hands on his hips, unable to comprehend how he had ended up in this position.

"You're saying this is *our fault*?"

"Who cares about *this*?" Kelly spat out. His eyes were wide, torturous. The veins in his neck bulged, his whole body straining against itself. If the couch and glass coffee table weren't between him and his parents, it would be disturbingly easy to imagine him marching across the room and strangling them both.

Jenna stood to one side, forgotten in the chaos of the moment.

"Kelly!" his mother cried out. "That's our family's crystal! Your grandfather got those—"

"You think I care about your plates and goddamn *cups*?"

Kelly shouted, vocal cords scraping against each other. "You left me! You just disappeared! Leaving me on my own like that, you don't get to tell me *anything*! Call yourself parents! You just *left* me! You left me there, sitting there waiting for years without a single call, waiting for you to come *visit* me in that goddamn prison!"

It wasn't until Patrick heard the word *visit* that he understood.

This wasn't about what was or what had been.

Kelly was railing about things to come. Stuck in that institution, locked away behind the white walls of an unnamed crazy house. Left to wonder what had become of the only two people with an unwritten duty to take care of their own. An abandonment so unimaginable that his parents hadn't even begun to contemplate what they would someday be capable of.

And Patrick couldn't bring himself to stop the accusations.

It didn't matter that it was impossible. That to allow this diatribe to continue was a tacit acceptance of all that Kelly believed to be happening. Every word was pure merit. The unspoken facts of Kelly's present life, a flawlessly decorated reflection of Patrick's own existence.

And so Patrick welcomed, gladly welcomed Kelly's madness, reveled in watching Kelly's parents draw close to each other in a terrified embrace.

"Kelly," his mother begged. "What are you talking about?"

"You'll find out," Kelly said, picking up his helmet from the fireplace and tucking it under his arm. "You know where the drinks are. Go help yourself."

He stormed out, past Patrick and out the back door.

Jenna was hot on his heels, and Patrick didn't bother dwelling on the McDermotts' inarticulate faces. He snatched up Kelly's gym bag and ran out to the car. Found Kelly starting it up, Jenna in the passenger's seat, waiting for him to join the fun.

"We've still got a deal," Kelly told him. "But just a warning, Patrick. I don't even know if I remember how to play this god-damn game."

"Just do your best," Patrick said, revolted at how meaning-less it sounded.

He jumped in the backseat, wondering how Kelly would ever bring himself to come back to that house. Shoving the thought aside, he buckled his safety belt. If there was still such a thing as later, he'd worry about it then.

Time being, there was the game to worry about.

It was quite a night for Wellspring Academy.

The stands were packed, brimming with spectators. Not just those from Wilson, a whole contingent of people had appeared just to see the state finals. Local news crews dotted the sidelines, along with CNN, ESPN, and MSN affiliates.

The school marching band was playing at full blast, cheer-leaders for either side kicking their legs up and somersaulting their way into people's fantasies. The time was drawing near, and Redwood had gathered the team together for a last-minute motivational tirade. Even Patrick, the team's unofficial, glorified gofer, was allowed to sit in on the prelude to blood, sweat, and tears.

"Starting now, we forget everything that's led up to this!" Redwood barked. "I don't care whether it was the blowout in Charlotte last week, or the game that got called for lightning last *year*. I certainly don't give a shit about any of your god-damn personal conflicts, even if they happened THIS AFTER-NOON!" Redwood's face ballooned into a red ball of pure, ambitious wrath. "Everything has been leading up to this, and as of this moment, none of it matters anymore! None of it happened as far as I'm concerned! I am calling for each and every one of you to say to yourself, I DO NOT MATTER! WHERE

I'VE BEEN DOESN'T MATTER. All that matters is the *game*. Nothing matters, except the *game!*"

As Redwood continued to talk, Patrick felt an unpleasant taste rising in his chest. More of a potent sensation, like fire-water. Clear, toxic liquid that couldn't be tasted. It could only be felt as it scorched the back of Patrick's throat. Spread to his thoughts, turning them poisonous.

Once you've gone too far, once the world is no longer the one it was yesterday–Patrick's angels reflected on what Bill had told him that afternoon–*it's very hard to go back.*

"Nothing matters, except the game!" Redwood repeated.

He'd heard it so many times, and never once believed it. Just accepted it, only now acceptance wasn't enough. Patrick found that he could barely tolerate it. Redwood's words weren't pep, weren't simple cuts of overused inspiration. They had become gospel. The word of God, coursing through the mind of every last player in the huddle, wet on the waiting lips of a packed stadium. The game was all that mattered. Sportsman-ship, teamwork, the noble tradition, none of it would be enough to replace the hysterical need for a *win*.

The shills for Wellspring Academy began to belt out their fight song:

"FIGHT, FIGHT, OUTTA SIGHT! KILL, PANTHERS, KILL!"

Patrick looked up into the stands, a swelling tide of faces, squirming larvae.

And right at the fifty-yard line, just a few seats up from center stage, were Patrick's parents. Dressed in school colors, wearing football jerseys the school sold along with bumper stickers sporting peace signs and selected quotes from MLK and Mahatma Gandhi. Grinning in anticipation, waiting for their substitute progeny to carry Wellspring Academy into the big time.

And Kelly's parents were nowhere to be seen.

In a single fluttering motion, everyone stood up and placed their right hand over their chest.

Patrick turned back to the huddle, only to find it had broken up. All team members side by side along the out-of-bounds line. Redwood standing at the end, face solemn as the crowd grew quiet. From far down the field, over by the south post, the marching band's conductor brandished his baton.

Drums rumbled, preparing the band for the first bars of the national anthem.

Patrick positioned himself directly behind Kelly and Cody as everyone began to sing.

Oh, say can you see…

Patrick saw Cody turn, ever so slightly, toward Kelly.

"You're not going to fuck this up, Kelly," Cody told him, lips barely moving. Barely sounding, just loud enough for Patrick to hear. "This ain't your house anymore. This ain't your game, this is mine. Don't make me take it from you. You hear me, Kelly? Don't make me take it. Don't make me do this, I'll take your little girlfriend for myself. Make her *know* she ain't yours anymore, Kelly."

Patrick glanced down and saw Kelly's finger tapping against his own thigh.

Getting through it all by simply tolerating it.

"This is stupid, Kelly," Patrick said, words overlapping Cody's repugnant taunts. He could barely hear his own voice over the off-key lyrics saluting Old Glory. Filling his lungs with a bit more ammunition, he began to repeat it over and over, voice rising: "This is stupid, Kelly. This is stupid, Kelly. This is stupid, Kelly. This is *stupid, Kelly!*"

Cody whirled around, hand still stitched to his heart. "Shut your hole, Patrick!"

Kelly turned on Cody, eyes livid. "Don't talk to him like that."

Before Cody could retaliate, Patrick simply repeated it one last time. "Kelly ... this is stupid."

Kelly gave him a questioning look, a reminder that this had been *Patrick's* idea.

Patrick simply nodded.

Kelly winked, and without so much as kissing Cody good-bye, he broke ranks.

Tossing the playbook aside, Patrick followed.

Though not immediately apparent, a gradual fold had taken place in the texture of the crowd. Barely noticeable murmurs spreading through the anthem like a virus, the sounds of a radio dial trapped between stations. Catching the ears of news crews; cameras like compass needles, tilting toward the two boys marching along the field with confounding strides.

Kelly stalked up to Jenna, standing at attention alongside her own brigade of gingerbread models.

Her chest hiccupped once, unprepared to see Kelly and Patrick before her.

"I was wrong," Kelly admitted against the final strands of music. "You were right. Patrick and I are getting out of here. And you're invited because you belong with us."

Sensing that their days on that field were numbered, Kelly and Patrick moved on. Heading for the exit as *the land of the brave* was overtaken by a full stadium rhubarb of bewildered sports fans. They passed through a split between the bleachers, stadium lights at their back. Falling into shadow as their number grew to three.

Patrick looked over and saw Jenna matching them step for step.

"Where are we going?" she asked.

Kelly turned to Patrick, and Patrick gave him the OK.

"We're going to get that goddamn memory card back."

19

An hour and a half after leaving Charlotte, Jenna came to a stop in front of the mailbox. Patrick and Kelly were out in an instant, doors closed as the car pulled away, heading west along the dark, empty stretch of country road. Crouched low, they stole down the driveway. As they kept close to the left side, the surrounding trees gave perfect cover, shielding them from the whitewash of a solitary lamppost just twenty yards down the street.

It was hardly the residential cluster of Verona's inner sanctum. Out there, large patches of forest and private fields kept neighbors well out of each other's business. The only stores in the area were gas stations. There were no sidewalks and, consequently, no pedestrians. And as a result, any and all suspicious activity fell under a very simple principle: if it was an activity, it was suspicious.

The driveway sloped down, widened, at which point Patrick and Kelly followed the line of trees around to the dark side of the house. First- and second-story windows bare like slates of marble.

"So far, so good," Kelly whispered.

The front-yard lights came to life, sent light sprawling over them.

Kelly grabbed Patrick's shoulder, yanked him back into the trees. He fell flat on his stomach, head buried between his arms. Dried leaves and pine needles poked at him. Breathing in the smell of dried forest bed and discarded bark, heart drumming in some dangerous time signature.

"Patrick..."

Raising his eyes, Patrick peered beyond the tree line.

A raccoon was scuttling across the flower beds, a stealthy blob on a brightly lit stage.

"Tripped off the motion sensors," Kelly whispered. "Once it leaves, we'll wait for the lights to turn off, head to the back. You're sure we can get to his room from there?"

Patrick nodded.

"You still got the crowbar?"

"Yes."

"Hang on to it, I don't want to be searching for shit in the dark."

"OK."

"You sure you still want to do this?"

"Shut up, already."

Without moving, they waited for the raccoon to leave.

Then for the lights to go.

Once their eyes had readjusted to the dark, Kelly led the way to the back. A couple of swift steps brought them to the base of a network of twisting ivy, weaving its way up the house along cross sections of cedar lattice.

Patrick pointed toward the far-right window jutting out over the roof. "That's Cody's room..." He then pointed to the window directly above and to the left. "That's Redwood's office."

"So we go in through there," Kelly concluded.

Patrick nodded.

Kelly didn't stand on ceremony. Securing his foot into the lattice, he hoisted himself up. In a matter of seconds, he had already scaled his way up to the roof. He waved down with an all clear.

Patrick glanced around, wary of any witness hiding in the dark. Nothing out there but the sound of crickets and the forest settling. He pulled the gloves Kelly had given him tight around his hands. Sheathing the crowbar between his belt and Armani pants, he reached up and hooked onto the wooden frame. Closed his eyes, visualizing the next step. Preparing himself, because he knew that would be the one that made it all real.

After this, no more kidding yourself, his angels cautioned. *This is actually happening.*

To his surprise, the thought had a calming effect. He tightened his grip and dug his toe in, lifting off as though he'd spent every morning for the past four years doing pull-ups. The crowbar tapped against his foot with every new foothold, flat ivy leaves brushing against his teeth. By the time he reached the top and took hold of Kelly's outstretched arm, Patrick's body was oversaturated with joyous adrenaline.

"Got you smiling now," Kelly chuckled as Patrick came to rest on the shingles. "How about that?"

They took a moment to enjoy the end of phase one. With

the woods surrounding them in quiet serenity, the two of them sat and basked in the glow of stars and a rising half-moon.

Patrick gave Kelly a pat on the back. "Let's do this."

"Right on."

Inching up to the window, Kelly fastened his arms around the screen. He glanced back and let out a breath. "This is going to be noisier than you might like," he warned before closing his eyes and ripping the screen from its home. It ended up taking two brutal yanks, each one accompanied by the pained creaking of metal. Then two harsh pops as the bolts tore free.

They paused, expecting a SWAT team to come sliding down a swath of suspended cables, semiautomatic rifles blazing.

A car sped past on Erwin Road, an oblivious metal trilobite.

Kelly laid the screen down beside him, reached back with his hand.

Patrick handed him the crowbar.

Positioning himself for a better angle, he rested the round end of the crowbar against one of the rectangular panes. Gave a few practice taps.

"What are you *doing*?" Patrick whispered.

"Going to break the glass. Unlock it from inside."

"I thought you were going to *pry* it open."

"Don't be ridiculous." Kelly tapped a few more times. "You can't pry open a window, that's doors you're thinking of."

"Then why not the back door?"

"You said there was an alarm system," Kelly whispered. "Whole downstairs is covered with motion sensors, wired to the front and back doors."

"How do we know this window *isn't?*"

"Well, *is* it?"

"I don't *know!*"

With a quick thrust, Kelly sent the crowbar through the window. It didn't shatter as much as crack apart. Large, geometrically confused pieces of glass came toppling down, no louder than the removal of the screen, but there was something about glass.

"Guess not," Kelly concluded, snaking his arm through the gaping hole.

Once inside, Patrick led them through the dark. He'd been in Cody's house on numerous occasions. Always with Kelly, of course, and Patrick had to wonder how much of this was coming back to the would-be time traveler.

Things versus events, Patrick's angels recalled.

The hallway was lit by the sickly orange glow of a scented plug-in. Now that they were safely inside, their concerns ebbed. Tiptoeing with a bit more abandon, they made it down to Cody's room. The door was ajar, and they opened it wide as they could to maximize the hallway light.

Patrick surveyed the room. It wasn't unlike Kelly's; hip-hop posters, clothes scattered about, dresser drawers agape, bookcases home to awards for athletic excellence. Imagining himself as a detective, he slowly approached Cody's desk. With an alert yet relaxed gaze, he took in every detail before moving in. Lowering into a crouch to get a different angle on things. He turned on a mental sound track, a few tunes from the album *Clifford*

Brown with Strings. Nothing more than a collection of standards, but the sound of Clifford's trumpet, set against the backdrop of a studio full of strings, always had that kind of 1930s detective feel to it....

"Got it," Kelly announced.

Patrick found him sitting on the box spring of Cody's bed. The mattress had been lifted at a corner, alligator jaw resting against Kelly's back. A large ziplock bag dangled from his hand.

Way to shine, Dick Tracy, Patrick's angels chided. *Wouldn't sell the farm if I were you.*

He approached the bag and peered through the plastic. There was the memory card, along with what appeared to be oblong pills of undetermined color. Patrick smiled, glanced up. "How did you know?"

"Remembered his secret stash," Kelly said, now holding up an issue of *Barely Legal,* in one of many skinny bags tucked farther down the mattress. "Thank you, Larry Flynt."

"So, one more time...," Patrick said, feeling more at home now that they had found what they were looking for. "Why did we bring the crowbar?"

"Just in case I was wrong and we had to do a little lock busting. Better safe–"

"–than sorry," Patrick finished. "There, we're *both* time travelers now."

"We should hang out more."

"What are these?" Patrick asked, pointing to the pills. "There's a lot of them."

Kelly closed his eyes tight, sorting through his limited memory. "Didn't Jenna say something about Cody acting a little more psychotic than usual?"

"Yeah?"

"Though that's a common misconception," Kelly muttered to himself. "Still, if Cody's predisposed to that kind of aggression—"

"You've seen the guy when he loses," Patrick interrupted. "I doubt there's an object on this planet he hasn't punched. What's the point?"

"Steroids."

"No."

"Cody's a little monstrous for a sophomore, don't you think?"

"Still . . ."

"Got any better suggestions?"

"Maybe they're just some kind of prescription—"

"Sure . . ." Kelly grabbed the rest of the porn mags, fanned them out like dirty playing cards. "And I suppose these are all past issues of the *Wall Street Journal*. They're here because they're contraband. Take my word for it, Cody's been juicing."

"Well, maybe Wellspring's got a shot at winning state after all. We've got the card. Let's get out of here before some squirrel calls the police."

"We're taking all of it," Kelly said decisively, folding up the bag and shoving it into Patrick's pocket. "If Cody finds just his card missing, he's going to know it was us."

"We take the whole bag, he's going to know anyway."

Kelly walked out into the hallway with Patrick in tow.

"Yeah, but now he can't finger us. Because he knows that if he does, we can just say, yeah...we came for a plastic memory card that happened to be in this bag filled with a controlled substance. We all go to jail together."

They made it back to Redwood's office, at which point Patrick stopped Kelly in his tracks. "I don't want to go to jail, *period*."

"For over forty years, the U.S. didn't want to disappear in a radioactive mushroom cloud," Kelly told him, shrugging. "They called it the cold war, and if mutually assured self-destruction worked for an entire planet, it'll probably work for us."

"The U.S. *still* doesn't want to disappear in a radioactive—"

"Then if I were you, I'd get the hell out of this country before the year 2012, my friend."

Even in the dark, Patrick knew his horrified expression must have made an impact.

"Just kidding," Kelly said grimly. "Looks like you do believe in time travel, after all."

"Asshole." Patrick exhaled, hand clutching at his chest. "Can we go now?"

"Hell yes."

The pair of them snuck back out the window, mindful of the broken glass.

Out onto the roof, where they shimmied back down their white lattice ladder.

Cutting through the forest, they came to the edge of Erwin Road, a strategically dark stretch between widespread streetlights. They kept to the trees, waiting. After a few minutes, they heard the sound of Kelly's car slowing to a stop across the road. Not another car in sight, and that was the icing on the cake. They sprinted across the road, and jumped into the convertible.

"Where to?" Jenna asked, checking to make sure all limbs were tucked safely into the vehicle.

"I, for one, could use a drink," Kelly said.

"Maybe a game of nine-ball?" Patrick added.

There was a momentary pause, and even the moon blushed with a fulfilled glow.

"I think I know a place where we can get both," Jenna said, switching on the headlights and hitting the gas.

#20

Kelly ignored the extinguished neon sign, the word OPEN reduced to a sooty, ashen color. Only one or two cars were parked along Broad Street. Scant traffic, especially for a Friday night. The funeral parlor across the street was on lockdown, green awning drooping like an eyelid.

There didn't seem to be much life coming from inside On The Rail, either.

Kelly was seconds away from knocking when a wooden door at the other end of the building swung open into the street.

Casper leaned out, arm flat against the door, fingers spread out.

"Oh shit, Kelly!" he laughed, grin of a practical joker wishing for *you to just* see *your face right now.* "You are a gosh-damn lunatic, man! Get on in here with your friends."

Inside, the house lights were off. Above the bar, a few nicotine-colored bulbs gave the immediate area a 1970s hue. The fluorescent lamps above the tables had also been turned off, save two or three. At one table, a pair of men in paint-spattered clothes were setting up a rack of nine-ball. The air was still dense with the exhaust from an evening's worth of

Olympic smokers, fusing to the music of Wayne Shorter, a little number from *The Blue Note Years.*

Kelly put an arm around each of his friends. "Can you dig it?"

"I can dig it." Jenna grinned.

"I can dig it," Patrick echoed, unable to remember the unease he'd felt when they'd first walked in there, just yesterday.

Casper strode behind the bar, downing the remains of a Pabst before slapping his hands down before his new invitees. "Glad you could make it, Kelly McDermott."

"I know that yesterday you told me after two," Kelly said. "But we were driving by, saw the sign turned off—"

"Closed up early!" Casper declared. "Kelly, what you pulled tonight ... Got to give you ten out of ten for style."

"What's that?"

"It's all over the news." Casper grinned. "Local, ESPN, MSN, *all over.* Star quarterback takes off in the middle of the *national anthem*! I'm surprised anyone even bothered to watch the game after that. Oh, and your team won, by the way."

"All part of my master plan," Kelly said with a wink.

"Lunatic!" Casper wagged his finger between Patrick and Jenna. "Which one of you is driving?"

Patrick laid his hand out on the bar, face up.

Kelly dropped the keys into his waiting hand, cool as could be.

"Beats the hell out of catching them upside your head," Patrick commented.

"Ha!" Casper smacked his palms together and crouched

down. He resurfaced with a squat bottle of bourbon. "May I interest the rest of you in a little Knob Creek?"

Jenna groaned, lowered her head to rest on the bar.

"Do you *sleep* in that outfit?" Casper asked her, leaning over to get a better look at her skirt. "Because that's just fine with me. There ought to be a law, far as I'm concerned."

"I *am* the law," Jenna informed him, voice muffled. "None for me, thanks."

"Kelly?"

"Can I get some ice with that?" Kelly asked, a wry smile saluting under tired eyes.

Casper shoveled some ice into two red plastic cups. He poured, setting one down in front of Kelly, raising his own high above his head. "To Kelly and his brass balls!"

The pair mashed their red cups together in a plastic toast and opened wide.

Casper grimaced with raw ecstasy, slammed his cup down. "Patrick!"

Patrick had been staring at a muted television screen situated on top of the fridge. "Huh?"

"Got my iPod hooked up to the speakers." Casper motioned with his head. "Get on back here and let's make ourselves a playlist."

Patrick felt Kelly's elbow dig into his ribs.

An hour or so later, the clock had drifted well past one in the morning. Patrick and Jenna were seated in a corner. The heavy wooden benches beneath them were built right into the wall, just below one of the sprawling front windows. A couple of sodas rested on the table before them. It was covered in stained green felt, for the benefit of any card players who happened to be looking for a game.

At the nearest pool table, Kelly and Casper were shooting some stick. Mixing liquor, fresh smoke trailing from Kelly's cigarette. Throwing money down left and right, gambling the night away.

"Patrick?" Jenna put her feet up on the edge of the bench. She wrapped her arms around her knees, chin cradled between them. "That was a good thing you did tonight."

Hearing it from Jenna gave him a momentary lapse in memory. "What do you mean?"

"Helping Edmund like that ..."

"Oh." Patrick reached for his drink. "Well, it wasn't much."

"It was quite a bit much. Illegal, dangerous, and ... I want to say, stupid, but ... still, it was good."

"It was Kelly, really."

"Maybe. Partly, sure. But Kelly's had twenty years to change. You've done it in less than three days...." Jenna scooted toward him. Shoulder to shoulder, turning her head to look at him directly. "I'm proud to be with you tonight, Patrick."

He looked over, elated to find how close her face was to his. Even his imagination had never allowed for being this close, so close he could actually see the fragmented color of her eyes. It was never supposed to happen, being this close, and yet, there was her breath, close enough to brush his lips.

"Do you actually think this might all be real?" he asked.

She smiled, glanced over to the pool table. "Up until now,

it's always sort of...been about Kelly, hasn't it? Our lives, everything, bonded to Kelly."

"That's not so strange, is it?" Patrick followed her gaze with lazy ease, carrying the memory of her face with him. "Lot of people like you, me, and Kelly, lot of friends with the same... thing."

"Before today, I couldn't have told anyone who Kelly McDermott is. I'd always say boyfriend, that's who he was. Even with Kelly, it might have been the same. Together for four years, and I'm starting to think that the only reason was... Kelly wanted someone to stay with. That if he wasn't with me, he knew he'd have to...party hard, screw around with anything on two legs, do all those things expected of him. With me, he was allowed to play the part without all that. The football star and the cheerleader, can't ask for a better way to keep up appearances." Jenna sighed, the sound of acceptance. "We all use each other, I suppose, to keep from having to...be anybody."

"It's hard to argue otherwise."

"Maybe that's why there was never really any you or me. I mean, it was Kelly and me. It was you and Kelly..."

"There was you and me long before there was ever Kelly," Patrick informed her.

Out of the corner of his left eye, he could see Jenna looking at him. Awaiting an elaboration he was now going to have to make good on. Patrick never doubted it would come. Watching Kelly take down a shot of bourbon, he sensed that there was no more Jenna and Kelly. Not the way it had been before. And although he wasn't ready to believe that Patrick and Kelly was a thing of the past, he knew that he and Jenna had only just found each other.

Whatever comes next, his angels counseled, *there are no guarantees.*

"I saw you in second grade," Patrick said, refusing to accompany his confession with anything other than a fixed stare, straight ahead. "And here I'll bet you didn't know I used to go to Jefferson Elementary."

"I didn't."

"Caught sight of you from my seat in the cafeteria. I was at the end of one of those long rectangles, right next to where each class would line up for the kitchen." Memories were tricky, and as the years went by, Patrick never put much stock into what he had seen that first time. A younger Jenna than the one he would eventually get to know, that's all Patrick had to go on. Standing in line, a body free of curves, face unwilling to let go of those remaining traces of baby fat; a thumbnail of what she would eventually grow into.

Patrick opened his mouth and let his angels speak for him. "Saw you standing in line that first time, and that was it for me. Every day, I'd sit at the same table. The same seat, good as behind home plate. I'd watch you stand in line. You'd stand in line, and that pretty much sums up my knowledge of you back then. Though I also knew, somewhere, that this would be as close as I would ever get to you. A girl standing in line. All that mattered reduced to a daily helping of indoor sunshine. A girl standing in line, trapped behind the half hour between twelve and twelve-thirty."

Patrick had a sip of his root beer, set the bottle down next to him. "I always thought that would be as lonely as it would ever get."

"If that was second grade," Jenna said quietly, "that means I was gone the next year."

"Children vanish at that age. Transfer to new schools. Parents get new jobs. They lose jobs, move across the country, out of the country. Sometimes they get in car accidents. . . . There was no telling where you had gone. In the years that followed, I just allowed acceptance to be my guiding light."

"And then, years later . . ."

"That's the part I think is really funny. . . ." Patrick wasn't about to laugh, but he was somehow able to let a quiet smile creep into the narrative. "You and Kelly met outside of school, right before it started. My parents ran into you two at the mall, and . . ."

"They didn't like what they saw," Jenna finished.

"They're cheap," Patrick told her grimly. "My parents are cheap people."

"Don't say that—"

"How could they possibly not like you?" Patrick aired his dirty laundry, shaking his head as he would a sheet in the wind. "You're kind, smart. Unaware of your own beauty, which I think only adds to the overall surplus you've got."

"That's not true."

"It is . . . But no matter, my parents didn't see it and . . . they just figured this girl from a working-class home, whose family split up, has no place in Kelly's heart. You do know, my parents introduced us to get you away from Kelly."

Jenna's feet hit the floor and she leaped back a little. Her eyes were wide, mouth open in a disturbingly accurate impression of a blow-up doll Patrick had seen at a party once. "*That's* what that was about?"

"That's wight, wabbit."

"You mean . . ." Jenna went back to drawing flies with her mouth, neck straining forward. "When they called me up and said, 'Oh, why don't you come over to our house for dinner with Kelly and our son, Patrick,' that was all–"

"A trick," Patrick said. "It was a trick to get you over to meet me."

"So I wasn't good enough for Kelly, but they had no problem foisting me on their *biological* son?"

"Not everybody's born with biological imperatives," Patrick sighed. "Someone today told me that you can rationalize just about anything. Kelly *is* their son. No DNA test on the planet's going to make them feel otherwise."

"So that dinner that was supposed to happen with you, me, and Kelly . . . Your parents said that Kelly, at the last minute, couldn't make it."

"They never invited him." Patrick was actually beginning to enjoy the bloodshot memories. "But could you put yourself in my shoes? There I was, years divorced from second grade. In my own house, when you come special delivery to my front door. You step in, my world goes head over heels. Before we can even be introduced, the first words out of your mouth–"

"Oh no!" Jenna cried, wrapping her arms around her head.

"That's right, were *Is Kelly here yet?*"

"No!"

"And my world quickly fell back into step," Patrick concluded with a smile and a sad shake of his head. "The instant I heard you say that, I already knew, it was you and Kelly for keeps."

"Baarg!"

"And all we talked about over dinner..."

"Much to your parents' dismay..."

"Was Kelly."

"Kelly!" Jenna screeched, jumping on the bench. "Everything you touch you destroy!"

Kelly swaggered over with the bottle of Knob Creek, two-thirds empty. He took a few steps back and forth to the Tom Waits song playing: "I'm a pool-shooting-shimmy-shyster, shaking my head. When I should be living clean instead."

"Where's Casper?" Patrick stood up, looking around. The two pool players had retired to the bar, beers clutched in chalky hands. Eyes glued to the close-captioned highlights on ESPN2.

"It's a surprise." Kelly winked, resting his ass against the bench's back.

The side door popped open, and Casper strode in with Kelly's car keys in one hand, Patrick's saxophone case in the other. He held it aloft, cutting behind the bar. The surface was wiped clean with a sweep of Casper's arm, the case set on top. He flipped it over, brass latches aimed in Patrick's direction.

Casper reached back and disconnected the iPod.

"Get on over here and get your horn set up," Casper told Patrick, voice echoing in the newfound silence. "You and I are gonna jam."

"All right!" Kelly raised his fist in the air.

"I don't know..." Patrick approached the bar with the hesitant hands of someone asked to hold a newborn for the first time. "I've never really played for people before."

"You're in the school band," Jenna said witheringly. "First chair since sophomore year, you've played every basketball game since we were freshmen."

"Yeah, but not for...real."

"He means he's never played for us," Jenna specified.

"This is as real as it gets, tonight," Kelly proclaimed, ambling across the room and leaning against the shuffleboard table. "I didn't travel twenty years into the past just to hear your sorry excuses."

"That's right," Casper said, heading for the back. "He didn't travel twenty years into the past just to hear your sorry excuses."

"I'll even put it together for you," Kelly offered, shuffling toward the case.

"OK, fine," Patrick relented, snapping the latches. "Just don't, Kelly, come near my saxophone. Stay right where you are and have another drink."

Kelly was happy to do as he was told.

Patrick opened the case and pulled out the strap, hung it around his neck. With his back turned, he went about assembling his saxophone with the same concentration that an aspiring student might read sheet music. He snapped the instrument onto the strap. Putting his lips to the mouthpiece, Patrick licked the wooden reed a few times, reveling in the familiar taste of tongue depressor.

Folding his bottom lip over his teeth and biting down on the mouthpiece, Patrick blew a few test notes. He winced, at sounds that seemed unwelcome in On The Rail's empty acoustics. He found himself projecting back to twelve years old, awkwardly cradling a heavy chunk of brass, wondering how the hell he could ever get this thing to actually make music.

By the time he'd turned around, Casper was already back. He'd dragged a chair over to table one, was seated with an electric guitar in his lap. Hooking it up to a small beige amplifier beside him, Casper began to tune up. Plucking at strings, twisting the keys. All kidding aside now, his rambunctious energy converted to solemn concentration.

"Nice horn," he said offhandedly.

Stringing a few more notes together that bordered on melody, Patrick made his way over to Casper's side. Casper adjusted a few dials and began playing. With his head tilted to the side, he settled into a bluesy groove.

Patrick stood by, waiting for him to finish warming up.

Looked up and saw Jenna and Kelly, both leaning against the bench.

"Don't just stand there, man," Casper prompted him. His head rocked to the rhythm, tending to the business of strings and frets. "Come on, let's hear it."

Patrick closed his eyes and slid his lips over the mouth-piece.

He went backward in time, slowly sifting through memories. The past four years cruising along with a disaffected ease. His story thus far, in rewind. Nothing but a collection of events, time spent at football games, dimly lit parties at whoever's house happened to be suffering from parental neglect on that particular weekend. Those rare dinners with his parents, Kelly's parents, the repetitive motions of silverware, repetitive topics of discussion about what the day had brought them all. A slew of repetitive days, no discerning difference between what preceded what. The classes, school meetings, band practices, the same hyperactive fight songs at every basketball game. Girls that floated in and out of focus, never close enough to kiss or even date, discomfiting thoughts of having to see them every day, interrupting the effortless poetry of his unchanging life. All that self-sabotage, insisting on maintaining such empty comforts. Patrick alone in his room, hostage to his brother's books, decorations, dresser drawers still half-filled with the clothes of a seven-year-old.

And these memories picked up speed, each one a yawning smear of nothing. Filled with nothing, just isolated symbols. Punctuated with ghostlike figures that took on temporary forms. His parents, his teachers, even Kelly and Jenna, a void that widened even as he remembered the music that filled it. Growing louder, brass wails sent out to replace all that which should have been there, culminating with the stark figure of his little brother.

Standing outside their school, tossing a football to himself.

Eyelashes batting away clumps of thick black hair, courtesy of his mother.

The last real memory of the days before music.

And without the applause from Kelly, Jenna, and two strangers at the bar, he might have kept on playing, without ever realizing he had already begun.

Raising his lids, Patrick peered through the dark veil before his eyes.

Casper playing along, really swinging his head now. Kelly with the bottle of Knob Creek perched on his thigh, head resting against Jenna's. Their arms linked, side by side, but that was OK, too. The house lights were off, the clock was keeping to its own rules. Even the indistinct, muted figure of Coach Redwood up on the television screen was just one more piece of a new night on earth.

Nobody bothering to read the choppy, misspelled black-and-white captions beneath his pleased, yet stern face.

WE DON'T KNOW . . . EVERYONE HAS BEEN WOR-RIED ABOUT HIM. WE HAVE . . . SUSPCICIONS

JUST WANT TO WAIT AND SEE . . . CHANCE TO TALKK TO KELLY MCDERMOTT . . .

Patrick didn't think twice about closing his eyes and returning to the music.

TODAY III

21

His eyes opened, and for a moment, Patrick didn't know where he was.

A sky-blue mattress floated just above his head, pressing down on thin wire mesh. Turning his head to the side, he got a worm's-eye view of a dark wooden floor. Beneath him was a green sleeping bag, gutted and spread out. From somewhere nearby, 1970s funk played at low volume.

Saturdays on 90.7 WNCU, Patrick's angels prompted.

It all came back to him then.

Patrick slid from under Jenna's bed, certain he'd fallen asleep next to it.

He stood up, stretched.

The blinds were drawn, gray light emanating from the edges of its vinyl borders.

Patrick got his bearings, eyes going from the empty bed to his coat draped over the stereo. He picked it up, slipped his arms into the sleeves. Realized that, sooner or later, he was going to have to replace the components of his new suit with something a bit less wrinkled. He walked over to Jenna's night table, took a close look at the clock.

One p.m.

He opened the door, thought he heard voices.

With uneven steps, Patrick headed down the truncated hallway, through the small living room, and into the kitchen.

Kelly McDermott was at the sink, washing dishes.

Face calm as a domestic servant with no name or birthday.

Jenna was pouring a cup of coffee, and upon seeing Patrick, her eyes lit up. Barely able to contain herself, she set down the mug and thrust an open envelope under his nose. Patrick took it from her hands, glanced down at the insignia in the top left corner. He looked up.

Jenna stood with her hands behind her back, a child awaiting the final assessment of the glitter-soaked drawing she'd made in art class.

Patrick removed the letter, several pages in length, and unfolded it.

There wasn't a high school student alive who ever needed to look past the first three words.

Patrick grinned. "You're off the wait list."

"They let me into Ohio State!" Jenna cried, leaping into Patrick's unprepared arms.

Well, swing her around a little, dummy, his angels insisted, and Patrick did so, wrapping his arms around her waist and lifting. She held on tightly, laughing. Uneven breaths escaping along the back of his neck.

"That's my girl" came the proud voice of Jenna's father.

Patrick hadn't even noticed him sitting at the small table crammed into the corner between the counter and the entrance to the kitchen.

"Good morning, Mr. Garamen," Patrick said, setting Jenna down.

"Good afternoon to you, too, Patrick...." He lifted his coffee to thin lips, hawkish nose dipping into the mug as he drank. His fine sandpaper hair was in full weekend mode, thistles sprouting at all ends. "Forgive my appearance," he added, tugging at his sweatpants and black Rolling Stones T-shirt. "And please, you can call me Al. Like the Paul Simon song. I know you don't come around that often, but it's going to have to stick one of these days."

"Right, sorry." Patrick reached out to shake his hand, as though meeting him for the first time. "Congratulations, Al."

"Oh fiddlesticks," he said with a humble turn of the cheek. "All I did was write the essay for her and slip the dean a couple hundred bucks."

"Dad." Jenna laughed, going back to her cup of coffee. She set it next to Kelly, who paused to take a sip then continued to wash with a dreamy smile. "Bribing the *dean*. What *will* the neighbors say?"

"They'll say please stop walking around the yard in your underwear, Al."

From the sink, Kelly let out a low chuckle. Placed a glass on the rack to dry.

"So have we got a trifecta yet?" Al asked, rubbing a light snowfall of stubble. He kicked at the chair opposite him, bringing it out from under the table. "Patrick, you heard anything yet?"

"Yeah, I got in," Patrick said casually, sitting down. "Got the letter back in January."

"Patrick!" Jenna held out her hands in a silent *What the hell, guy?*

"I take it you're revealing state secrets," Al said, sipping his coffee.

"But you got a letter saying..." Jenna glanced over to Kelly, then remembered he didn't remember he didn't remember. Turned back to Patrick. "You got a letter saying you were wait-listed."

"Faked it," Patrick admitted. "Easy as pie, once you know the magic of Photoshop."

"But why?"

"Just trying to postpone tomorrow for as long as I could." Patrick shrugged. Remarkably at ease with his accumulated disasters. "I also might have gotten into Juilliard, but my parents are holding the letter hostage."

"Patrick!" Jenna threw an oven mitt at Patrick's head. "I have to hear this from my dad?"

"You just heard it from me...."

"You know what I mean."

"Well, you're hearing it now," Patrick said. "Juilliard is actually the only place I didn't get accepted to immediately. I've been hunting for that letter, too, but we all know the story with that now."

"They don't want you to go," Al concluded with a disappointed frown.

"Ohio State or bust," Patrick sighed. Hunched over, elbows on his knees.

"You know, I was called out by them, once." Al leaned back, put his arms behind his back. "Your parents. Had a problem with a leak up over the kitchen. Turned out to be a problem with the pipe coming from the upstairs sink. Gave 'em a good deal, on account of you being friends with Jenna and all. Never got a call back, though..."

The conversation dead-ended for a while. Pleasant and unassuming silence accompanied by the sound of running water and the soft rattle of knives and spoons.

"So are you going, then?" Jenna asked, hips flat against the counter. Eyes on Patrick's socks. "Are you going to Juilliard?"

Patrick scanned the pictures on the refrigerator. "I don't know."

"I mean, if you got in, which I'm sure you did."

"I don't know...." Unable to stop himself, Patrick looked up at Jenna.

She lifted her face up from the floor. Slowly, as though raising a drawbridge. Her eyes met his, still new to the practice, but nonetheless able to understand what remained unspoken. She quietly set aside her acceptance letter and crossed her arms, slowly rubbing her shoulders.

"So..." Al's voice was soft, gently sliding between them. "Prom's tonight. What do you kids have planned for today?"

Patrick leaned back, taking a cue from Al's relaxed slouch. "Kelly..." He looked over to the sink. "Are you still here?"

"It's still today," Kelly replied, shutting off the water. He picked up a green towel and dried his hands with thorough rubs. "And we've got some unfinished business."

He reached into his pocket and pulled out the small gray memory card.

"Try finishing your coffee first," Al recommended. "You look tired."

Kelly didn't need to be told twice.

#22

Edmund stepped out into the muggy afternoon. He seemed genuinely surprised to see Patrick. The screen door slammed behind him, and he looked around the front porch with trademark suspicion. Leaned to the side, checking out the walkway.

"Where's Kelly?" he asked.

"At the playground." Patrick pointed across the street. "He didn't want to make a big deal."

Edmund's eyes narrowed. "Big deal of what?"

"Of this..."

Despite the unsettling nature of Edmund's mistrust, Patrick had to hold back a smile.

Edmund appeared unable to place the memory card in his mind. He stared, confused, as though Patrick had just ambushed him with a diamond engagement ring. His Adam's apple worked once, twice against his neck before he could manage to ask: "What's that?"

"Our half of the bargain."

Edmund didn't move.

He doesn't want to believe, his angels nudged silently. *He's lived it for so long, he can't begin to imagine there's anyone left on his side.*

"Go ahead," Patrick encouraged. "Take it."

Edmund took the memory card gingerly between his thumb and index finger. Held it close to his face. He turned it over a few times, thoroughly examining both sides. The action was purely arbitrary, but it came through as absolutely necessary. Searching for evidence of an elaborate practical joke, enemies everywhere.

"Thank you," he said cautiously.

"Don't," Patrick replied. "I don't have a leg to stand on. This whole thing was as much my fault as it was for the rest of those numb-nuts on the team."

"Yeah . . . Still, though, thanks."

Patrick thought he detected a question mark punctuating the appreciation. He couldn't blame the kid, though. With a simple nod, he put his hands in his pockets, turned to walk down the front steps. Back on solid ground before he heard Edmund pipe up: "Do you think Kelly would mind if I went over and talked to him?"

Patrick turned, shrugged. "Not at all. Now that we're all squared away."

Edmund took to the steps, and the pair of them started off across the street.

"You guys going tonight?" Edmund asked, trying for casual. "The prom?"

"Maybe. We were supposed to share a limo with some of the guys from the team." Patrick shook his head with a slight laugh. "Don't think *that* part's going to be happening."

"What do you mean?"

"Just saying, if you thought *you* were unpopular before last night..."

Patrick didn't think Edmund had even heard about the game. Still, the thought of a football player rating below Edmund on the social ladder brought the dark outline of a smile to the sad outcast's lips.

They reached the two-foot concrete barrier that surrounded the park, keeping erosion at bay. Stepping up, they rode the small slope up to where the grass leveled out. A collection of wooden play sets greeted them; slides, ladders, monkey bars.

Kelly and Jenna were sitting on the swings, swaying back and forth.

Toes twisting in the scattered cedar chips all around.

"Edmund." Kelly saluted. He nodded to his side. "I'd like you to meet Jenna."

"Hi, Edmund."

He clearly wasn't expecting a girl, and Edmund flustered his way into a mumbled greeting. For a moment, Patrick thought Edmund might even try hiding behind him, the comforting sanctuary of a mother's skirt.

"It's been a big day," Kelly said. "Glad you could make time for us."

"I–I wanted to see you," Edmund stammered.

"Thank you."

"No, you shouldn't..." Edmund cleared his throat. He began anew, taking a firmer stance. "I thought I should tell you that I wasn't entirely on the level. Yesterday, when it came to the time-travel thing."

"Do tell."

"I mean, it's all just theory." He began to speak more rapidly. "And I don't even understand most of it. All I presented yesterday was an assortment of ideas, things that I'd read about in periodicals and stories. Some of it doesn't even have any direct scientific bearing, I was just... trying to tell you things I'd thought you wanted to hear, because I thought that if I didn't... I mean, there's time loops, and wormholes, and the actual nature of time—"

"I liked your theories," Kelly assured him. "They gave me a lot to think about."

Edmund let out a shaky breath, struggling against Kelly's sincerity.

"Edmund..." Kelly hesitated, then took the plunge. "Edmund, what was it you even saw?"

For a moment, it looked as though Edmund was about to weave himself yet another defensive cocoon. The darkness returned to his eyes, fists balling up.

Patrick was on the verge of saying something, anything, to bring him back into the fold.

And then, incredibly enough, Edmund fought back, somehow calling upon himself to ignore the ingrained misgivings that came with every human interaction. Muscles relaxing. Eyes lucid once more.

He shook his head. "I don't know."

"If you still think I'm not on the level..."

"I mean, I *don't know what I saw*...," Edmund explained. "I'm staying late in the science lab one afternoon, rooting through the supply closet, when Cody comes in with some guy I'd never seen. He was an older guy. White guy, with a crappy beard and big, dumb gold chains. I guess they thought they were alone, because Cody gave him some money, and the guy gave him a bottle of something."

"Guess they found you out," Kelly said, shaking his head.

"It's like something out of Kafka... I don't even know what I saw."

"Well... what have you got in your hand there?"

Edmund glanced down, memory card resting in his open, sweaty palm.

"What's that still doing in one piece?" Kelly smiled.

"I'm sorry I didn't believe you," Edmund mumbled, head downcast.

"You had no reason to."

"I didn't want to be made an idiot... again."

"We've got the camera right here," Kelly offered again. "If you want to take a look at the pictures on that card, make sure it's really the one Cody–"

"No ..." Edmund shook his head. His voice dropped to a whisper. "I believe you."

Kelly nodded. "Then have at it."

The memory card fell to the ground. Edmund raised his foot and brought it down in a slow grind, twisting the tip of his brown Hush Puppy. For good measure, he switched to the heel, biting down on his lower lip as the plastic snapped, broke apart.

"Sweet music," Kelly murmured, grabbing on to the swing chains and tilting his head back. Eyes closed in anticipation of what felt like an approaching rainstorm.

Edmund let go with a long, exhausted sigh, body trembling with unexpected release. Patrick saw his lower lip quiver. Tears ran down Edmund's face, dotting the ground around the decimated memory card, all that was left of that squalid afternoon by the flagpole.

And it was something special when Edmund finally smiled.

That's satisfaction you're feeling, Patrick's angels informed him.

He reached out to pat Edmund on the back.

Edmund didn't flinch, even as Patrick gave his shoulder a reassuring squeeze.

"So what happens now, Kelly?" Edmund asked, looking up from his kill with a satisfied sniffle. "You going to disappear into a white flash of light, like the guy from that old *Quantum Leap* show?"

"Don't think it's going to go down like that." Kelly straightened himself. "I was just thinking, maybe if I actually got some sleep. Maybe then."

"So maybe it's time to get some sleep," Edmund suggested.

"All in good time," Kelly said, getting up from the swing. He brushed off his pants. "There's one more thing I'd like to take care of."

They waited for him to elaborate.

"Head on home, Edmund," Kelly advised, stepping forward and shaking his hand. "You don't have anything to worry about anymore."

Edmund seemed loath to let go, keeping a firm grip on Kelly's hand.

"You're a good man, Edmund..." Kelly gave it one last squeeze and let go. "You should stay that way."

Patrick thought about offering his own handshake, but simply gave a small wave as Edmund turned and made his way back across the park.

The three of them watched him go, then headed over to Kelly's car.

"So it looks to be around two," Jenna remarked, scanning the sky. "What do you want to do now, Kelly?"

"Think it's time we paid Patrick's parents a little visit," Kelly said, opening the door to his Ferrari. He caught Patrick's eye, and motioned for him to get in. "A little overdue, don't you think?"

Patrick silently agreed.

He jumped in the backseat, finally ready.

#23

They parked the car out front and walked up along the stepping stones to Patrick's house.

"You always do this," Kelly casually informed Patrick, taking a look around. "Nobody else in this neighborhood comes in the front way except—"

"We've had this conversation," Patrick said dully, stomach tightening up.

"Oh."

Patrick slipped the key into the lock, twisted the knob, and pushed.

There was no need to announce his presence. Seated on the plush maroon couches were Patrick's mother and father. Side by side, their heads turned to the front door, away from the television.

"Where have *you* been?" Patrick's mother demanded, shooting up. A flowered throw pillow slid off her lap and onto the floor. "Do you know who we just got off the phone with?"

"I was out last night," Patrick said evenly. "I wanted some time—"

"Not you, Patrick." His father jammed his thumb on the remote, muting the television. He joined ranks with Patrick's mother, sent a finger pointing past his son. "We just got off the phone with your parents, Kelly."

Can't even get punished properly when their firstborn's around, Patrick's angels spat. *They don't even realize they're changing the subject.*

"Guess what, Mr. and Mrs. Saint?" Kelly said, crossing his arms. "My life happens to be none of your business."

"Please, Kelly, it's Harris and Elizabeth," Patrick's father insisted, even as Kelly cut past his bogus attempts at intimacy: "Oh, so suddenly you two have names."

"What do you mean, none of our business?" Patrick's mother asked, trying to catch up. Covering her shock with a ludicrous grin. "Kelly, we're like parents to you."

"No, you're actually quite a bit like Patrick's parents to me."

"Kelly, what—"

"Hey!" Patrick yelled, bringing the babble to a sudden halt. Never thinking it was possible to command any kind of attention in his own house, with his own parents. Feeling it for the first time, remembering all the stolen moments that should have been his. Kelly had been right.

"I got into Ohio State . . ." In the brief seconds following his announcement, Patrick sensed this was his one chance at their undivided attention, and he took full advantage. "I actually got in ages ago, early acceptance. I forged the wait-list letter and . . . I've been getting to the mail before you-all, every chance I got, just to intercept any additional letters OSU might've been sending. I also applied to Juilliard for early acceptance, as you've both figured out. I scheduled my audition to coincide with the band trip to New York. Back in December, but...I guess I didn't do so hot, it was the only place that really wait-listed me. I never told you because...because I wanted to see if I could just *get into* Juilliard. If I ever even had a chance. And maybe I have, maybe I haven't. But if it turns out I didn't, you both win. I got into Ohio State, and I'll go there. If I have to."

And even though the television was muted, its alien hum filled in for what should have been a frenzied burst of congratulations. Instead, Patrick's parents remained glued at the shoulder, stuck in the middle of stationary gestures, a pair of deactivated robots. Unsure of what they'd heard, but it was more than that.

They don't even know what to say.

"They don't know what to say," Patrick agreed, almost amazed at how right he was. "You two don't even know what to say. You don't even know whether to be happy or not. This was all you said you wanted, for me to go to OSU with my replacement brother."

The concept seemed to jar Patrick's mother from her paralysis, enough to blink, at least. "Of course it's what we wanted..." She stopped short, realizing she was going to need more.

"Because you can't admit *anything*." Patrick pressed ahead, unraveling. "It's all been one nonstop act since Casey died. And if your remaining son gets into Juilliard, you might have to actually realize that there is no plan, nothing you can do about *anything*."

"Patrick, I said we'd talk about Juilliard when—"

"No, we've got to talk about it now."

"You've got something that belongs to Patrick," Kelly said, brushing his way past the sofas, toward the kitchen. "Where is it?"

"In her bag," Patrick said. "I doubt she's even thought about it since yesterday."

Patrick's father held out his hand. "Kelly—"

"You don't *talk* to me!" Kelly spun around, filling the kitchen doorway with his body. "My aunt died in that accident. And I thought that was bad, all that weight on my shoulders. But you two. You two are sick, you know that? Your son is dead. Casey's dead. . . . And Patrick isn't."

He didn't wait for their reaction. Kelly contented himself with a quick exit into the kitchen.

Patrick turned back to his parents.

His father reached out, cupped his hands around his wife's shoulders.

She shrugged them off, breathing deeply.

Refusing to be affected.

Jenna moved to Patrick's side and scooped his hand into hers.

Patrick wasn't sure what any of it meant. There had been times, in his room. Making music, making sure his parents weren't in the house, because they hated the sound. Blasting enraged melodies, imagining what this moment would be like. Anger turning to relieved tears, mellow notes as his parents broke down and admitted their transgressions, begging to be forgiven for their sins. Years of neglect struck down with a single blow to the Achilles' heel. The silver bullet.

"Patrick," his mother began, taking a small step forward. "Where were you last night?"

Now that he'd said his piece, Patrick found the question to be strangely appropriate. He was almost thankful at the opportunity to move on.

Even still, there was something unnerving about it. "I was with Kelly."

"All night?"

Patrick bristled. "I don't understand what this—"

The front doorbell rang.

Harris held his arm out, as though trying to will Patrick from answering the door. "Patrick, if we tell them they don't have a right to come in without a warrant, or question you without an arrest, then it's going to look bad."

"What are you talking about?"

The doorbell rang once more.

"Where were you last night?" Elizabeth repeated. "We need to know. Now."

"I dropped them off," Kelly said, once again standing at the kitchen door. "I dropped them off at Jenna's house. Then I went out for a while. Then I went back to her house, and we stayed the night there."

Everyone turned to look at him.

"Say whatever else you want," Kelly said, backing through the kitchen door. "But remember what I just told you."

He backed up into the kitchen, leaving the rest with another chime to be reckoned with.

Patrick turned and opened the door, still uncertain as to what was about to happen.

Through the screen door, two men in suits raised their chins in an abbreviated greeting.

#24

"The back door is open," Donahue called out from the kitchen. He walked back into the living room and sent his thumb over his shoulder, bringing the point home. "Just thought you'd like to know."

Detective Donahue was a broad man, dark-skinned. A Latino-Anglo cross-pollination, not a trace of an accent either way. Not southern, not northern; not second-generation anything. Dark hair trimmed so close, there was no telling the texture. No telling whether he was politely reserved or inadvertently suspicious. His sentences defied punctuation, mixing periods, question marks, and ellipses.

Detective Randal sat in the easy chair across from Patrick and Jenna. Undoubtedly, a man of manners, though he was also no easy fit. His white cheeks carried a flush that would have passed for embarrassment, anger, even panic if there had been some context to him. As it were, he asked his questions with the same routine ambiguity as his partner.

"Kelly's parents told us you two are lawyers," Donahue said, walking around to Randal's side.

Patrick's parents sat on the couch perpendicular to their son.

"That's right," Patrick's father told them. "I'm a tax lawyer and Elizabeth's a civil lawyer."

"Thank you for making this easy," Donahue told them. "Ordinarily, you-all can't wait to let us in on that. Not you two, specifically. I guess my point is, usually, in my experience, lawyers can't wait to tell cops that they're lawyers. Telling us to watch our step, informing us of the law. In my experience."

"My father was a textile worker," Patrick's mother informed him. "I don't have a chip on my shoulder when it comes to my job. And I'm glad to see you don't have a chip on yours. I've found police officers to get a little touchy when it comes to the law. As though they're the only ones involved in it. In my experience."

"So Kelly just left." Randal leaned forward with the curious smile of a seven-year-old. "Went out without taking his car?" Before anyone could answer, he tacked on the name of his witness. "Patrick?" He looked over in Patrick's direction, as though noticing him for the first time. "Hey, nice suit."

Patrick glanced down, almost pleased with the compliment over what had fast become his second skin. "Thanks."

"Maybe it's time to send it to the cleaner's, though."

Patrick absently tugged at his pants. "You were asking about Kelly?"

"Yes, any ideas where—"

"He was going for a walk," Patrick told him. Taking comfort in the fact that his lies were so much less extraordinary than talking about a time-traveling mental patient. "He's been having some issues."

"Yes," Donahue agreed, stretching out the word as he pulled out his notepad. "From what I understand, talking to Mr.

Redwood, he's been acting erratically in school. Missing classes, causing scenes. He told us that Kelly had even skipped class to go to a pool hall and have a few beers."

He let the litany hang, waiting. Staring at Jenna now.

"Is that a question?" she asked.

"No, just what we've been told ... Though I would like to hear about the fight."

"What fight?" Jenna asked.

Randal stepped up, scratching his nose. "It seems that him and Cody Redwood had a bit of a ... I guess, rivalry happening? There was a fight, just yesterday, during school. Mr. Redwood said he didn't know what it was about, Cody just said that Kelly's been acting kind of ... off balance. Do either of you know what was going on between them?"

Jenna shrugged.

"Patrick?" Donahue asked. "Any ideas?"

"I'm sure you two know Kelly's been top dog on the team for a few years now," Patrick said. "Cody's about to take his place. He's very competitive, and players, you know ... The closer they get to the end zone, the more they can't wait to get there."

"Don't you think the opposite would hold true?" Randal asked, a question that seemed better suited for Donahue. His flushed cheeks bunched above his grin. "I mean, Kelly's about to give up his throne, right? Don't you think that would be reason for him to try to defend it? Lot of people don't like to let go."

"I don't know why Kelly would want to hold on to all that, when he's headed for greater things at Ohio State."

"I see you've been watching the news," Randal said, pointing at the muted screen. "Kelly's walk off at the game last night has become a big story."

"Ohio State's looking a little lean, as far as Kelly's future is concerned," Donahue explained.

"Could you please tell us what this is all about?" Patrick asked, knowing full well that officers were never sent to investigate sports anomalies.

"There was a break-in at the Redwood house last night," Randal informed them. He almost seemed unconcerned, as though years of delivering worse news left him with little passion for breaking and entering. "Happened during the game. Got in through a second-story window."

"And you think Kelly did it."

"As we were saying, him and Cody had a bit of a—"

"*That's* why you think Kelly broke into their place?" Patrick asked, hoping straightforward would do the trick.

"You know, there's a lot of false posturing that comes with being a cop," Donahue said. He sat down on the arm of the easy chair, tucked his notebook away into his jacket. "Did you know that police officer doesn't even rank among the fifty most dangerous jobs in the United States? Most of them fall to municipal workers. The guys who work the sewers, construction crews. Now that there's a war going on, you've got a better chance of dying simply from being a volunteer.... But the one cliché that's never going to change is that this job exposes you to the weirdest shit you can imagine. Pardon my French, of course, Mrs. Saint. My point is, we can't rule anything out, and even though we don't think it was Kelly, we have to check up on this."

"Wait." Jenna shifted in her seat, sagging between two cushions. "You *don't* think it was Kelly?"

"I don't *think*." Donahue smiled. "That's what my wife tells me, at least. The fact is, the only things missing from the house were in Mr. Redwood's safe."

Patrick forced all emotion from his face. "What's that mean?"

"Well, the point of entry was the window to his office," Randal piped up, pulling out his notebook and leafing through it. He tilted his head, as though trying to read someone else's penmanship. "And his safe was cleaned of five thousand dollars . . . some of his wife's jewelry . . . and a folder of paperwork involving past donations to Wellspring Academy."

"Granted, the money's nice," Donahue added. "But Mr. Redwood's got a nice safe there. Not top of the line, but close enough. I think it's a bit far-fetched that Kelly broke in on a revenge kick, then managed to crack the safe. . . . Especially if Cody's the one he wanted to hurt."

"But that's not enough to clear him," Patrick's father said, keeping his professional opinion to himself. "I mean, you've still got a motive, it seems."

Donahue sighed. "Yes, we do. And we're rustling up a warrant to search his car."

"And his house, I imagine," Elizabeth added.

"We didn't need one." Randal stood up and stretched. "His parents let us search their house. Just a superficial glance at everything. Kelly didn't go back there last night. Can I get some water?"

"Yes..." Elizabeth motioned toward the kitchen. "So wait, his parents just let you—"

"Frankly, the things that make our life easier sometimes surprise even us," Donahue sighed, standing up as well. "I just wanted to go over this one more time.... Last night?"

"Kelly drove us to my house," Jenna said. "He wanted some time alone, and took off for a while. He came back. We sat around talking..."

"About?"

"We graduate in a few weeks," Jenna told him. "Our lives are a little shaky right now, Detective Donahue."

The detective gave an appeasing nod. "Between you and me, I don't think Kelly did it...."

"Thank you." Jenna smiled best she could.

"Hey, congratulations!" Randal exclaimed, walking back into the living room. He wandered behind the couch and slapped Patrick on the back. "I hear Juilliard's the place to be if you're the musical type."

Patrick balked. "Huh?"

"Saw the envelope there on the table. Looks mighty thick for a rejection."

"Randal..." Detective Donahue rolled his eyes. "Please tell me you didn't congratulate—seriously, get his hopes up just based on the envelope."

Randal's cheeks remained flushed. And while there was no way to tell what that meant, he quickly apologized. "Hey, I'm sorry. I'm sure you were probably looking to open it up with your parents."

"No," Patrick said curtly. "No, I actually have no intention of doing that."

Donahue and Randal exchanged looks as Patrick stood up. His parents looked mortified that their son would even dream of bringing up family business in front of two strangers, policemen at that.

"Patrick," his mother coughed. "I don't think–"

"I don't care," Patrick told them, stalking toward the kitchen. He was tired of his parents and, once again, felt the time was perfect to have his way with them. He took the letter off the table and strode back into the living room.

"Look," Donahue was saying, "we don't want to keep you-all any longer..."

"You don't get to know," Patrick told his parents, ignoring both detectives. His heart was racing, blood pumping pure anger, fear, and regret. Almost seething as he brandished the envelope in his mother's face before stuffing it into his jacket. "No matter how much I want to open this right now, I'd rather have you two stuck wondering how you ended up without *either* of your sons sharing this moment with you."

Jenna came to Patrick's side, a heartbroken cringe tainting her features.

Patrick's mother and father remained silent, unable to air their dirty laundry in present company.

Which was all that Patrick wanted from them at the moment, and he turned to their guests, doing what he could to squeeze out any remaining civility for the sake of an easy exit. "Detective Randal, Donahue, may we please continue this conversation some other time?"

Donahue nodded appreciatively. "With any luck, we won't ever have to continue this conversation. We'll be back to search Kelly's car, of course, but in the meantime . . . you and Jenna are free to go."

"Thank you," Patrick managed.

This was echoed by Jenna as the two of them opened the screen door and stepped outside. It slammed behind them, even as Donahue called out for one last moment of their time.

"If you see Kelly," he told them, brown eyes narrowing through the pollen-encrusted mesh, "let him know that if he's in the clear, then he's in the clear. And he should think about giving us a ring."

Patrick gave him a weak thumbs-up, and headed down the walkway, Jenna by his side. Head throbbing, knees like rubber. Vaguely sensing tears beneath his eyelids as they left the rest to talk about their young, as adults tend to do.

25

The rest of the day crept by with a heavy limp. Whenever Patrick glanced at the time, it was either seconds instead of hours or hours in place of seconds. Stop and go, nothing stayed consistent.

Patrick and Jenna had returned to her house.

Jenna's father, Al, was waiting for them in the living room, standing in front of the television as though his team were down twenty points in the last quarter. He nodded at the screen. His daughter joined him, followed by Patrick. The three of them stared down, all a little alarmed to find that Kelly had made the local news.

Once again, he is only wanted for questioning, though sources within the department have told us that there is concern for his well-being. Last night, Kelly McDermott, starting quarterback for Well-spring Academy, surprised his teammates, students, and teachers when he abruptly walked off the field in the middle *of the* national anthem.

The screen cut to footage of Redwood after the game.

As for that, we don't know what happened. Everyone has been worried about him. We have our concerns and suspicions. We don't want to speculate. We're just going to have to wait and see . . . wait for a chance to talk to Kelly McDermott.

At that point, Al turned off the television, invited them into the kitchen.

Patrick and Jenna then told him everything about the previous night. Al's concern never went past justifiable limits. His frowns and interjections were welcomed and reasonable. After all was said and done, Al let them know that he had been asleep when they had "arrived" last night, since eight-fifteen. Whether it was true, or if he was saying it for the benefit of any future questioning, Patrick wasn't sure.

"You two should stay here for tonight," Al advised them. "I'm helping a friend with their house today, so I've got to be heading out soon." He stood up, taking steps toward his room. Stopped at the kitchen door and pointed at the envelope in Patrick's hand. "You going to open that?"

Patrick looked down, turned it over in his hands.

Al sighed. "Well, I think you two did a good thing last night, anyway."

That took them through to four in the afternoon.

And so the minutes lurched forward with a frustrating inaccuracy.

Patrick tried to pass the time in front of the television, with limited results. He couldn't stop himself from flipping back to the reports, checking in on the Kelly situation. Sneaking updates that weren't really updates, just the local news filling time.

Jenna wandered around the house, looking out the window every now and then.

Though occasionally remarking on each other's presence, they hardly interacted.

It was Jenna who finally suggested they go for a walk.

"What if Kelly shows up?" Patrick asked glumly.

"There's this car down the block," Jenna said. "I think the cops are keeping a lookout for Kelly. And I think Kelly's too smart to come here."

"Then what are we even waiting for?"

"We're not." Jenna opened the door with an irritated tug. "We're going for a walk, so stop moping around."

Patrick took exception to that, though he could manage little more than a weak sneer. Hoisting himself off the couch, he turned off the television and went to join her. Upon stepping outside, he was surprised to find that dusk had settled. Another one of time's little tricks. Projecting back three seconds, he was certain the house he'd left had still been awash with that day's gray, ethereal light. Now the sky was a dull plum color, clouds protruding from the black in ominous billows.

And now, the hungry rumble of thunder could be heard overhead.

Patrick threw a quick glance down the block.

Sure enough, just out of reach of the tangerine streetlights, a single car was parked. Whether or not it was a stakeout would be answered soon enough.

They walked away from it, eyes on the sidewalk. Sharing slow, contemplative steps, they reached the corner before hearing a car door open, then close.

"Guess one of them's following us," Patrick said.

"Guess so."

They walked in silence, accompanied by further sounds of an eager sky. No words as they rounded the next corner, porch lights turning on as they made their way past flat single-story houses.

It wasn't until they'd passed the second corner that the raindrops began to fall, and Jenna finally broke their unspoken vows. "Where do you suppose Kelly is?"

Patrick held out his hand, feeling for rain with an apathetic shrug. "I don't know."

"He can't stay hidden forever.... What do you think is going on with what Donahue told us? All that stuff he said was missing from Redwood's safe, what do you think that was about?"

"I don't know."

"Kelly said he took those steroid pills from Cody's mattress as insurance. To exchange them in return for not telling, just in case Cody told on him. Do you think Cody hasn't even looked..."

"I don't know, I don't *know*," Patrick snapped, stepping in front of Jenna and facing her. It was audible now, raindrops tearing through the trees, smacking against leaves in a rustling symphony. "Jenna, I don't *know*. I don't know where Kelly is, I don't know what's going on, I don't know what I'm going to do. I'm sorry but I can't just *know* what's next."

"Patrick, what..." Jenna took a moment to catch her breath, dragging her hand through her hair, already growing wet with rain. "I don't expect you to know, I was asking–"

"Everyone expects me to know!" he shouted. "Everyone's always talking about the goddamn future like they're so sure of it!" He felt a few drops splat against his envelope, glanced down.

Jenna's supplicating tone shifted, grew demanding. "Is that why you haven't opened that yet?"

Moving quickly, Patrick shoved it into the back of his pants.

"That's it, right?" Jenna asked, voice loud to compensate for a long stretch of rolling thunder. "You don't... You know you got in. You know you got in, and you don't want to open it and find out you have a choice!"

"Choice! Like *you* weren't nipping at Kelly's heels, applying to Ohio State."

"Like Kelly McDermott wasn't your boyfriend also, you little tagalong!" Her face was dripping now, water spraying from her lips with every other word. "And now that Kelly's chances at Ohio State are ruined, you turn to me!"

"You?"

"You're in love with me, you idiot!"

Patrick drew his head back. "What?"

"At least, you'd better be, because if it's just some pathetic excuse, then you're no better than your parents! Yelling at them, talking about how they can't get past... Getting mad at them for how they took Kelly in... Nobody *forced* you to be friends with Kelly, Patrick!"

"I certainly never *asked* for it!"

"You went along for the ride because it was the easiest thing to do, just like everyone else!"

"Oh, *that's* it!" Patrick gave a condescending bow. "Rah-rah, sis-boom-bah, cheerleader. Ohio State's got one *hell* of a therapist headed their way."

Jenna sprung forward, darting her hand around Patrick's waist, gunning for the letter.

Patrick grabbed on to her arm, felt the slick skin under his fingers.

"Give me that!" Jenna grimaced, sending her other arm around Patrick.

Jenna pressed against him as the two struggled in the downpour, a pair of writhing bodies. Accusations reduced to scattered gasps and heavy breathing. Faces pressed together, side by side, as Jenna fought to look over his left shoulder, then his right. Wet faces sliding against each other, and for one agonizing moment, Patrick felt her lips on his, the full force of her breath, searing, filling his mouth.

Her fingers curled around the letter, and the two of them were face to face again, locked in a tug-of-war with Patrick's impending acceptance. Turning sideways, Patrick gave a final tremendous yank. His shoulder rammed against her, and Jenna went down, landing hard on her ass.

Patrick stood over her, the now shapeless envelope clutched in his fist like an unlit torch.

Jenna sat with her hands planted in the soft dirt behind her. She looked around, mouth open, like a tourist gawking from the top of the Empire State Building.

There was no sense of triumph for Patrick, and he immediately bent over to help her up.

"Go away," she said, batting his hand and rising to her feet.

Patrick licked his lips, swallowed. "Jenna—"

"Fuck off!" she yelled, arms crossed, shoving past him. *"I'm* going."

Patrick leaped after her, pelted by bloated raindrops. "Where?"

"To find Kelly."

"It's pouring!"

"Leave me alone!" she yelled, and began to run.

"What are you doing?" Patrick was sure he heard the sound of footsteps slapping the pavement some dozen yards behind him. "The guy can still follow you!"

She whirled around for an instant. "We'll see who catches pneumonia first," she shot back, before breaking into a full sprint, crossing the street and not looking to stop.

Patrick shoved the letter into his pocket and ran to the corner. He looked after Jenna, blinking rapidly against the rain as she disappeared from sight.

For some reason, Patrick kept going back to something Kelly had said. Several things he had said, in fact. All those times, over the past few days, when Kelly had suddenly burst out with a simultaneous reading of what other people were saying. The lecture from Principal Sedgwick. The specials at Spiro's. Capping off Edmund's concluding dissertation on time travel.

Those isolated moments repeated themselves over and over as Patrick burst into Jenna's house. Transmitted by his angels in a hypnotic loop, not a one bothering with their usual analysis. Doing all he could to avoid their chatter, Patrick froze in the middle of the living room. He looked around wildly, dripping wet, trying to remember where he'd left his keys.

The land line began to ring, an unwelcome distraction as he ran into the kitchen.

Patrick closed his eyes, tracing that afternoon's activities.

The answering machine clicked on, and without the whine of the phone, Patrick remembered. Darted toward the fridge, leaped up, and took his keys down from on top. He was almost at the door when something made him stop.

"Good evening!" the voice on the machine cried out in a high-pitched, bizarre English accent. Bad English accent, and Patrick moved toward the machine. *"This is Madame Saint James, calling about the advert for a nanny. You may call me at my current place of residence, the number being—"*

The number being one that Patrick recognized to be Kelly McDermott's cell.

He rushed to the phone, picked it up. "Kelly?"

"Are you alone?" Kelly's voice crackled through the phone.

"Yes, Kelly, where have you *been*?"

"I'm at the BP phone booth, on Ninth," he said. "I wanted to wait until it was dark. I've been . . . I couldn't remember anybody's number, I had to find a phone book, this was the only one listed."

"Kelly, I need to go get—"

"Patrick, listen to me." Kelly's voice was low, urgent. "Can you get to Jenna's computer and go online?"

"Yes, but—"

"Go, there's something you need to see."

Patrick glanced toward the front door, still ajar.

"Patrick, are you there?"

"Yeah," Patrick said, running into Jenna's bedroom. He kicked the chair away from her desk and hunched over, wiggling the mouse. The screen came to life, and he double-clicked on the EarthLink icon.

His ear was suddenly filled with a deafening collection of garbled electronic screeches.

"Damn it!" Patrick yelled over the noise. "Kelly, she's still got dial-up!"

"Check your e-mail and call me back!"

"What's the number?" Patrick yelled, scrambling to grab hold of a pen as Kelly began to read it out. With no time to bother with paper, Patrick carved the digits into Jenna's desk. He hung up and gave the double click another go.

The gravelly scream came back, unimpressed with Patrick as he impatiently bounced on his feet.

The connection was finally established, and Patrick logged on to his school account.

Among the unread e-mails, Patrick immediately knew which one Kelly was talking about.

SENDER: REDCOD

SUBJECT: SMALL PACKAGES

It was from Cody, complete with an attachment.

What's more, it had been sent out to every last person at Wellspring Academy.

With his heart sinking, Patrick clicked on the e-mail.

Well... His angels had returned with their usual attitude. *What made you think Cody* wasn't *going to upload the damn picture onto his computer?*

"Kelly *told* him not to!" Patrick cried out to the empty room.

But of course, that had been before. Just a few days ago; Edmund tied at the stake, everything going according to plan. It had been unthinkable that Cody would have disobeyed Kelly's orders to not upload the picture. But years had passed within those few days, and Patrick had forgotten to adjust to a world where Kelly McDermott no longer commanded any respect, and Cody Redwood was beyond anybody's control.

And now, it seemed, Patrick and Kelly were going to have to make some *major* adjustments.

A sick little whine escaped his lips. Patrick reached back, arm flailing in hopes of pulling up a chair. He gave up, and continued to stare at the attached photograph. Knowing how well it would play among the students. Maybe not the few who turned their heads in polite protest when such things occurred, but what difference had those silent few ever made? There was something about the duct tape wrapped around Edmund's body. The combination of his bottom half exposed while his shirt remained in place. Worst of all, the perfect expression; jaw jutting out with an absurd underbite, one eye half-closed, the other half-rolled up in a fit of desperation. Patrick couldn't deny it; just a few days ago, he would've been on the floor, trapped in the throes of irrepressible, mean-spirited giggles.

Another whine escaped his mouth, and he reached up to cover his mouth with his hand.

Don't puke, his angels commanded in a rare bout of clarity. *Call Kelly, right now.*

Patrick dialed the number.

Another maddening shriek stabbed at his ear.

"Damn it!"

He hung up and logged off, struggling to get the cursor where he wanted.

Patrick redialed, and Kelly picked up on the other end. "You saw?"

"Yes."

"Edmund's number is unlisted," Kelly told him. Even over the phone, Patrick could hear the roar of the storm. "If you can't find Jenna's student directory, you're going to have to go to his house. Go, check on him. Find out if . . ." Kelly paused. "If he's there, just do what you can to talk him down."

"What if he isn't?" Patrick mewled.

"If he isn't . . ."

For a moment, Patrick thought the line had gone dead.

He was about to hang up and redial when he heard what had to be the most frightening words anyone had ever spoken to him. "Find out if they own a gun."

Patrick closed his eyes, ran a hand down his clammy face. "Please tell me you didn't—"

"Patrick, we don't have time—"

"No, Kelly, *talk to me.*"

A massive thunderclap exploded outside, through the

phone, in stereo. Patrick felt a hot, bilious liquid rise to the back of his throat. "You really think..."

"Yes, or worse."

"What do you mean *worse?*"

"Patrick, I just don't KNOW!" Kelly yelled over the phone. "Now go! Go, get to his house, and then call me! And whatever you do, *don't pick me up, they'll be watching—*"

The line went dead.

Patrick was left alone. Holding on to the cordless phone in the sickly light of a desk lamp Jenna must have turned on while he was too busy not paying attention to the time.

26

Rachel-Ann opened the door, not a bit surprised to see Patrick. Her eyes were sloped with concern, body language perfectly clear under her purple bathrobe.

Patrick burst into the house, heading for the steps. "Is Edmund here?"

"No," she replied apprehensively.

Patrick turned to face her. "What happened, do you know where he went?"

"It was strange, because he just walked downstairs, and right out of the house." She pointed up the stairs, retracing her son's steps with a guiding finger. "There was a cab waiting for him. He must have called for it before even–"

"Mrs. Radcliff..." Patrick put a comforting hand on her shoulder, sure it wasn't much to make up for his own breathless expression. "Did he mention anything?"

"A name," she said tentatively, tightening her robe around her ample body.

"What name?"

"I don't... It began with a *C*, I think."

"Cody?"

"Yes..." Her face grew concerned at the very fact that

Patrick seemed to know what was going on. "It was Cody, I think."

Patrick didn't want to think what that might mean.

Or worse, his angels reminded him, glad to do the thinking for him.

"May I use your phone, Mrs. Radcliff?"

She nodded and led him into the den. The furniture was all antiques, or at the very least two generations past the current trend. No way to tell with the couches, as they were all covered in white sheets. The Radcliff house was hardly a mansion, but Patrick couldn't help thinking of the Havisham house from *Great Expectations.* Everything at a standstill.

With the exception of a working phone, thank God.

Patrick picked it up, dialed the number.

It had been so long since he'd heard a busy signal, he almost didn't know what he was hearing.

"Public *phone.*" He grimaced, slamming the receiver down. Doing his best to recoup, he pulled out the pen he'd taken from Jenna's desk and scrawled out the number on a yellow sticky note. "Mrs. Radcliff, please keep calling this number, every two minutes. You remember Kelly?"

Rachel-Ann's chest swelled, operatic lips parting. "What's the matter with my son?"

"Nothing, if you just do as I say . . ." Patrick underlined the number twice. "When Kelly picks up, you tell him everything you told me. And let him know I'm headed for the prom."

Patrick dashed for the door, then stopped.

He turned, glad to see Mrs. Radcliff picking up the phone, all ready to redial. "Mrs. Radcliff?"

She looked up, eyes distant. "Yes?"

"Do you own a gun?"

She looked as though she had been caught with a case of C-4. "His . . . his father kept one up in the safe. But it's locked, and . . . Edmund doesn't know the combination."

Patrick let out a shuddery breath. "What *is* the combination?"

"My birthday."

The Internet's got a lot to teach this older generation about safety, Patrick's angels lamented.

He steadied himself against the threshold, resisting the urge to slump back against the wall.

"Take me to it," Patrick told her.

Rachel-Ann's naïve decision to use her birthday for the combination was just as apparent in her willingness to take Patrick directly to the safe. It might have been the influence of the past few days—the deception, the suspicion, the double-crossing— but Patrick couldn't help thinking of the many ways he could take advantage of Rachel-Ann, simply by implying that Edmund might have gotten to her gun.

Of course, two minutes later, and the proof was right in front of them.

"Oh God." Rachel-Ann tried to stifle a moan with her hand.

Patrick turned his back to the empty safe. "When was the last time you opened this?"

She didn't answer, eyes plunging to the safe's shallow depths.

"Mrs. Radcliff..." Patrick resisted the impulse to grab her by the arm and shake. *"When was the last time you opened your safe?"*

"I don't know..." She stared at the top of the closet door, thinking. "Weeks, no... months. Maybe even a year."

Patrick's angels drew in a breath. *Just how long has Edmund been holding on to that piece, waiting?*

"Keep calling the number by the phone," Patrick told her, gearing up. "Just keep dialing. When Kelly picks up, tell him *everything* that's happened tonight. Understand? *Everything."*

Patrick didn't have the time to see if his orders had sunk in.

Without the slightest urge to find out just what was awaiting him at the prom, Patrick tore down the stairs, burst through the front door, and ran out into the night. Leaped into his car, and pulled out into the overflowing streets, heading downtown for the Marriott Hotel.

#27

He left his car near the Downtown Film House, figuring it might save him the trouble of dealing with an overcrowded parking garage. He charged through the puddles, past orange construction cones lining the gutter, listening to the sound of his own breath under the static of semiautomatic raindrops.

The entrance to the Verona Marriott was right around the corner, on Davies Street. A semicircular driveway curved toward the revolving doors, sheltered by the building's over-hang. A pair of security guards were stationed outside, passing the time with a busy doorman. Patrick had the presence of mind to slow down. Using his fingers as a comb, he breezed past the cops with a how-about-this-weather smile radiating just above his frigid skin.

Patrick slid through the revolving doors and into the lobby, pausing to get his bearings. The ceiling was raised high, chandeliers dangling like decadent earrings, diffuse and purely decorative. The off-white wallpaper, encrusted with ornate, semidiscernible gold patterns, was almost pulsating under the brilliant white light that seemed to have no actual source.

Already he saw several Wellspring students strolling by. Tuxedoed boys arm in arm with their pirouette girls. There was nothing subtle about the looks, the whispered asides. Patrick was representing Kelly, his very presence akin to a traitor in their midst.

The one who had almost cost them the state championship.

Patrick started over to the front desk, a wide alcove carved into the far left wall, before catching sight of the hallway to his right. Double doors were set into either side at lengthy intervals. From farther down, Patrick could hear the dampened sound of music.

He trotted down the hall, past more wandering teenagers floating about like mismatched chess pieces, looking to take a break or score some weed. Following his ears to the end of the hallway, Patrick arrived at a set of open doors leading into a large ballroom. He had less than a moment to take in the flash of red, yellow, and green lights before a hand fell on his shoulder.

"Bill," Patrick gasped, hand folded over his chest.

"Jesus, Patrick," Bill said, withdrawing his hand. He was dressed in black pants, forsaking an actual suit for one of those shirts with a tuxedo design drawn on the front. "You're soaked."

"It's raining," Patrick explained, glancing back into the room.

"You're in a lot of trouble, Patrick," Bill told him, though his voice was far from retribution. Worried expression behind his glasses, secretly asking if everything was all right. "Are you here with Kelly?"

"No, but . . ." Patrick didn't know where to begin. Decided it was best to skip straight to the appendix. "Have you seen Edmund?"

"Edmund Radcliff?" The question took him by surprise. "No, I didn't expect...I mean, there's a lot of freshmen who don't show up, I just didn't think he'd be here."

"Bill, I don't know how I can ... stress this without making it a big deal but...Just look out for Edmund. Tell the rest of the staff, chaperones to look out for Edmund. If you see him, could you just pull him aside—"

"Patrick—"

"Keep him on lockdown, whatever. Something bad is going to happen, *you have to find Edmund.*"

"Where are you going?" Bill asked, gently taking hold of Patrick's arm.

"I've got to find Cody."

Patrick knew this would only raise further questions, and he ducked into the party. Tables were set up on both sides, white tablecloths glowing a radioactive purple under the gleam of black lights. A few heads shot up from their refreshments. Some mortified, others flabbergasted. A few angry ones, hurling insults that never reached Patrick's ears under the blanket of...

He caught sight of Principal Sedgwick, standing over by a large plastic bowl. Midway through ladling a glass of punch when their eyes locked across the room. Even from across the room, Patrick knew this wasn't Sedgwick's usual glare of oversensitive outrage. Kelly was a wanted man, and Sedgwick was now blessed with a luxury he rarely indulged in: confidence.

Tossing the ladle into the punch bowl, he began to make

his way over, navigating between the tables. A self-assurance that bordered on menacing.

No time for cocktails, Patrick's angels sang. *Somebody's going to die.*

Patrick threw himself into the gulf of dancers. Weaving between the thicket of hips, arms, and strobe-lit faces, he cast his sights around. Keeping an eye out for Edmund, Cody, Sedgwick, the whole damn world. It was like maneuvering through a snake pit, expecting a shot to ring out at any moment, send everyone tumbling to the ground.

And, suddenly, Patrick was face to face with Cody.

Well-fitting tux showing off his broad build.

"Welcome to the party!" he yelled, immune to the undulating bodies around him.

"Cody!" Patrick yelled back. "You've got to get out of here!"

Cody cupped his hands around his mouth. "Come with me!"

Not bothering to explain the why or wherefore, he began to slip away, into the crowd.

Patrick glanced over his shoulder, thought he saw Sedgwick's graying head floating above the fray.

Two roads diverged in a yellow wood, his angels screamed over the music.

Patrick plunged in after Cody. The jungle of warm bodies had grown thicker, and he was practically hacking his way through them when he burst out on the other side.

Cody was waiting for him at shore's end.

He took Patrick by the arm and led him to an emergency

exit. They slipped through, emerging into a dimly lit hallway, walls and floors made of rough concrete. A fluorescent buzz, coupled with the hum of electrical wiring, took over as the door slammed shut behind them.

"Alone at last." Cody grinned, cracking his neck and straightening his lapels.

For a moment, Patrick thought he was about to get decked.

Cody reached out and ran a hand through Patrick's hair, ruffled it with a pleased smile. "I guess you heard we won anyway."

Patrick drew back a little. "Yeah, I heard."

"It's kind of funny..." Cody motioned for Patrick to follow, and the two started down the endless hallway. "What with Kelly running away like that, right in front of all those cameras... Well, there's not a sports fan in this whole country now that didn't see us take Wilson down."

"Cody..."

"I'm sure you know I've never liked Kelly that much...," he continued. The hallway turned at a right angle, and he beckoned with an unnecessary wag of his finger. "A little too high and mighty. He never really was part of the team, you know? Not a real leader. He never really had it. I sure as hell ain't surprised he freaked the fuck out, you know?"

Cody came to a halt before another door, red exit sign buzzing above.

Directly across from that, an open doorway led to the laundry room. Dryers clattered, washers made wet sopping sounds.

"Why did you have to send the picture out?" Patrick asked

him. "Why'd you have to e-mail it to every last person in the *school*?"

"Kind of self-righteous for a petty thief, aren't you?" Cody winked. He pushed on the door, which lead into an empty stairwell. "Forgive this roundabout route, but what with the breaking and entering, you and Kelly are the catch of the year, and I don't want Principal Sedgwick getting his hooks into you."

Patrick followed him up two flights, the dry scrape of their footsteps echoing up through a thirty-flight rectangular spiral. They exited onto the second floor, a quiet hallway with the same wallpaper, same green and red carpeting as the lobby.

They headed toward the elevators.

Cody the very model of sophisticated fashion.

Patrick plodding along in a ruined Armani suit.

"Why did you *do* it?" Patrick repeated, growing angry.

"You don't want to get too excited there..." Cody pressed the Up arrow on the brass panel. "The only reason you're not in jail right now is because I don't want you there. You have no idea how lucky you got, Patrick.... Luckier than Kelly, anyway."

"What about Kelly—"

"Shhh..."

Cody waited with his arms folded in front of him. Humming tunelessly, making a little elevator music. Knowing well and true that Patrick was in a corner. Enjoying the perks of absolute immunity.

The doors to the elevator slid open.

Cody and Patrick stepped in.

Cody pressed the button for the second floor from the top.

The doors slid closed.

Patrick didn't even feel the lurch of the elevator as Cody's fist slammed into his stomach.

A sorry wheeze rushed from his mouth as he doubled over, fell back against the elevator wall. His tailbone rammed into the flat brass railing, sending infuriated screams to his brain. Breath gone. Eyes bulging, ludicrous thoughts of Harry Houdini, dead from a sucker punch to the stomach.

"That's for breaking into my house," Cody told him, grabbing him by the hair. "And this one's just 'cause Kelly ain't around to stop me."

The second punch caught him in the face, a straight jab that sent his head snapping back. Skin splattering against his cheekbone. A few knuckles knocked his eyeball back into the socket, lights flashing, instantly becoming an agonizing throb.

Patrick felt himself sliding to the ground.

Cody caught him, hoisted Patrick to his knees as though he were stuffed with feathers.

"You think I don't know what you were doing?" Cody asked flatly. Patrick blinked against reflexive tears, straining to see. Cody's face was a contorted wet thumbprint. "You could've just taken the card. But you two thought you'd take the pills in hopes that I'd be too afraid to tell on you."

Patrick couldn't think past the wailing in his head. "He's still got 'em, you dumb shit."

"Maybe...," Cody mused, unaffected by the rebuke. "But they're his now."

"They're *yours*."

"Not so much anymore. The cops found the pills in his car. They let us know about it, asked about it. I denied it up and down. They should be running tests on them even as we speak. Kelly's going to be the user, not me."

"They'll test him," Patrick shot back, regaining his composure through the obnoxious throbbing. "He's going to come out clean. When Kelly tells them they were yours—"

"He'll have to tell them where he got them." Cody stepped back, let Patrick stand on his own. "I'll be tried as a juvenile on a minor possession charge. Kelly as an adult for breaking and entering. Same as you, Patrick."

Patrick glanced up at the round numbers above the elevator doors.

Couldn't make out just what floor they were passing.

"As for testing?" Cody continued, preparing himself for their final destination. Straightening his suit, combing his hair. "Don't be too sure Kelly's going to come out clean."

Patrick drew himself up, shook his head.

"Oh, you really are *pathetic...*" Cody shook his own head, a relaxed smile on his face. "Kelly's been using for about a year now."

"No."

"Yes," Cody replied simply.

"Kelly would have remembered."

Cody laughed. "Oh, you mean in his little trek through time?"

Before Patrick could even begin to wonder where Cody was getting this from, his angels began to repeat Edmund's words verbatim: *He's rationalized it, you see. In his head, he's told himself it's OK. It becomes nothing to him. As a result, when he comes back in time, that whole part of his life is erased along with everything else.*

Yes, Kelly could've had any number of skeletons floating about in his closet that he would never even have begun to touch upon.

The door slid open and Cody grabbed Patrick's arm, dragging him out into yet another hallway. Patrick stumbled along, shaking his head. A fresh shot of pain with each movement. "Why would Kelly *do* something like that?"

"Because *that* is how it *is*," Cody replied, tapping a finger against his temple. "That's what athletes *do*. Kelly was always a wet blanket, but he knew what was expected of him. Kudos to him for *that*. At the very least, he understood *that*."

"If Kelly goes down," Patrick threatened, weaving toward a wall before Cody jerked him back onto the straight and narrow, "then he'll give you up, too. You won't pass a test."

"Look at you with your little threats. You can't even walk straight."

"You'll test positive, Cody."

"And why's that?" Cody asked pleasantly, coming to a halt in front of room 2507.

"Because..." Patrick suddenly felt very unsure of what he was about to say. "Because you're using, too."

"I've never touched the stuff," Cody said with a superior grin. "I come from good stock, you've seen pictures of my dad when he was my age."

A nauseating tumor began to grow in Patrick's mouth. "But the pills..."

"*Idiot,* I was keeping those pills for *Kelly.* I *bought* them for him. Methandrostenolone, better known as Dianabol. Better known as Reforvit-b down in Mexico, where the dealer I bought them from *gets* the shit." Cody leaned close, cupping a hand alongside his mouth with theatrical secrecy. "You dumb, stupid asshole... Kelly just broke into *my* house to steal back his *own... fucking... stash.*"

The tricks the mind plays, Patrick's angels lamented.

Patrick realized he was bleeding from his mouth.

Didn't care, could hardly stay on his feet. "So what Edmund saw..."

"What Edmund saw was me, buying *Kelly* his anabolics. I saw Edmund witness the deal. I told Kelly. And Kelly came up with that little plan to photograph Edmund's little soldier." Cody nodded with sound approval. "Got to hand it to him. It's the only time I ever saw Kelly acting like a man of his means should."

Cody placed his hand on Patrick's shoulder. "But you ain't got a thing to worry about. Neither does Kelly, truth be told. Not much, anyway. After the cops take him in, my father's going to ask to speak to him, alone. After he leaves, he's going to tell the cops that Kelly didn't do it, and that he doesn't want to press charges. The cops won't have found the missing files and money stolen from my dad's safe anyway."

"That money was never stolen, was it?"

"We just thought it would give the cops a reason to search

Kelly's car, maybe his house. But all he's going to have to worry about is the steroid charge. Like I said, he did us a favor not playing in that last game. Sedgwick gets his sacrificial lamb, gets to make an example. And since we won the game without Kelly, we get to keep our trophy. Not to mention hefty contributions from rabid alumni."

"Got to admit..." Patrick let out a pained laugh, covering for the sobs he felt welling up inside. "You're not the brainless wonder I always took you for."

"Too bad for you."

"No, too bad for you," Patrick retorted. Spat some blood onto the carpet. "You shouldn't have sent Edmund's picture out, man. There, *you* fucked up."

"Kelly made me do it," Cody sang with mock innocence.

"I came here to *warn* you," Patrick hissed. "I don't know why the hell I still am, but there's a *very* good chance that Edmund is coming after you."

"I'm not the one Edmund wants," Cody assured him, the way an adult might tell a child that Mommy and Daddy's divorce wasn't his fault. "This really isn't your night, is it?"

The chill of central air was beginning to make Patrick tremble. "What are you talking about?"

"Well, not everybody believes in killing the messenger," Cody said with a sly smile. "Sure, *I* sent out that e-mail, but what do you expect? I've always been an asshole, right? A brainless wonder? I'm just doing what I do.... But what Kelly did, man, that's just cold."

"What Kelly did, *what*?"

"Way Edmund figures it, Kelly's the real mastermind here. Wasn't enough he had to take that little snapshot. Wasn't enough he went ahead and sent it out to the whole school. No, Kelly befriended Edmund, gave him some wild story about time travel. He gained Edmund's trust, even showed him the memory card, let him destroy it. Kelly gave him all that hope, just so he could dash that poor kid's soul to pieces...."

Even Patrick's angels couldn't begin to put it all together.

"Betrayal stings like a bitch, Patrick," Cody said, knocking on the door to 2507, three times, then once. "So if you were Edmund, who would *you* be after?"

And for the first time, Patrick heard the sounds coming from beyond those numbers.

The clank of bottles. Loud, raucous laughter.

All mixed with the heavy bass and synthetic loops of hip-hop.

All of which grew louder as the door to 2507 opened.

Patrick barely had time to place Zack as the one who opened the door when a rough shove from Cody sent him stumbling into the room.

"HEYYYYYYY!" came the manic, sarcastic cry of what had to be the entire football team.

Patrick brought himself to a halt and fell back against the wall.

Through the eye that wasn't rapidly swelling shut, he saw a large room. Soft recessed lighting, a desk and table littered with beer bottles. The entire football team was there all right, dressed to the nines like a flock of gym-class penguins. The familiar faces; bodies of Wellspring Academy's most popular girls lined the walls with their slender, sequined curves.

And there, sitting at the round drink-laden table, was Edmund.

Decked out in an oversized tweed jacket. Drunk grin on his face.

Sitting next to him, with no particular flair or fanfare, was Jenna Garamen.

28

"You're back, baby!"

For a moment, Patrick thought Jenna was talking to him. He could feel a simpering grin blooming along his battered face as he saw Jenna rise from her chair. Damp hair hanging over a wet shirt, she opened her arms. The swish of her hips propelling her across the room, and for a moment Patrick thought this might have all been one large surprise party for him.

Cody brushed past him.

Patrick watched in a sickening state of limbo as Jenna threw her arms around Cody.

Drew him close for a loathsome kiss, full on the mouth. The fact that she was a good two inches taller didn't help how absurd the two looked.

Cody broke away with a loud smack. He turned to Patrick, one arm around Jenna, the other brandishing a beer that had somehow appeared in his hand.

"Funny how life works out," he told Patrick, taking a swig of Sam Adams. "We were in our limo, headed to pick *you* up, of all people. And who do we see stranded in the rain?"

"Me!" Jenna declared proudly with a vampy grin.

"Seems like she was in the mood to party!" Cody declared, raising his beer.

Jenna let out a loud whoop, the rest of the room joining in.

Including Edmund, but Patrick was going to do this one step at a time.

"Jenna..." He tried to regulate his breathing, forget that he was trapped between four walls and a window leading to a twenty-five-story drop. "What are you doing?"

"Uh..." Jenna put on a vapid expression. She pressed a finger against her cheek. Twisted it, crossing her eyes before going back to normal. "Having a good time!"

Patrick felt blood trickling down his chin. "Jenna... Kelly—"

"Screw Kelly McDermott!" she lashed out. "*And* Patrick Saint. I'm sick of the both of you." She spun around drunkenly, addressing the whole room. "Kelly actually thinks he's from the *future*!" She was greeted with boisterous laughter, though it was clear they'd been enjoying this little joke for a while now. "He thinks he's come back to *right the wrongs*! Make better what once was worse!"

"Fucking true to that!" Edmund announced with a crass, uncharacteristically nasty selection of words, courtesy of what was looking to be quite a drinking binge. He raised himself out of his chair, all elbows. The hand he was using to support himself went slipping across the table. Beer bottles fell like dominoes, drawing cheers from the rest. Edmund raised a bottle of tequila to his lips and took a swig. "I mean, what kind of idiot travels through time and *fucks* things up the way he has?!"

"Edmund..." Patrick glanced around, still unable to piece it together. "What are you..."

"He's looking for Kelly!" Cody laughed. "Looking for the man of the hour!"

"Looking for Kelly," Edmund slurred.

"My guess?" Cody walked over and slapped his new friend on the back. "Kelly should be coming out to play any minute."

That's why he sent the picture! Patrick's angels screamed. *He did it to draw Kelly out in the open, get him arrested. It was* Kelly *Edmund was after when he left the house. The name he said didn't being with a* C. *It began with a* K. *He must have come looking for* Kelly, *and–*

Patrick opened his mouth, when–

Don't warn them about the gun. You tell them he's got a gun, there's no telling what Edmund might do, there's no telling what or worse *could be.*

"You can't change history." Edmund grinned, taking another swig of tequila. "Can't be done."

"Yeah!" Jenna said, sauntering across the room and nabbing a handle of Aristocrat vodka off the night table. "Think about it! Kelly trying to change destiny! Can't happen! We're all stuck with what is and always has to be!" She took what appeared to be a mammoth swig from the plastic bottle, head tilted at a ninety-degree angle.

Cheers erupted around the room.

Patrick frowned through the disruption.

There's no air bubbles, his angels whispered frantically. *She's not really drinking.*

"Here's a thought..." Jenna sauntered over to Edmund. "And I'd like to ask our resident genius what *he* thinks."

"Yeah, genius!" some girl cried out.

"If someone traveled back through time . . . ," Jenna postulated, swaying aggressively. "And if that person found themselves doing some weird-ass shit like . . ." Jenna burped. "Like maybe if they screwed their own mother or something . . . If the time traveler didn't disappear right then and there, wouldn't that mean he was always, without knowing it, his own father? Edmund, what say you?"

"I say . . ." Edmund put his arm around Jenna, under orders from Jose Cuervo, joining her in storm-tossed motions. "I'd say that if Kelly were doing something like that . . . Well, that means it's all happened already, hasn't it?"

The jury of drunk athletes let loose with deep *ooooohs*.

"It's already happened!" Jenna declared, slinking toward Patrick.

Her steps were drunk and wavering, but her eyes were suddenly serious. Piercing, the look of someone doing all she could to send an SOS across a crowded room.

"Already happened," she repeated, stepping close to Patrick. "It would mean that Kelly is only doing what he was supposed to do. What he was *meant* to do, sexy." Jenna reached around and grabbed Patrick's ass, pressing her body against his. "Don't feel bad, baby. Kelly's a goddamn nutjob, that doesn't mean you can't step up."

Jenna took the back of Patrick's head and drew him in for a deep kiss.

The leftover traces of vodka burned Patrick's lips, mournful realizations that this was how he would be forced to remember their first kiss. He closed his eyes, unable to be swept away with the staged motions of Jenna's tongue.

"Look at that slut!" Cody's voice called out in the darkness, pleased as punch. "Look!"

Jenna slid her lips across Patrick's cheek, began chewing on his earlobe.

"We've got to get out of here," Jenna whispered through her mouthful of cartilage. "Patrick, we've got to get out of here before Kelly shows up. Cody's got it in Edmund's head that this is all *Kelly's* fault."

Patrick stared over Jenna's shoulder, saw Edmund watching with curiosity. Whatever enraged euphoria had previously gripped him, it was gone now. Already receding, beginning to stew. Maybe thinking just how sweet that *bang-bang* would sound, watching Kelly's blood redecorate the beige walls an oily red.

But if Kelly dies, Patrick's angels screamed in a frustrated chorus, *then how does he ever manage to come back after twenty more years on this sorry planet?*

Patrick squeezed his eyes shut, screaming back to his angels, *There is no such thing as TIME TRAVEL! It just couldn't be REAL!*

You know what is real? Patrick's angels whispered. *Edmund's gun is real, my friend.*

Jenna drew away, slipping once again into her promiscuous role.

Eyelids drooping as she plopped onto the bed.

Patrick didn't know how much longer she would be able to

keep this up. Didn't know how much longer he could pretend to be just another bystander. Under the cover of his own broken face, he scanned the room for possibilities. The room was lined with large bodies, grinning faces gathered like spectators at a ritual killing.

The only thing standing between him and the door was Zack.

Two hundred and forty pounds of Zack.

Cody's own personal Patrick Saint.

A distraction, something to distract them all...

All five million of them, his angels despaired.

"Hey, Pat..." Jenna leaned back on the bed, absolute vixen. She slid her hand along the comforter, licking her lips. "Why don't you come join me?"

Through the rumbling approval of his jailors, Patrick knew that she had the same idea.

He felt his bile rise, disgusted with the vile stares, grins that seemed razor sharp.

"What do you say, boys?" she called out. "Who wants to see me do Patrick?"

The crowd roared with enthusiasm.

Patrick couldn't play along, looking about wildly at the surrounding mob. Beers raised like torches, a slow chant rising over the blast of rap music.

"FIGHT, FIGHT, OUTTA SIGHT! KILL, PANTHERS, KILL!"

Even the girls, straight out of *Girls Gone Wild.*

The only holdout was Edmund, who stood by, drunk and

impassive. Staring into nothingness, backstage to a life flashing before his eyes.

"You can stop this, Edmund," Patrick pleaded. Wasn't able to get through, didn't get anything other than that lost, remote stare. "There's a part of you that knows you can't do what you're thinking of doing, Edmund, you *know they're just using you–*"

"Patrick!" Cody shouted.

Patrick looked over, saw Cody's lips pulled back in a lecherous grin.

"Don't be such a pussy," he said. "Just go on and fuck the bitch."

And so Patrick's angels became demons.

There might have been a scream. In that moment, Patrick was almost certain something had torn from his body, bursting through his chest, slinging him across the room, and sending his hands around Cody's neck.

It didn't last.

For all his diabolical wishes, Patrick didn't have a chance to get his licks in. He found himself surrounded, torn away by Cody's willing teammates. Eager to blow off a little steam. They threw him to the ground, and Patrick prepared himself for a deadly thrashing. Vague hopes that the sudden slowness he was experiencing would give Jenna the chance to bolt for the door. Refusing to believe that it was Jenna he was seeing, leaping ferociously onto the nearest running back. Breaking character, screaming for them to stop.

It was only then that Patrick noticed he was well past the

first in a series of blows meant to land him in the emergency room. Maybe he'd gotten lucky so far, hurried fists falling short of a direct hit. No telling how long that would last.

His angels went into shock, rocking back and forth.

Humming the comforting melody of his favorite Coltrane tune: "I Wish I Knew."

And though there was no real clarity in the events that followed, one of his angels did manage to break free from the shock and awe. A single angel who witnessed the whole thing.

A single angel who heard the door to the room burst open.

A single angel who saw Kelly elbow Zack in the face. The blurry outline of a Kelly-shaped figure, mad with panic. Crazy, some might say, and most would remember. Not within any rational scheme of perception, but most would remember the unhinged eyes of an already broken madman.

Few would see what that one angel saw.

The face of a sad and desperate nobody, finally deciding exactly where all that rage belonged. Woodchuck features contorting, blinded by a life of obscurity and hideous derision. Reaching behind him, under his oversized tweed jacket, the closest thing he could find to fit the occasion. A flash of black steel, brandished by a floppy, inexperienced, fifteen-year-old hand.

And one of those fists finally made direct contact.

Busting up against Patrick's skull, sending everything into a vibrating blur.

But that one angel held on.

Saw Kelly rushing forward.

Reclaiming his past as a dynamite football player.

Charging at full steam.

Head down, as they always said.

Arms wrapping around Edmund, both of them careering toward the skyline of a city doing all it could to develop into a thriving, competitive metropolis.

It must have taken some kind of force to break that glass.

And the blood-curdling shriek would have been preferable to the grotesque silence that followed.

That one lone angel saw it all before drawing back to join the rest.

And Patrick lost consciousness amid the howling chaos in his head.

#29

*F*irst, there was sunlight.

A whole lot of afternoon delight for so late in the night, pouring through the leaves of springtime trees. Kaleidoscope wedges tumbling in the breeze, through the luminous fog now starting to lift. Bright curtain pulling back to reveal the wide expanse of lawn in front of Jefferson Elementary.

Children dotted the space like sheep, holding on to brightly colored lunch boxes. Cheap book bags bouncing off their backs as they trotted alongside their parents, recounting their day with high-pitched excitement.

Cars rolled by along the residential street, crawling well below the speed limit.

From a nearby parking lot, a fleet of yellow school buses came to life, engines grinding.

Patrick reached up to rub his eyes and felt something bump against his chin.

He blinked, face to face with a lunch box sporting rosy-cheeked cartoons.

Pokémon, Patrick thought lazily. *I'm holding a Pokémon lunch box in my hand.*

He heard a voice to his left ask: "Where's Mrs. Sheldon?"

Patrick looked down and saw Casey standing next to him.

His Redskins shirt hung just above the knees, green shorts barely peeking out from beneath. Eyelashes batting away at clumps of thick black hair, courtesy of his mother. Hands held out as he tossed a football to himself.

One last catch before looking up and repeating his question: "Where's Mrs. Sheldon?"

"I don't know," Patrick heard himself say. Heard someone else say, this wasn't his voice. Wasn't his body, he was almost sure of it. Not sure enough to actually check, though, and his mind accepted it with mushy approval. "What time is it?"

Casey looked down at his watch, squinting. "It's three-forty."

"How much is it until four?" Patrick asked with an encouraging smile.

"Twenty, duh."

"You're getting smart."

"Nobody's smarter than Mrs. Parker."

Patrick couldn't remember the name. "Who's that?"

"My teacher, *duh . . .*" Casey rolled his eyes. "Anybody home?"

"I don't know," Patrick said, trying to focus. "I think I'm supposed to be in a room."

"You're weird."

"I think I'm supposed to be in a hotel room."

"You're *so* weird," Casey amended, turning to the sound of three loud honks. "Hey, look!"

Patrick saw a gray car stuck in the middle of the road. Through the open windows, he saw two children. One in the backseat, one in the front, waving and crying out for them to get over there.

Without thinking, Patrick picked up Casey's book bag and fastened it onto his back. Reached out and took hold of his brother's hand, trying to account for how soft and small those fingers felt.

By the time they got to the car, the back door was already open.

Patrick sent his brother in first, then slid in, closing the door behind him.

"I thought I told you to wait for us at the side entrance," Mrs. Sheldon scolded from the front seat.

From where he sat, Patrick could just make out a quarter-profile of orange foundation and gray hair, all up in a bun. He glanced into the rearview mirror, saw nothing but a series of deep creases along a large forehead.

Patrick giggled.

"It's not funny, mister," Mrs. Sheldon admonished as she pulled away from the school. "We were waiting back there this whole time."

"Patrick's going to get in trouble!" came a singsong voice from the front seat.

Patrick couldn't see who it was, wondered why he was having so much trouble remembering. With the car picking up speed, he turned and fastened his safety belt. Caught sight of the world blurring past the open window, unable to see the road from his vantage point. The wind rushed in, gale force throughout the car.

This is fun, Patrick thought, before feeling his brother tug at his sleeve.

"Do you know what we did in class today?" Casey asked.

"Nope," Patrick replied, felt the car go over a few ugly bumps.

"We got a new hamster!" Casey held out his hands, cupped them together, as though trying to re-create the fuzzy little beast. "He's small and brown. And do you know what his name is?"

Patrick smiled. "No."

"Mr. Ears!" Casey cackled, eyes alight. "Mr. *Ears!*"

"That's a funny name."

"It's just silly," Casey explained.

"Did you get to play with him?" Patrick asked.

"Not yet . . . but do you know what we saw him do today?"

Patrick heard the sound of a cell phone going off some-where in the car. He heard Mrs. Sheldon say the d-word, and saw her hand reaching between the front seats, into her purse.

"I said, do you know what we saw him *do* today?" Casey repeated.

"No," Patrick said, putting an arm around his brother.

"We saw him run in his wheel!" Casey raised his voice, competing with the ongoing sound of the phone, even as Mrs. Sheldon continued to rattle around, looking to put a stop to the whole thing. "He got onto it, and started running! Real fast! But he didn't get anywhere! The whole thing kept going round and round and round! It was so silly! And I finally had to ask him–"

"–*where do you think you're going?*" Patrick finished in perfect unison with his little brother as the car picked up speed, and seconds neared the brink of extinction before he managed to add: "I love you, Casey."

As for what came next, someone would just have to tell him about it.

#30

His first thoughts were of Kelly.

How much he loved him.

The crippling, unfortunate love he felt for the best friend he'd known for just a few days now.

Then there was Jenna, crying images of her playing the whorish cheerleader in a mournful attempt to save them all.

And somewhere in there, he thought he saw his brother.

Seven-year-old smile fading fast.

Cross-fading against a room filled with police officers.

One in particular was kneeling down, troubled eyes under bushy brows.

"All you son right?"

A bright flash of light went off nearby. Patrick blinked. "What?"

"Are you all right, son?" the officer repeated.

"Where's Kelly?"

"They're taking him down to the station."

Patrick shook his head, edges of the room stretching out like cellophane before returning to the shape of a hallway. He was seated against the wall, face and head a collection of aching knobs.

"Have I swollen much?" Patrick asked.

"We got a guy from the EMS who already looked at you," the officer assured him. "Had to scamper off to take care of a broken arm, but he said you seem fine. Just bruises."

"He's down at the station?" Patrick mumbled, doubling back. "Where's . . . what about Edmund?"

The officer didn't answer, looked down the hallway.

Patrick did the same.

Caught sight of a few of the football players, huddled together.

Saw Zack talking to Detective Donahue, shaking his head and pointing directly across from where Patrick was sitting. He followed the signs, eyes landing on the entrance to room 2507. Two more uniforms on either side of the door, standing guard.

Patrick lurched to his feet and staggered forward.

The guards moved to stop him, but it wasn't necessary. Patrick stalled out halfway there. Staring through the open doorway. Taking in the small yellow markers sticking out all over the surrounding space like price tags for the visually impaired; large, bold, single-digit numbers printed on each one. A trove of empty bottles still littering the floors and table. And beyond that, a gaping hole in the window opened out into the night. Jagged circumference like large, uneven teeth.

Patrick could feel the breeze billowing through, smell the humid aftermath of the storm.

A photographer stepped into view and snapped a flash picture.

Took a note on a clipboard hanging from his arm.

All that procedure to piece together a five-second event.

Then Detective Donahue was by his side, leading Patrick away. There was no resisting. He would be going back under any minute now, Patrick was sure of it. Expecting handcuffs to snap around his wrists just before the world went black.

"What happened?" Patrick managed.

"Jenna's downstairs," Donahue told him, dismissing the question. They stopped at a set of elevators. "We've already talked to her, she told us her version. The short version."

Patrick swallowed hard. "I probably shouldn't talk without a lawyer."

"You're not under arrest. Unless there's some other crime you'd like to confess to, I can almost guarantee it'll stay that way...." The elevator arrived, and Donahue helped Patrick in. "In case you're still worried, though, Jenna called your parents."

The doors closed, sent the elevator on its way down.

Patrick suddenly remembered what happened the last time he was in that elevator.

"If you'd like to press charges against any of them, you can...," Donahue told him. "For what they did to your face. If you can specifically identify any of them, that is. But I wouldn't recommend it."

"Are you allowed to tell me stuff like this?"

"No...So if you like, you can press charges against me." Donahue sighed. "But I wouldn't recommend it. I'm just giving you two nickels' worth of free advice."

"So why shouldn't I?"

"Because this is a real mess as it is...Because Cody's going to talk about how you jumped him, and the entire football team's going to have his back. And these aren't happy times at the DA's office, either. With the coverage Edmund's death is going to get, you bring in this extraneous charge, and it's going to be like Duke Lacrosse all over again–"

"Wait," Patrick interrupted. He had been lulled by Donahue's reasoning tone, right up until he'd mentioned Edmund's name. "Edmund?"

"Oh shit…" Donahue shook his head, rubbed one of his eyes with the back of his hand. "I'm sorry, Patrick. We're still trying to sort it out, but Edmund started shooting. Managed to get Cody pretty good, he's at the hospital now, in critical condition–"

"But *Edmund*," Patrick insisted.

"Kelly tackled him. Accidentally, it appears, sent Edmund through the glass…Kelly managed to let go before…I mean, to stop himself from…grab hold of the metal frame before… I'm sorry, Patrick, but Edmund is dead."

It was all lost to him as the image of that window came back to him. A window twenty-five stories above the resting place of Edmund's final thought. If it could have even qualified as a thought, when the final seconds before were spent in a massive riptide of rushing wind, without hope of a peaceful end.

Patrick was mortified to discover he was about to yawn.

He covered his face with his hands. Sharp jabs of pain shot through his brain, and he played through. "What about Kelly?"

"We called Mr. Redwood to tell him about some pills we

found in Kelly's car.... I think Redwood expects the worst. He told us that even if Kelly did end up confessing to the break-in, he wanted all charges dropped, so—"

"Kelly and *Edmund*," Patrick insisted. "What's going to happen to *Kelly*?"

"I don't know..." The doors slid open at the fifth floor. A collection of guests were about to step in when Donahue flashed his badge. Enough said, and the doors closed once more, leaving them alone for the rest of the trip. "I'm going to need you to corroborate Jenna's story. I understand you two came to be here through different means."

"Please don't listen to anything Kelly tells you," Patrick said miserably.

"I'm afraid that's my job."

"He's not well."

"I know."

The doors slid open into the chaos of the lobby. More officers; students scattered about with shock a common expression. Beyond the hotel doors, a police line had been set up to keep the press back. Lights flashed, glared from shoulder-mounted cameras.

"How long was I out?"

"A while...," Donahue said, concerned, motioning to one of the boys in blue. "You actually came to for a few minutes, that's how you got out of the room and into the hall.... Do you not remember that?"

Patrick shook his head, drowning under all that activity.

"OK, we're going to have the EMT take another look at you. If he gives the OK, I'm going to take your statement. If he doesn't, you can go to the hospital and I'll catch you later."

"I just want to get out of here."

"You can always try lying to the EMT," Donahue said. "Though unless you get one who's been working a little too hard, it won't do much good. . . . And I wouldn't recommend it."

From out of the crowd, Jenna appeared, running toward him.

His face exploded with pain as she fell into his arms. He didn't mind. Could've done with a lot more of it, considering what the following days might bring. Even that realization couldn't make it real, and, time being, he pressed his face against Jenna's neck.

"They're here," she said, pulling back and looking across the room.

Not wanting to, Patrick cast his sights with Jenna.

There, standing by the convex corner leading to the grand hallway, were his parents.

And in the end, Patrick did lie to the EMT.

"We have to go to the station," Patrick's father said. He adjusted the rearview mirror, framing his son in its reflection. "Kelly's parents are already there. Your mother and I wanted to see if we could help."

"We're going to drop you off at home," his mother added from the passenger's seat, motioning for her husband to start the car.

"I want to go with you," Patrick said sullenly, staring

through the window and up at the Verona Marriott. A helicopter buzzed overhead, spotlight dancing. "I want to see Kelly."

"It's going to be a while before you see Kelly."

Patrick turned away from the window. In the seat next to him, he saw Jenna do the same, a siren going off to match the flash of red and blue police lights.

"What do you mean?"

"He's going to be there for a while, is all..." His father started the car. "There hasn't been an official arrest, and with our help there probably won't."

"We'd rather you didn't..." His mother paused. "It would be best for Kelly if you simply went home."

"Why?"

"We're only trying to save Kelly."

"*Save* Kelly?"

"Patrick..." His father eased out into the street and headed out from the downtown area. "You have to trust us. You may not remember, but just today, you were questioned in connection with breaking and entering. *Now* you want to show up at the police station where Kelly is being held for what hasn't yet been ruled out as a *homicide*? It won't *look* good."

Patrick's head was killing him. Plain and simple, he couldn't think straight. Of all that had happened that evening, of all the signs he had missed, nothing seemed more important than what he was hearing.

But what he was hearing made for a very seductive rationale.

He turned to Jenna for help, silently asking for advice.

Jenna shook her head, unsure.

"Let us take you home." Patrick's mother twisted in her seat to face him. "Can we please, Patrick, just take you home."

Jenna's hand slid across the seat, held on to his.

"Take me to Jenna's," he ordered, as though just stepping into a New York cab.

Patrick's mother wrinkled her nose, but the battle was done.

"Can you tell me how to get there?" his father asked.

"Jenna's still here," Patrick said, turning back to the window. "You can talk to her."

31

The clock on the coffeemaker read 3:15 a.m. Its green glow was the lone light source from within the kitchen. A slim shaft of illumination came in through the window, compliments of the back-porch bulb. From the living room, the television's blue sheen reflected off the walls, made them move with breathing life.

None of it managed to find Patrick or Jenna, seated at the kitchen table since eleven.

They had run out of things to say over two hours before.

Grasping at straws, Patrick looked down into the cup before him. "I can't believe I'm actually drinking coffee."

"How do you like it?" Jenna asked.

"I don't think I get it."

It was too dark to see her expression. "Are you awake?"

"Yes."

"Then there's nothing more to get."

The house continued to settle around them.

The digital clock ticked off another minute, bringing them to 3:16.

"Patrick?"

"I'm here."

"Why don't you just open the letter?" Jenna asked, sliding the twisted wreckage of Patrick's envelope across the table.

Patrick picked it up.

Turned it around in his hands, trying to determine which end was which.

"Honestly," Jenna insisted. "What's stopping you?"

"I don't feel right saying this.... Not now, it's not the right time..."

"Then answer my question.... Is it because of me?"

Patrick looked down into what little he could see of his coffee. "I don't know."

"I'll admit, maybe there's something happening here...," she told him. Mournfully unemotional, her voice didn't match the words. "You and I, us two, I mean. Maybe there's something but... We're not going to figure it out tonight. Maybe not for a long time, so Patrick, just—"

The phone rang in a sudden surprise attack.

The two of them jumped, chairs scuffing the floor.

They waited for the confirmation of a follow-up ring.

There it was, and now neither one of them could bring themselves to answer.

"You still want me to open it?" Patrick asked, too apprehensive to be truly snide.

From the living room, they heard Jenna's father rise from the couch and step around the small wood-framed coffee table. He picked up the phone just before the answering machine could report for duty.

"Hello?"

Patrick strained his ears with unrealistic hopes of picking up the voice on the other end.

"Yes, I'm Al, Jenna's father. . . ." He coughed. "Yes, we met once. Would you like to talk to your son? . . . Oh, you're *Kelly's* parents. Never mind, I can guarantee you we haven't met. How is Kelly . . . ?"

In the silence that followed, Jenna put her hands together. Head bowed in a silent prayer.

Patrick watched her, unable to surrender just yet.

"Are you sure you don't want to . . ." Al's shrugging shoulders could be heard in his voice: "All right, if you want, I'll tell them. . . . No, please don't call back tonight."

Then the muted beep of the phone turning off.

Al shuffled into the kitchen. In the wan light of the television, his bathrobe had the appearance of a prehistoric animal pelt. His face was hidden, but the disillusionment in his words made eyesight an undesirable afterthought.

"They found Edmund's gun, and Kelly's being released."

In the time it took for Patrick to even consider why such somber tones for such good news, Al shut it all down.

"His parents are driving him to Saint Sebastian Mental Hospital."

Patrick looked over at Jenna.

Watched as her hands parted slowly, and spread out along the edges of the table.

"Just in case, is what they said. Just in case they missed something, just in case the police call him back in, and that leads to an actual arrest this time around. They said it would help to have him diagnosed as not being of sound mind . . . just in case."

"Kelly's not crazy...," Patrick said. Dazed, not comprehending that convincing Al would solve absolutely nothing. "Kelly is *not* crazy. Where were *my* parents in all of this?"

"It was their idea."

Patrick felt the air rush out of him. If he hadn't been sitting down, there was no question he would have collapsed right there on the kitchen floor.

"My parents did this?"

"Honey?" Al asked, head moving slightly to the left. "Are you all right?"

With her head still bowed, Jenna whispered yes.

"We'll find out more in the morning," Al told them. "In the meantime, I have to get to bed. Patrick, please stay here tonight. Or for as long as you like," he added, understanding that it might be a good while before he met Patrick's parents again.

"Do you think Kelly's crazy?" Patrick asked, voice sinking.

"I think you're all crazy," Al said sternly. "But please don't forget that my daughter and her friend Patrick were almost killed tonight. I'm an adult, and this is my job. So don't take it personal...I'm going to bed." Al turned, rubbing his head. "Be sure and clean up before doing the same."

His footsteps faded to the back of the house.

"Patrick?"

Patrick nodded, though he wasn't sure if Jenna would pick up on it.

"Come on," she said quietly. "Just open the letter."

With air trembling past his swollen lips, Patrick held the envelope before his face, searching for the edge before simply ripping into it. No point in preserving the integrity of the letter; it was just a piece of paper. Just a piece of paper with another fork in the road, and Patrick gnashed his teeth as he finally managed to tear the thing wide open.

Chest heaving, he held the mutilated letter before his eyes.

"The light switch is on the wall behind you," Jenna said.

Patrick turned, felt along the wall, and caught hold of the protruding nub.

The fluorescent overheads burned into his retinas, and he had to squeeze his eyes shut against the glaring white wall before him. With one eye open, he swiveled around, back to the table. Before he could scan the letter for the only sentence that mattered, he froze.

It was the first time in hours that he'd gotten a good look at Jenna.

Her hair was a nest of brambles, falling woefully over almond eyes that had the appearance of having drooped at the ends, so much that he expected them to slowly slide down along her ashen cheeks. Her hands and elbows were bruised and scraped. The earlier rainfall had stretched her clothes out. She appeared almost shapeless under her wrinkled blue-striped shirt. Lips pressed together in a thin purple line.

"You look like a different person," Patrick said.

"You're no prize, either," she informed him.

He lowered his eyes to see whether Juilliard agreed with her. The time was now 3:25.

THE LONG WAIT FOR TOMORROW

"**M**ore coffee?"

"Yeah. I like this blend, it's good."

"Like you'd know good coffee from a bucket of tar, Patrick."

"I'm getting the hang of it, Al. . . . I am getting the hang of it."

It was bright outside. Dynamite bright, even through the kitchen windows. A wide sheath of light cut through the room, spotlight on the linoleum floor. Felt as though it was the source of all warmth that morning. Good warm. Cozy and soft, the welcoming embrace of a well-worn comforter.

Patrick took a sip of his coffee.

Jenna's father did the same. He stared over the rim of his cup, raised his eyebrows.

"What?" Patrick asked, putting down his mug.

Al didn't answer all at once.

The radio was tuned to NPR, news at the top of the hour. Impartial reports of suicide bombers in Iraq. Numbers without names. It was an ugly thing, enjoying a cup of coffee half a world away from the other half of the world.

"You hear that?" Al asked him.

"The news?"

"Guess it goes to show . . . ," he said.

"Goes to show what?" Patrick asked, dipping back into his coffee.

"And here I sit, on my daughter's graduation day..." Al gave his Saturday morning scruff a once-over with his hand. "I'm so very proud of her, Patrick."

"You've got every right."

"And I guess it doesn't mean much... The ceremony, I mean. The ceremony doesn't really mean that much, but along with all these things... Happy, sad, proud, worried. I don't know, maybe I just kind of thought I'd be watching her walk across that stage. Cap, gown, the whole nine, right?"

The news went local, reports of another scorcher all across Verona.

"Am I being selfish?" Al asked.

"Not without reason," Patrick assured him. "And I'm sorry if our decision's hurt you."

"Nah... It's not hurt. Thing is, it makes more sense to me than that whole graduation nonsense. I think it's admirable. I'm proud of both you two. Guess there's no stopping reflex, though."

"Ain't that the sad truth...."

Al motioned to a white envelope sitting alongside Patrick's coffee. "Been meaning to ask..."

"My homeroom teacher dropped it off a few days ago. It's for Kelly, care of me."

"How are your parents?"

"They are how they are."

"Mmm."

Patrick caught sight of white ceramic peeking through the thin layer of coffee. It was his turn, and he walked over to the coffeemaker, dislodged the pot. He poured them both a fresh cup, wondering what the hell he was thinking that one morning, knocking the coffee out of Kelly's hand.

Busting up his parents' collection of rare crystalware.

Patrick waited for his angels to comment, but they were content with their silence.

He sat back down, looked at Al.

Al smiled at him.

Patrick smiled back.

Jenna popped her head around the corner. Her hair was damp, stuck together in thick stalks.

"Just about ready to go," she informed Patrick.

"OK," Patrick told her.

She vanished, back from whence she came.

"You two will keep in touch," Al said with all the assurance of a casual prophet, decked out in sweatpants and a Rolling Stones T-shirt. "Can't stop something like that."

"We've still got the summer," Patrick reminded him.

"It'll go by fast. . . . I dare you to blink, it'll go by that fast."

Patrick blinked.

Al laughed, deep lines forming parentheticals around his smile.

Then Jenna was standing at the entrance. Dressed in jeans and a sunflower blouse. Purse hanging over her shoulder, signaling their present departure.

The men stood up, leaving their coffee behind.

Patrick picked up the envelope while Al walked over and hugged his daughter. Blessed her forehead with a kiss.

"Proud of you, baby," he said.

"I know, Dad." Jenna squeezed him tightly, eyes closed.

"It's been one crazy, stupid trip, hasn't it?"

"It has."

Al turned and shook Patrick's hand. "I'll see you both later. We'll go grab some dinner."

Patrick nodded.

He reached into his jeans and pulled out the car keys.

"Let's go," he told Jenna, heading for the door as the radio did what it could to put their life in context: "June seventh, nine-forty-five a.m., here on NPR."

The drive took the good part of an hour.

They spent the ride in silence. Neither one moved to speak or turn on the radio. There was nothing uncomfortable about it. Meditating along the winding road, sun still low, shade from surrounding trees keeping it comfortable.

They reached the gates of Saint Sebastian at eleven. A security guard signed them in, sent them in the proper direction. They parked in a near-empty lot, the only ones apart from a long line of employee cars stationed near the front of the estate.

At a glance, the grounds looked no different from a slice of campus life.

The inside proved to be just as unremarkable.

There was no doubt the place had been remodeled several times since the 1800s, but apart from casual hints of bygone infrastructure, it was like any other hospital. A front desk, painted white, matched the uniform of the attending nurse.

"We're here to see Kelly McDermott," Patrick told her.

Wondering if he should add anything about what landed him in there.

"OK," she said pleasantly enough, handing them a clipboard.

As they filled in their information, the nurse flagged a passing doctor. A very *doctor*-looking doctor, tall and balding. He wore wire-rimmed spectacles and sported a beard that screamed *psychoanalyst.*

"Oh good." He pulled out a handkerchief and wiped his nose. "I'm Dr. Sandler."

"Please empty all personal items," the nurse instructed, plunking two plastic bins onto the counter.

They didn't have much, and by the time they were done, the nurse had already finished filling out their guest passes. She then checked out their various belongings, decided there was nothing there of any worry to the hospital, and handed it all back.

"He's been looking forward to this," Dr. Sandler told them.

"Thank you, Doctor," Patrick said, unsure if this was actually a compliment.

"You look a bit like Oliver Sacks," Jenna told him.

"I'm no Oliver Sacks," the doctor said, eye hinting that, yes, he knew this was where he was supposed to smile. "Thank you, though."

Dr. Sandler led them to a thick, heavy-looking door.

Patrick was expecting him to remove a key ring from his belt, maybe undo a few locks. This wasn't the case, and he simply opened it, doing a gentleman's job of ushering them through.

After that, it was down a casually populated hallway and under a large archway.

Patrick marveled at how ordinary everything seemed.

It was, basically, a large recreation room. Long windows allowing for generous amounts of sunlight. Patients dressed in what appeared to be everyday clothing, not a straitjacket in sight. Board games abounded, paper and crayons spread out amongst the collection of plastic tables, plastic chairs.

Before any of the details could sink in, Patrick spied Kelly McDermott. He was seated at a table. By himself, by the window. Dressed in jeans and a white shirt. Hands folded, calm as the light pooling on the table before him.

It was the first time Patrick had seen him, really seen him, since that last day at his parents' house.

Barely a month ago.

He felt Jenna take in a breath, filled with the same compulsion to rush forward. Grab hold of Kelly and never let go. Absurd thoughts of shuffling him out of the hospital in hopes that nobody would notice a six-legged human composite drifting past the front desk.

Instead, they walked over with the slow and expectant steps of a child face to face with its very own pony. Each one petrified of getting a blank, sedated stare upon saying his name.

"Hey, guys," Kelly said, looking up with a soft smile. "They said you'd be coming by."

He rose from his seat, and they did all fall into that three-pronged embrace.

Six eyes, all closed tight.

Kelly was the first to break away.

He took a look at them, saw that Jenna had already sprung a leak. He reached out and brushed the tear with his thumb. Sighed and shook his head with a proud smile.

"Shouldn't you two be graduating right about now?"

"It's just a game," Patrick said, smiling to the fullest extent that he remembered how.

"Let's sit."

They did, and Patrick noticed a blank sheet of paper, paired with a single red crayon.

"What have we got here, Kelly?" he asked casually.

"Just wanted to show you guys something," Kelly replied. "All in good time, though."

They looked at each other for a bit, unsure how to move forward.

Patrick pulled out the letter from his pocket. "This is from Bill."

"Neat," Kelly said, taking the envelope and setting it aside.

"You going to open it?"

"I think I'll wait on that." Kelly gave Patrick a knowing look. "You know how that can be."

"I hear you."

"How are your parents?" Kelly asked.

"Fine, I guess..." Patrick shrugged. "I've been staying at Jenna's ever since that night."

Kelly nodded, keeping his approval right there in the middle.

"How's your dad?" Kelly asked Jenna.

"He's good."

"They treating you all right in here?" Patrick asked awkwardly.

"Well . . . ," Kelly sighed, moving his hands over the surface of the table. "Haven't put me on any serious meds yet. Some stuff to help me sleep every now and then . . . So I finally have slept."

Jenna swallowed. "So . . . you still in there, Kelly?"

"I thought about lying to you guys," Kelly said matter-of-factly. "Crossed my mind while I was sitting here, before you showed up. Just for a second, I thought I'd let you all enjoy the . . . shared sanity that the outside world is privy to. But what's the use, I tried that once before, didn't I?"

Patrick and Jenna smiled slightly, remembering Kelly's ludicrous attempts to refashion himself from time-traveling madman to all-American jock.

"Want to see something fun, Jenna?" Kelly asked with a sly and tired grin.

Jenna nodded softly. "Sure."

"Say the first thing that comes into your head. Doesn't matter how ridiculous."

"Uh . . ." Jenna tried clearing her thoughts. "Elephants don't—"

"—*happen quite like they used to,*" Kelly finished in tandem with her. Before anyone could say anything, he kept right on.

"To think there was a time when that kind of thing actually surprised us . . . Yeah, it's been happening more and more lately. Scares the bejeezus out of the doctors."

Kelly laughed, even as Patrick and Jenna remained anchored in worried uncertainty.

"I'm OK . . . ," Kelly assured them. "I've just had a bit of time to think. A lot of time to think, really. And I kind of understand it all now. That little trick I just pulled turns out to be the key to everything."

"Kelly . . ." Patrick glanced around, trying not to imagine him as another one of these wandering inmates. "What do you mean?"

"Think about it," Kelly told them. "All those times, it wasn't as though I was finishing someone's sentences. It's like that paradox theory. If I finish someone's sentence because I know they're going to say it . . . well, then I stop them from saying it, so how could I have ever known they were going to say it? It's Abraham Lincoln at Ford's Theatre, all over again."

Patrick felt his mouth go dry.

"Nope," Kelly continued. "All those times, I was saying those things at the *exact same time.* Kind of stands to reason, now that it's . . . kind of all over. It got me to thinking, that I wasn't predicting anything. It wasn't any kind of foreknowledge. I was saying those things when I did, because that's what happened the last time I came back through here. And the time before that. And before that, like two mirrors held up to each other . . . Each time thinking that I could change what was

going to happen, never realizing I'd already tried. And failed..."
Kelly tilted his head, remembering something. "Hey, what happened to Rachel-Ann?"

Patrick was disgusted that he didn't immediately recognize the name of Edmund's mother, even as Jenna replied: "She sold her house. Moved. Nobody knows any more about it."

"Did you go to the funeral?"

Further self-recrimination as Patrick shook his head.

"I did...." Jenna twisted her knuckles together, lips tight. "Whole school did."

"Even the football guys? Cody and the rest?"

"Yeah..." Jenna scratched her nose. "Well, Cody couldn't, he... Edmund shot him through the spine, and he's not going to be walking... Ever again, they say."

Kelly shook his head sadly. "Jesus."

"I know... There's nothing he did, I feel, deserving of that."

"Yes."

"It's strange to say it, but I think maybe they might have... Well, as far as the football team, students, teachers. I guess everyone's been treating each other a bit better lately."

"We'll see how long that lasts," Patrick muttered.

Kelly turned to him, hesitating to ask. "Patrick?"

Patrick's stomach knotted. "I couldn't go to the funeral."

"Why?"

The gnarled mess in his abdomen only worsened. "Same reason I couldn't go to graduation."

Kelly chuffed without any serious offense taken. "And here I thought you came to see me."

336

"I get this image in my head," Patrick said quietly. Head bowed as though confessing to all the world's atrocities. "This image that looks all sunny. That football field, filled with folding chairs. Folding chairs filled with ghosts in caps and gowns. *A proud milestone,* I imagine Sedgwick saying that. Standing before the graduating class of 2008. He's got that mushy expression on his face; working so hard to make sure everyone knows just how he's feeling.

"And then he starts talking about Edmund, and I see the graduates looking all sad. I know they mean it, and I know that the principal means it, because Sedgwick isn't a monster. None of them are. . . . But then I hear Sedgwick talk about Kelly McDermott. Bowing his head. Talking about the need for a strong community, even as the rest of the football team watches from the stands or in their chairs, bowing their own heads. I see the tassels dangling from their caps, brushing against their faces. Every last one of them absolved, while Kelly . . ."

Patrick paused, hands bundled in his lap.

"I see Sedgwick regretting every last thing that led up to this, but I can see his thoughts, too. I can see him crying tears of relief over the bullet Wellspring Academy managed to dodge. That the 'steroids' turned out to be legal, that Cody's dealer was just running a scam, passing legal performance-enhancers as something more. I hear him blessing the skies that Edmund had a gun, that his killer acted in self-defense. And that this killer now sits here as a shining example of how a stronger community will stop such things from ever happening again. . . .

"And still, even behind *that,* I see real regret. I *know* that he cared. But then, behind that, more opportunistic thoughts. Then actual love, then cynical manipulation, and so on, until I can't tell what's what. And I can't be there, because if that wheel stops spinning, and my thoughts settle on all the inexcusable things they did to you, I might end up right here with you....

"And then I wonder if that's not where I belong."

"Patrick..."

Patrick looked up, well aware that there were tears in his eyes.

"It's just Wellspring Academy...," Kelly said with a heart-broken smile. "They're going to keep doing what they're doing. Forget about them."

A sob caught in Patrick's throat, choking him. "Kelly..."

"Forget about them... and forget about me."

Jenna glanced up, stunned.

"Maybe I'm wrong," Kelly told them. "Maybe it won't happen the way I think. After all, I've got memories past these walls. I know my parents aren't going to be of any help, I know that I'm going to end up working in a bakery. In Louisville, someday. I know I'm going to develop a taste for alcohol and cigarettes. But maybe, come twenty years from now, I won't be drifting off to sleep in some other asylum for God knows whatever reason I ended up there. Maybe I won't wake up twenty years in the past, or just a couple of weeks ago, if you want to look at it from our present position. Maybe it won't all happen again."

Kelly looked at Patrick, looked at Jenna.

Both knowing what was next.

"But I don't think I am wrong," Kelly lamented. "It's like

that common thread Edmund told us about. Moments when there's nothing that can change, where things are simply set. And I just happened upon that path, going along for the ride.... There's a Kelly-shaped hole in the universe that needs to be filled, that's been hollowed out specifically for me to fill. And twenty years from now, I'm going to end up right back where this whole thing started."

Kelly took in the dismal faces of his friends.

"I was going to draw you a diagram," he said. "But I think you've got the gist of it, don't you?"

Patrick shook his head violently, unabashed. "I don't believe we're stuck. I don't believe we don't have a choice. *I refuse to believe it's all been decided.*"

"I don't think it *is* the same for everyone...," Kelly mused. "After all, if you two stay away from me, very far away from me, if you can just move forward without me... well, there's a good chance every decision you make is going to be your own."

Patrick began to panic.

Looked over at Jenna, horrified to find her sitting with a defeated complacency.

"Jenna, you can't seriously sit there and let him *say* this!"

With a quick glance out the window, Jenna swallowed and asked: "Why?"

Kelly looked genuinely confused. Not by the question, it turned out, but by the mere fact that they hadn't figured it out. "Well, for you two, obviously."

"What?" Patrick was almost outraged at the gross oversimplification. "All this so that Jenna and I would get together—"

Kelly laughed, halting Patrick in mid-rant. "Oh no, Patrick. No. That's not important. I mean, it's great. It's wonderful, and I do have a great feeling about you two as a couple, sure...."

Jenna looked away, but she wasn't blushing, and she wasn't smiling.

"This didn't happen for you two as a couple," Kelly told them with a soft, reassuring tone. "It just happened for you two. Patrick. Jenna. Look at where you-all were headed before all this happened, how you both, all of us, lived our lives."

At the very thought of such a pure outcome, Patrick felt himself preparing to fight it.

"Stop," Kelly told him. "You both know you're not the same people you were."

"That can't be the reason," Patrick whispered.

"It is."

"But how do you *know?*" Patrick whispered harshly.

"We don't get to know about this...." Kelly's face was calm and penitent. "We will never know if anything good came out of this. Just like we don't really know whether I'm simply stark, raving bonkers. The question isn't whether you can deny the change all this brought about. It's obvious the both of you have changed, and only for the better. The real question is ... do you *believe* me?"

Patrick couldn't bring himself to look at Kelly's face any longer. Lowered his head down and to the left, a baby refusing that last spoonful of strained peas.

"Jenna?" Patrick heard Kelly say. "Do you believe me?"

The quiet, reluctant word was almost buried under its own weight. "Yes."

"Patrick, do you believe me?"

"No . . ." Patrick raised his chin. Not in defiance, not with any intent to surrender. He simply thought he'd give Kelly the respect of looking him right in those blue, eternal eyes. "I'm not ready to say goodbye."

"Well, hell . . ." Kelly's smile was wide and honest. Taken aback by how serious he'd allowed things to get. "You can come back to visit me tomorrow. And tomorrow there's no need for a sudden goodbye. If you really want something to look forward to, look me up in twenty years. Come and see me. See what ever did happen to that older McDermott before he jumped back through time. . . . You can hold on to that. Though sooner or later, I suspect you'll get around to knowing what's best for you."

It was powerful stuff, what Kelly McDermott was capable of, because with that small bit of homespun wisdom, the shroud lifted from them.

Leaving its mark, that much was certain, but gone long enough for Kelly to hug Jenna. Long enough for Patrick to feel at home in his own parting embrace with Kelly McDermott. Long enough to allow them both to leave him standing by the sunlit window, gracing them with a final, unassuming wave.

Long enough for Patrick's angels to wake up, and whisper: *We're still here.*

Patrick and Jenna were seated on the swings. The sun had long since turned orange, with plans for a glorious setting. The trees were full and green. Birds sang. From some unseen corner of the world came the soft sound of music grazing blades of grass. A pair of children ran along the grass, parents watching from a cautious distance. A cyclist breezed down the street, bell ringing. Right past a sad, uninhabited house, the word SOLD was plastered over a now debunked FOR SALE sign in the front yard.

Train whistle in the distance, and Patrick let it all soak in.

"I love you," he told Jenna.

Jenna tilted her head to one side with a demure smile. "I know." .

There it was.

Jenna stood up from the swing and faced Patrick.

"We can go and visit him tomorrow," she said, extending her hand.

He took hold of it, not a second thought as to whether that would be the case.

"Tomorrow," Patrick agreed, and the two of them took slow steps across the park, wandering with open eyes and great reluctance into the arms of another life.

JOAQUIN DORFMAN was born in February of 1979, and since then, very little has changed. He is a film-school dropout, and graduated from New York University with a degree in synchronicity. Soon after, he made New York his home for several years. Once the money went away, he retreated to his hometown of Durham, North Carolina, where he currently resides.

He is the author of *Playing It Cool*, a New York Public Library Book for the Teen Age, and, with his father, Ariel, *Burning City*.

His best friend is a cat.

Visit Joaquin at www.joaquindorfman.com.